THE MAN I HATE

SCOTT HILDRETH

Scott Hildreth

SCOTT HILDRETH
PUSHING BOUNDARIES SINCE 2013

This dedication is twofold:

First, to all those whose lives have been turned upside down by COVID-19, this one is for you. In this time of being confined to your homes, may you find a way to love those within your reach just a little more.

Secondly, if, through the course of your work, you were required to expose yourself to others, be them infected or not, thank you. Working at 7-Eleven, as a first responder, a nurse, Wal-Mart shelf stocker, or Cedars-Sinai Hospital surgeon matters not. Thank you. Throughout this pandemic, you are the true heroes.

AUTHOR'S NOTE

The acts and actions depicted in the book are fictitious. Any similarity between the characters and real persons, living or dead, is merely coincidental.

Every sexual partner in the book is over the age of 18. Please, if you intend to read further than this comment, be over the age of 18 to enjoy this novel.

This book is a work of fiction. Names, characters, places, and incidents are the product of the author's imagination or are used fictitiously. Any resemblances to actual events, locales, or persons living or dead, are coincidental.

Cover design by Jessica

Follow me on Facebook at: www.facebook.com/sd.hildreth

Like me on Facebook at: www.facebook.com/ScottDHildreth

Follow me on Twitter at: @ScottDHildreth

Sign up for my newsletter here: www.scotthildreth.com

PROLOGUE

When I was 18 years old, a surprise visit to my boyfriend's house turned ugly when I found a naked cheerleader hidden in his closet. Experiencing infidelity in all three of my relationships left me wondering what I'd done wrong.

My mother swore that good men were out there. Her advice in securing one was simple. I should be more cautious with the men I offered my heart.

In hope of bringing me out of my broken-hearted funk, she plucked her favorite movie from the collection she kept in the cabinet beneath the television. Although I'd never seen it, I knew the movie all too well. The 1976 version of *A Star is Born* was as much a part of my mother's life as Sunday Dinners, decorating for holidays, and feigning excitement each time my father presented his newest hot rod.

She pushed the VHS tape into the machine and reached for the remote. "Anna, I'm telling you," she said, barely able to contain her excitement, "you're going to absolutely love it."

"Mom, I just...I'm," I stammered. "I'm sad. I don't need to watch—"

"It's the best love story of all time," she argued, gesturing to a massive bowl of fresh popcorn she'd placed on the center couch cushion. "It's time you see it. Sit down. We'll watch it together."

"Is it going to make me cry?" I asked. "You're in here bawling every time you watch it."

"Yes," she replied, placing her hand on my knee. "But the tears will be therapeutic."

John Norman Howard and Esther Hoffman's version of the movie did make me cry, but it did little to cause me to believe in anything, especially love. Twenty years later, however, Jackson Maine and Ally Campano changed things.

"They remade *A Star is Born,*" my mother declared. "It has Bradley Cooper in it. Your father isn't interested. Do you want to go?"

At the time, I was on the heels of an ugly divorce. Unwilling to believe that men were anything but unfaithful pigs, it was highly unlikely the movie would do anything to convince me otherwise. I was mature enough to enjoy it, regardless.

"Sure," I said. "I'll go."

Entering the theater, I had minimal expectations. Lady Gaga could sing, but her ability to act had yet to be seen. So many musicians had tried the big screen, and as many failed. Most did so miserably. I told myself if nothing else, Bradley Cooper's blue eyes were enough to carry the film.

Although I already knew the story, I rode an emotional rollercoaster throughout the entire film. Lady Gaga did a remarkable job bringing her character, *Ally Campano,* to life. At the end of the film, her performance of *I'll Never Love Again* reduced me to a blubbering wreck. Her contributions, both vocal and acting, transformed me into a different woman. I left the theater believing in my heart of hearts that one day love would find me.

I simply needed to wait until a real-life Jackson Maine stumbled into my life.

1

ANNA

I was the only child in an extremely close-knit Midwestern family. We went to church on Sundays. *Please* and *thank you* were second nature. We took vacations as a family, every summer. My father coached my softball team. My mother taught me to cook the same recipes her mother prepared a generation earlier.

She cried the day I left for college.

Although I moved away after completing my education, I didn't go far. Nevertheless, the fifteen miles that separated us caused her tremendous grief.

It provided me with a sense of self-worth.

After graduating, fifteen years quickly passed. During that time, many things happened. My mother learned to accept my absence. My butt grew. I purchased an affordable building on a corner lot and opened a small exotic car dealership. I got married to a successful man. My father turned sixty-five. My business flourished. Wrinkles became prominent. I got divorced. My father retired.

Immediately following his retirement, my father announced his intention to move away. Not thirty miles or even one hundred.

They'd purchased a home 1,443 miles west, in Los Angeles, California.

"You need to come out here," my mother said. "It's wonderful. They call it the land of dreams and drought."

She said it as if the *dreams and drought* moniker would attract me.

"What does that even mean?" I asked.

"It never rains," she replied. "Because it doesn't rain, the sun shines every day. That's the drought. The streets are lined with palm trees and there are celebrities everywhere. That's the dream. You should really consider moving here."

Although it sounded like an interesting enough place to visit, I didn't go immediately. Life, as always, got in the way. Then, on afternoon before I planned to visit their new home on the palm tree-lined street in the land of dreams and drought, I received a phone call.

The detective gave me a virtual pat on the shoulder.

"At least they died in their sleep," he said.

The condolences he expressed did little to ease the pain of losing both parents before I gave them grandchildren or even so much as visited their new place of residence.

Deciding what to do with their home wasn't a simple task. I had two options: stay in Oklahoma and pay a mortgage or move to California and live mortgage free. To many, the decision would be easy. Personally, I couldn't find many redeeming qualities about Los Angeles. The only one that repeatedly came to mind was the weather.

I meandered through the living room. The furnishings were in complete contrast to what I was accustomed to seeing in my mother's home. I imagined her explaining how much she enjoyed choosing each thoughtfully positioned contemporary piece that was placed in the room.

I gazed through the window that faced the street. According to my mother, the view was picturesque.

Compared to the one-acre tree-filled lots I was accustomed to seeing, the sight was far from scenic. The view consisted of the neighbor's two-story home on a postage stamp-sized lot, four unhealthy-looking palm trees, a shallow driveway filled with cars, and a neon green AstroTurf yard.

I couldn't help but wonder what drew my parents to California. Or, what drew anyone to California for that matter. The sky was hazy and never quite clear, the traffic was horrendous, and everything was overpriced. People didn't wave, they rarely spoke, and everyone was in a hurry. The streets weren't lined with palm trees, they were littered with homeless.

Hungry, frustrated, and uncertain of where I was going to call home, I snatched my purse from the end table and sauntered toward the front door. In the ten days I'd been in Los Angeles, eating out had become a guilty pleasure. It saved me from being alone in a home that did nothing but remind me of losing my parents much earlier than I had expected. Eager to beat the morning rush, I locked the front door and turned toward the driveway.

The sun peeked over the top of an adjacent salmon-colored Mediterranean-style home. Positioned midway between Beverly Hills and North Hollywood, along what the locals called the four-oh-five, Sherman Oaks was filled with two-story homes situated on lots barely large enough to encompass them. Many had swimming pools. Very few were fitted with garages. None could be obtained for less than seven figures.

I rolled down my windows and drew a long breath of the cool morning air. After tossing my purse in the passenger seat, I adjusted the rearview mirror and started my playlist. With Lada Gaga's *Shallow* my morning's inspiration, I reached for the gearshift.

"Get out of the car!" a gravelly voice demanded from my left side.

Paralyzed by fear, I gripped the steering wheel like a vise. The smell of pot and stale sweat wafted into the car. My stomach convulsed. Ever so slowly, my eyes drifted toward the voice.

A bald man in a black hoodie loomed over the side of the car. A five o'clock shadow covered his sunken pale cheeks. His neck was littered with awful looking tattoos. With a gun in one hand and my door handle in the other, he glared right at me. His massive pupils made one thing perfectly clear.

He was a wacked out lunatic.

"Get out of the fucking car," he said through clenched teeth.

Overcome by the thought of what might happen if I didn't relinquish my vehicle, I stared mindlessly at my attacker. The bitter smell from his clothes and fear of the inevitable merged. Bile rose in my throat. Despite my desire to thrust open the car door and run as far and as fast as possible, I couldn't convince a single muscle to move.

Frustrated at my lack of compliance with his concise demands, he yanked against the door handle. "Now, bitch!"

Be it a blessing or a curse, the automatic door lock prevented him from opening the door. If I couldn't figure out how to release the steering wheel and let him have the car, the tattooed psychopath was going to plaster my guts all over the interior of my new Mercedes-Benz.

Less than two weeks after the death of my parents, I was destined to draw my last breath in their driveway. The fact that no one was going to attend my funeral came to mind. Crippled by that thought, I choked the steering wheel and stared straight ahead.

He pressed the barrel of the gun against the side of my neck. "Get. Out."

"I'll give you one chance, asshole," a second voice said, enunciating each word clearly. "Drop the gun in her lap and take two steps away from the car."

Relief tickled its way up my spine. In hope of the lunatic complying with the stranger's demand, my eyes darted to the gun. The carjacker's knuckles went white as he gripped the gun firmly in his shaking hand.

Obviously, he had no intention of releasing it.

I peered over my left shoulder. The distracted hoodie-wearing thug blocked my view. I glanced in my rearview mirror. A black Range Rover was parked in the street behind me.

The carjacker took a step back. A long shadow darkened the concrete beside him. I conjured up the countless possibilities of what was going to happen next. My heart raced to the point of making me sick.

While I fought the urge to vomit, the carjacker was yanked away from my car. A flurry of movements followed. The dull *thud* of someone's head being hit with a fist caused me to cringe. A gun skidded across the driveway.

My eyes darted to the left. A well-dressed man stood behind my would-be assailant with his right arm wrapped tightly around the car thief's neck. Immobilized by the chokehold, the bug-eyed lunatic flailed for an instant and then went limp.

A sickeningly handsome suit-wearing stranger had singlehandedly disarmed and subdued my attacker. In sheer disbelief of what I was seeing, I stared mindlessly.

My gray-haired protector lifted his chin slightly. "Would you open the trunk, please?"

The sincerity in his eyes diffused the situation enough that I was comfortable complying with his request. I glanced around the car's interior, completely lost as to what I should do. I'd opened my trunk countless times. Despite that fact, I couldn't seem to recall how to do it. Being held at gunpoint in my driveway had taken a toll on my ability to reason.

I craned my neck toward the street. My savior was dragging the unconscious man toward his SUV.

I swallowed a baseball-sized lump of nervousness. "My trunk?"

"There's a button on your door panel," he said calmly, pausing at the back of his SUV. "Beneath your window switches."

Mildly confused, I lifted the silver switch. The trunk shot open. Relieved that the task was complete, I glanced out my car window.

Choking the carjacker with one arm, the well-dressed stranger rummaged in the back of his SUV with the other. A few seconds later he produced several long white plastic straps. Perplexed, I watched as he zip-tied the ankles and wrists of the semi-conscious thug.

No differently than if he were taking an armload of groceries across Target's parking lot, he dragged the tattooed thug toward the back of my car. I gawked in disbelief as he tossed him into the trunk with a *thud*! After situating things, he carefully closed the lid. Obviously, subduing bad guys was tritely familiar to the suit-wearing badass.

With some hesitation, I got out of the car. The courteous stranger took a step in my direction and then paused. He brushed the wrinkles from his suit. Once satisfied, he looked up.

His presence was undeniable. He just as well held a neon sign that flashed the words "KEEP YOUR DISTANCE", yet there was something about him that I found extremely comforting.

He offered an apologetic smile. "Sorry about all of this."

I glanced beyond him, at the attacker's gun. I'd witnessed a few drunken barroom brawls in the bars while in college and seen two cowboys get in a fistfight at a rodeo once, but I'd never been directly involved in any kind of violent act. I wiped my clammy hands against the fabric of my dress.

"It's not your fault," I replied.

"I live next door." He reached inside his jacket pocket with his left hand and extended his right. "Braxton Rourke."

I was bewildered by his calmness. I cupped his hand in mine and shook it. "Thank you...for everything. I'm uhhm...my name is Anna," I stammered. "Anna Wilson."

He gave me a thorough once-over. One side of his mouth curled up slightly. "Nice to meet you."

"Is this a common thing?" I glanced at my car. "Being carjacked?"

"In Sherman Oaks?" He tapped his finger against the screen of his phone. "No." He raised the phone to his ear and turned away. "Attempted carjacking. Yes. No. He's been subdued," he said matter-of-factly. "Yes." He glanced at the carjacker's pistol, which was ten feet away on the edge of the concrete. "With a pistol. No. Yes. 15021

Valley Vista. I'll be standing beside a white Mercedes E-Class. Sure. Braxton Rourke."

He slipped the phone inside his jacket pocket and faced me. "The police will be here in a few minutes."

The suit he wore accentuated the shape of his very athletic body. A trim waist, broad chest, and well-toned arms were hidden beneath the fine Italian fabric. His silver hair was disheveled from the scuffle yet managed to look perfect. I wondered how many pictures of him were floating around Instagram with #silverfox attached to them.

Thousands, I decided.

Overcome by everything, I muttered my response. "Okay."

I was nearly shot to death. A criminal was locked in the trunk of my new car. I was now waiting on the Nation's most trigger-happy police force to show up, and there was a loaded gun in my driveway ten feet from where I stood.

I was a bundle of frayed nerves.

Braxton Rourke, however, acted as he had just called in a dinner reservation.

My thoughts went to the pistol that was sure to be the focal point of the soon to be arriving police force. Visions of overzealous officers with weapons drawn screaming demands came to mind. Me dying in a hail of gunfire while a ten-year-old with an iPhone recorded the atrocity from his second-story window would be the closing chapter on my life.

I glanced at the gun and then at him. "Are you going to pick that thing up before they get here?" I asked. "It's making me nervous."

"I'll leave it there." He curled his fingertips toward his palm and studied his fingernails. "Don't worry," he said calmly. "Everything will be fine."

I wished I had his sense of being. While he repaired an errant cuticle, my heart was thrashing against my ribs. I couldn't decide whether to scream, cry, or ask my sexy neighbor for a mercy fuck.

"Are you always this calm?" I asked.

"Depends on the circumstances," he replied, not bothering to look up.

"These circumstances," I squeaked, coughing out a nervous laugh as I spoke. "A Saturday morning carjacking. Disarming a pistol wielding maniac. Choking someone half to death and then locking him in a trunk?"

He shifted his gaze from his fingernails to me. His face, which had remained rather emotionless, now seemed slightly amused.

"I spent nearly fifteen years being shot at by people I often couldn't see." He raked his fingers through his silver locks. "Surviving that makes this seem like a cakewalk."

"You were a soldier?"

"A Marine," he replied.

His fast hands and calm demeanor now made perfect sense. I wanted to thank him for his service but didn't want to sound like the countless others who I was sure had already done so. I glanced at his feet and then looked up.

"I like your shoes," I murmured.

Where the hell did that come from?

He laughed. "Thank you."

Before I could continue to make a fool of myself, a fast-approaching police car screeched to a stop behind Braxton's SUV. The driver, a young-looking officer with closely cropped red hair thrust open the door and strutted toward the driveway.

His much younger partner cautiously followed close behind.

The first officer immediately recognized my handsome neighbor. "Braxton Rourke," the officer announced, seeming amused. "Didn't know what he was in for when he tried to carjack you, did he?"

"It wasn't me he was after," Braxton replied, tilting his head in my direction as he spoke. "He was trying to steal her Mercedes."

The officer glanced at me. "I'm officer O'Malley. Are you okay?"

"I'm just...yes, I'm fine, thank you."

He offered a shallow smile and then looked at Braxton. He

pushed the brim of his hat up with his thumb. "Do I need to call an ambulance?"

Braxton shook his head.

It appeared the police were privy of Braxton's ability to disarm criminals. A blanket of intrigue encompassed me. I wanted to know more about the soft-spoken, suit-wearing, Range Rover driving badass.

O'Malley glanced left and then right. "Where is he?"

Braxton nodded toward my car. "He's in the trunk."

"Handcuffed?" the officer asked.

Braxton shrugged one shoulder. "More or less."

O'Malley gestured toward the carjacker's gun. "Is that his piece behind you?"

"It is," Braxton replied dryly. "Glock .40 cal. It's loaded."

"Secure that weapon," O'Malley said, directing his request to his partner. "Take pictures before you do." He walked to the back of my car, drew his weapon, and looked at me. "Ma'am, would you mind opening the trunk?"

A police officer had his gun drawn and was waiting for me to reveal the wild-eyed tattooed lunatic that my handsome neighbor tossed into my trunk. Beyond him, his partner was carefully picking up a gun from my driveway with a pencil.

The entire event was utter madness. Nevertheless, I forced myself to smile and took hesitant steps toward the car. "Sure."

I pulled the trunk release and quickly stepped to Braxton's side.

O'Malley peered inside the trunk. Upon seeing the thief, he let out a laugh. "Nathan fucking Travis. How long you been out? Two weeks?" He slammed the trunk closed and shook his head. "This asshole's been out of the joint for two weeks, tops. This'll be his third strike. He'll do twenty-five to life for this one."

A mental sigh of relief escaped me.

"Listen, O'Malley." Braxton cleared his throat. "She's kind of shaken up by all of this. If you don't mind, we'd like to get to breakfast. We can stop by the station and fill out the report on our way back."

"I don't suppose that'd hurt anything," the officer replied. He looked at me. "Enjoy your breakfast, ma'am."

My emotions were riding a runaway rollercoaster. In ten minutes, I'd been carjacked and saved by a handsome stranger. Now, I was accompanying him to breakfast. While I tried to process just what was happening, Braxton got my purse out of the car and handed it to me.

"May I have your keys?" he asked.

He was as polite as he was good-looking. I gave him my keys on the heels of a half-hidden smile. "Here you go."

"Lock her car when you're done and take the keys to the station," Braxton said, tossing the officer the keys. "We'll pick them up when we come in."

O'Malley gave a sharp nod. "See you in the station, Rourke."

Braxton moved aside and gestured toward his vehicle. "After you."

I stepped around him. "How did you know I was going to breakfast?"

He smirked. "Good guess."

I walked past him. A hint of his cologne tickled my nose. He smelled like he looked.

Striking.

He followed me to the SUV and opened the door. As I struggled to pull my five-foot-two frame inside, he pressed his open hand against the small of my back.

"Here," he said. "Let me help you."

My life had been dick-free since the vow of celibacy that followed my half-assed failed marriage. Subsequently, I hadn't had a man touch me in years. Upon having Braxton do so, fiery desire shot through my veins.

One hand cupped my waist. Another pressed against the back of my bare thigh.

Every inch of my skin itched with want.

He lifted me effortlessly and then released me into the comfort of the fine leather seat. Feeling lightheaded, I glanced in his direction.

His hazel orbs expressed his interests with unclouded clarity.

Braxton Rourke may have been hungry, but it wasn't breakfast he was hungry for.

2

BRAXTON

Anna buckled her seatbelt. "How did that police officer know you?"

A typical day for me might include removing crucial evidence from a crime scene, erasing surveillance footage, or manipulating a witness to give an alternate testimony. I worked for the police as much as anyone. Admitting the truth to Anna wasn't in my best interest.

"I trained some of the officers in close quarters combat techniques. He was one of the officers that took the course."

"Oh." She seemed surprised. "I didn't realize Marines trained police officers."

"I received specialized training in the military," I responded. "After I retired, I offered a course to teach that same training. I was approached by the police chief to train the officers. Fortunately, I was the low bid on the contract."

"What kind of specialized training?"

I merged into traffic. "Disarming attackers. Close quarters combat. Strategies to survive an ambush. Things like that."

"Do you still train police officers?" she asked. "Is that your job?"

"Not any longer."

"What do you do now?"

"I solve problems."

She laughed. "What kinds of problems?"

I chewed on my response as I maneuvered through the early morning traffic. After wedging the vehicle between a Prius and a Tesla, I gave her a response that I hoped she'd find satisfactory.

"When people with financial means do something that they later regret, I make the evidence of their regretful act disappear."

She gave me a blank look. "Have you practiced that response?"

"No."

"It sounded canned."

"It wasn't."

Traffic went from eighty miles an hour to a near stop in an instant. Curious, she gawked at the freeway ahead. While she was distracted, I looked her over.

The left side of her dress was caught in the waistline of her emerald green laced panties. I took a few admiring glances at her well-toned legs before shifting my attention to the road. "How's the traffic where you live?"

"Not like this, I can tell you that much," she complained. "In Tulsa, I can drive fifteen miles in ten minutes. Here, fifteen miles takes two hours."

"How long are you staying?" I asked.

"I'm leaving on Tuesday." She gazed through the side window, watching the traffic inch past. "I'll decide before then what I'm doing with the house. Right now, I'm afraid I'll probably sell it. Carjacking might be uncommon in that neighborhood, but it happened. The more I think about it the more it bothers me."

"It's definitely a more common occurrence here than it is in Oklahoma," I admitted. "There's over four million people here. We're bound to have some criminals in the mix."

"Back to what we were talking about." She shifted her attention from the traffic to me. "What types of people have the financial means to hire you for your services?"

"All kinds."

"Anyone famous?"

"I suppose."

"Name one."

"I'd rather not," I said. "It's best if I keep the extent of my work confidential."

"Okay. Work-related or not work-related, I don't care. Have you met..." She rocked her head back and forth. "Oh, I don't know. Tom Cruise?"

"No."

"Brad Pitt?"

"No."

"Britney Spears?"

"Yes."

"Lady Gaga?"

"Yes."

"Holy crap." She gasped. "Really?"

"Yes, really."

Her eyes lit up. "Was she nice?"

"Extremely."

"I'd give my left arm to meet her," she said. "I'd let them hack it off at the shoulder."

"Your entire arm?"

"Uh huh."

I didn't get wrapped up in admiring the actors, actresses, or really anyone, for that matter. In my eyes, we were all the same.

"Sever and arm?" I looked at her like she was crazy. "Just to meet someone?"

"Not *someone*. Lady Gaga, for Christ's sake. The part she played in A Star is Born? It changed my life." She glanced at me. "You've seen in, right?"

I'd seen the one with Kris Kristofferson, but not the most recent one. I shook my head. "I haven't," I admitted. "Not the new one, anyway."

"Oh, wow. That's crazy. Well, Lady Gaga did a marvelous job. I guess I really want to just thank her for putting her heart and soul into the part she played. Her character gave me courage."

She looked away for a moment but then appeared to have an epiphany. "What about the cute one? She was married to Ben Affleck." She snapped her fingers a few times. "She does the credit card commercials."

"Jennifer Garner?"

"Yes," she said. "Her. Have you met her?"

"I have."

"Was she nice?"

"Very."

"Oh my God." She shook her head in disbelief. "This is bananas. My mind is going a million different directions wondering what they must have done that they needed your assistance."

"To be fair to everyone involved, I generally don't speak about my work. For the sake of clarifying matters, I do offer services other than erasing regretful acts."

"Like what?"

I felt like I was being interrogated. The women I typically spent my time with talked very little and asked even less about my profession. She was cuter than hell, but her incessant prying into my private life was going to become unnerving if she didn't slow down.

"Security services," I responded. "Surveillance. Things like that."

"Like a bodyguard?"

"I suppose."

"Everything makes sense now," she said.

I hoped she was right. If everything made sense to her, maybe the questions would stop. I grinned in anticipation. "Everything?"

She nodded. "Pretty much."

Regardless of her claim, she had no idea of what types of situations I got myself into. If she knew, I doubted she'd be in the car with me. We definitely wouldn't be going to breakfast together.

Satisfied—at least for the moment—she glanced around the car's interior. Now seeming more interested in the vehicle's gadgetry than with me, she traced her fingertip along the edge of the dash.

"Is this the Autobiography Edition?" she asked.

"It is," I replied. "I'm surprised you noticed."

"I own a car dealership in Oklahoma," she replied. "I specialize in exotics."

I wouldn't have guessed her for an exotic car dealership owner. She was an extremely attractive thirty-something who dressed like a successful businesswoman and drove a new Mercedes-Benz. Considering that her auburn hair was fixed differently on each day that I'd seen her and that her makeup was nothing short of perfect, my guess would have been a high-end hairstylist.

I glanced in her direction. "I didn't know people in Oklahoma drove exotics."

"We drive the same cars you drive we just do it with smiles on our faces," she said in a snide tone.

"I was joking."

She shot me a playful glare. "I wasn't."

I chuckled. "Not caring for California?"

"Are you aware of my parents?" she asked. "What happened to them?"

Initially, I believed Anna was a realtor planning to sell the home. Upon seeing the out of state plates on her car, I realized she was the child of my two deceased neighbors.

Her parents moved from Oklahoma to Los Angeles, hoping to retire in a location JoAnn described as paradise. After unpacking the last box from their move, she and her husband Randy traded in his restored vintage Suburban for a new Toyota 4Runner.

They intended to use the new SUV exploring the state, visiting Joshua Tree National Monument and the Mojave Desert at their earliest convenience.

On the night they obtained the vehicle, their new purchase was celebrated with dinner out on the town. Upon returning, Randy parked the Toyota and walked away, not realizing the new *keyless* SUV was still running.

With the key fob in his pocket, he and JoAnn retired to their bedroom, fell asleep, and never awoke. Carbon monoxide from the vehicle's exhaust suffocated them while they slept at each other's side.

"I am," I said, glancing in her direction. "It was tragic. I'm so sorry."

"Thank you." She shifted her gaze to the side window. "I came here not knowing whether I was going to sell their home or not. I decided I'd make the decision after I got here and looked everything over. After being here for a while, it's obvious this place isn't for me. People are in too big of a hurry and everyone's an asshole." She looked at me. "Except for you."

"It's a different lifestyle, that's for sure," I admitted. "And, for what it's worth, I'm an asshole on the inside."

"What does that mean?"

"If you take away the suit, the car, and shitty little grin, what you're left with is me." I looked at her and laughed. "I'm a prick."

"I don't think you're a prick." She gave me an admiring look. "You saved me from that stinky asshole who was trying to steal my car. A prick wouldn't have done that."

I'd intervened because it was the right thing to do. It didn't dismiss the fact that the entire time I was zip-tying the asshole and throwing him in the trunk of her car that I hoped she'd find my actions heroic enough to offer me gratuitous sex in exchange for saving her.

"It was second nature," I argued.

"Your Marine training?"

"I suppose."

"Well, not everyone would have done what you did." She reached for her purse. "Because of that, I say you're not an asshole."

I was, but there was no sense in arguing with her. If she was leaving in six days, she wouldn't have time to find out on her own. I'd let her continue to believe what made her happy.

I offered her an appreciative grin. "Thank you."

In the midst of adjusting her makeup, she checked her reflection in her compact and then smiled in return. "You're welcome."

I exited the freeway and came to a stop at the traffic light. "The restaurant is right up the street."

"Good," she said, shifting her gaze to the side window. "I'm starving."

I stole a glance at the side of her ass. "Yeah," I said. "Me, too."

3

ANNA

People like Braxton didn't exist in Oklahoma. Completely astonished by what I'd learned, I gazed at him with admiring eyes. Soon, I became lost in the heady scent of his cologne. Half a dozen scenarios came to mind, each of which ended with him being naked and me being happy.

After gawking much longer than I probably should have, I emerged from the carnal fog that encompassed me. I pierced a potato wedge and raised my fork to my mouth.

He motioned toward my hand with his eyes. "You're shaking."

He was right. It had nothing to do with the incident, though. To be honest, all thoughts of the event had been temporarily replaced by mental images of Braxton and me doing the dirty.

I wasn't about to admit that I was enthralled by him or that the fascination was likely the cause of my nervous energy. I glanced at the tip of my fork and feigned surprise.

"I guess I am," I said. "I don't know what's going on."

He leaned forward. "Come here," he said, his voice nearly a whisper.

Excluding a half-assed smirk from time to time, Braxton didn't exhibit much emotion on the joyous side of the spectrum. His look wasn't stern or angry, it was simply one of a serious nature. Having him playfully approach me with a whisper was intoxicating.

Overcome with curiosity, I set my fork down and met him at the center of the table. "Yes?"

"I've got an idea," he whispered.

He was close enough to kiss me. His breath was nearly as sweet as his cologne. I was captivated.

"An idea?" I asked.

"Of sorts. I want you to make a bet with me," he explained. "It ends with one or the other of us taking off our clothes. It should help take your mind off whatever's making you shake."

If one of us was going to end up taking off our clothes, I'd be an idiot not to play. Regardless of which one of us was going to strip to our skivvies, things would be headed in the right direction. My knees wagged back and forth in anticipation.

"Okay," I breathed.

"So, you want to do it?"

Incapable of hiding my excitement, I nodded eagerly in agreement. "Sure."

"I'm going to guess the color of your panties," he said flatly. "If I get it right, you're going to take them off and put them in your purse. If I guess wrong, I'll strip down to my boxers and finish breakfast."

As if it wasn't bad enough already, he tossed gasoline on the sexual fire that was burning between my legs. I expected him to smirk, laugh, or to say that he was joking. The look on his face was as clear as his request.

He was dead serious.

The odds of him guessing the color of my panties was minuscule. My heart raced at the thought of seeing him half-naked.

I swallowed heavily. "All the way to your boxers?"

"Boxers and socks," he declared. "I'll give everything else to you."

I would have given him a hundred bucks to see him without his shirt on. It seemed like a fair bet. Nevertheless, I wanted to negotiate for more.

"If I'm going to risk losing my panties, you're going to have to sweeten the pot."

His gaze narrowed. "Like what?"

"Strip to your boxers and socks and tell me about Lady Gaga," I said. "How you met, and what she was like. The entire story."

He let out a sigh of frustration and leaned away from the table. After studying me for a long moment, he gave a regretful nod. "Fine."

I offered my hand. "I'll take that bet."

He started to shake my hand and then hesitated. "How close do I have to get?"

"What do you mean?"

"For instance, would I have to guess the specific color, or could it be orange instead of tangerine, mango, or pumpkin?"

I laughed. "If you get the color right, it'll be good enough."

He crossed his arms and looked me over. His hazel eyes glistened mischievously. Feeling as if he'd hypnotized me, I stared blankly into the abyss of his green and brown speckled orbs.

"Take off your green panties and put them in your purse," he said.

I blinked. "Huh?"

"Green," he said. "Your panties. They're green."

"How did..." I stared in disbelief. "I feel like you sucked that information out of my soul."

"Am I right, or am I wrong?" he asked.

I forced a sigh. "You're right."

He leaned against the back of his seat and playfully wagged the tip of his index finger at me. "Get busy."

I wasn't opposed to taking my panties off in the restaurant. Not by any means. In fact, if it was going to get me one step closer to having sex, I'd likely strip naked if he asked me to. I reached under the table and hiked my dress to mid-thigh. As if it were a common occurrence for me to remove my undergarments while eating breakfast, I pushed my panties to my knees.

I glanced nervously around the restaurant. The small diner was filled with people, all of which were obviously more concerned with eating their breakfast than watching me undress. Pleased that I'd worn a presentable pair of underwear, I was brimming with nervous excitement.

Without further hesitation, I slid the panties along my calves and past the heels of my shoes.

In a rather theatrical display, I flopped my purse onto the table and propped it open. Then, I lifted the lace undergarments above the bag and paused. Contrary to what he may have thought, I had no intention of dropping them in my purse. I was going let him keep them for a souvenir, hoping they'd provide him the inspiration to act on whatever urge prompted him to have me remove them.

The green fabric dangled from between my thumb and forefinger. A few seconds ticked off the clock.

His eyes twinkled with satisfaction.

I tossed them at him.

With the speed of a bolt of lightning, he plucked them from the air before they landed against his suit. Wearing a slight smirk, he reached inside his jacket and tucked them in his pocket.

"How do you feel?" He nodded toward my lap. "Right now?"

I writhed in my seat. My pussy was soaked. Braxton, the other hand, seemed unaffected. Maybe when he wasn't saving women from vicious thugs, he was torturing them with his handsome looks and playing games that required them to relinquish their underwear.

I didn't know what he expected me to say.

"Liberated," I said.

My response seemed to amuse him. He almost grinned to prove it.

Almost.

He raised his chin slightly. "What else?"

"You just asked me to take off my panties in a public restaurant and I did it," I said. "I'm sure you're aware that you're an extremely attractive man. What do you expect me to say?"

He gave me a quick once over. "Do you feel better?"

Obviously, he wasn't getting my point. I rolled my eyes. "I'm not bothered by the idiot who tried to take my car. To be honest, I wasn't even thinking about him."

"I didn't say you were," he replied. "I asked if you felt better."

I fidgeted in my seat. "Better? About what?"

"You were clearly sexually frustrated earlier," he said in a flat tone. "Do you still feel that way?"

I was sexually frustrated. I took exception, however, to him claiming that I exhibited the frustration prior to that exact moment. "Earlier?" I snapped. "When?"

"Ten minutes ago, when you started to eat that potato." He gestured toward my fork. "The one you still haven't eaten."

It seemed he already knew the truth. There was no sense in lying about it. "Okay. What if I was? You're sexy, I'm single, and it's been far too long since I've had sex." I mentally cocked my hip. "So, yeah. I was sexually frustrated."

It was a little more information than I would have normally given on a breakfast date, but he crossed *normal* off the list when he asked me to ditch my panties.

He gave me a confused look. "Taking off your panties didn't help matters?"

I was wallowing in a puddle of proof that peeling off my panties in public made matters much worse. "No," I said in a sarcastic tone. "It sure didn't."

He arched a playful eyebrow. "What do you think might?"

"Might *what*?" I asked. "Ease my sexual pain?"

He gave a nod. "Yes."

I had only one solution. I hoped his thoughts mirrored mine. Not knowing whether I was going to sink or swim, I dove in headfirst.

"If you'd fuck me," I responded. "All my problems would be solved."

He leaned away from the table. After eye-fucking me twice, he met my hopeful gaze. "Is that what you want?"

His voice lacked emotion. His face was without expression. He was enjoying himself far too much. It was time to put his little mind-fuck game to an end.

"Are you enjoying this?" I asked, my tone thick with frustration.

"Enjoying what?"

"Torturing me. Is this fun for you?"

He smirked. "Immensely."

His playful resistance was making matters worse. I could feel my heart beating in places I had never felt it before. Namely, between my legs. I tossed my napkin over my plate and reached for my purse.

I tilted my head toward the exit. "Let's go."

He grinned. "Where?"

I flipped two twenty-dollar bills out of my wallet and onto the table. "You're either going to fuck me and then take me to the police station, or you're going to take me to the police station, and then fuck me. But we're having sex."

He stood. "Are we?"

"Yes," I said. "We sure are."

I reached for the seatbelt. Unreeling it was more complicated than a Chinese calculus textbook. My panties weren't the only thing that was missing. Apparently, I'd lost my ability to reason altogether.

Braxton started the vehicle and turned on the air conditioner. Upon realizing the depth of my mental struggle, he laughed. "What are you doing?"

"I'm trying..." I continued my inspection of the foreign-looking device, silently laughing at my inability to perform the simplest of tasks. In no time, my lap was filled with every inch of seat belt strap the British SUV had to offer.

"I'm trying to remember how one of these things works," I muttered.

He pulled off his jacket and tossed it in the backseat. "I thought you wanted to fuck."

My lower region flushed with excitement. Giddy at the thought of fucking in the car, I excitedly glanced around. A sunshade covered the windshield. The side windows were a dark enough tint that only those curious enough to peer inside would be able to see what we were doing. Having sex in a public parking lot wasn't on my conscious to-do list, but it wasn't on my to-don't list, either.

I released the seatbelt. All ten feet of it sucked into the retractor with a *thwack!*

"Here?" I asked, just to make sure we were both singing off the same song sheet. "You want to fuck here? In the car?"

"I thought you said you were sexually frustrated." His brows pinched together. "How bad is it?"

I'd hit the freaking jackpot. There was no sense in wasting any more time. I pulled the hem of my dress to my waist and wagged my index finger toward his lap. "Get those pants off, Mister."

He unbuckled his belt and pushed his slacks to his knees. His boxers came next. When they cleared his lap, his gorgeous cock sprung to attention.

Apparently, he was as excited as I was.

I stared at it like it was a two-headed unicorn. "Is there anything about you that isn't attractive?"

He chuckled. "I'm pretty ugly when it comes to relationships."

"Yeah," I said. "Me, too."

He stretched a condom over his massive member.

My lust-filled eyes met his. I didn't need a written invitation or any verbal instructions. Eager to feel his massive girth inside me, I crawled onto his lap, facing him. At the instant I came to the realization that I'd never had sex in a car, he raised his hips.

With the tip of his God-given gift resting against my soaking wet folds, he paused.

"Oh!" I exclaimed. I exhaled a long breath. "Wow."

His eyes narrowed. "Are you going to be okay?"

"Uh huh."

"Are you sure?"

I could have responded in the affirmative, but I chose not to. At that juncture, I felt actions would speak much louder than words. I sank my teeth into my bottom lip and released my weight. His thick shaft penetrated me.

Surprised by his girth, I paused.

We locked eyes. I forced myself to take him into me, slowly. As I began to wonder about my physical limitations of accepting his entire length, the tip of his dick collided with my cervix.

The breath shot from my lungs.

My gaze fell to my lap. I had no idea the cervix was an erogenous zone. The men I'd been with in the past hadn't had the ability to bring it to my attention. Braxton, on the other hand, couldn't help it.

Proud of my accomplishment, I replaced my look of pleasure with a guilty grin. I met his gaze. He looked like he'd see a ghost.

"Oh, yeah. I'm doing just fine." I let out a breath. "What about you?"

"Jesus." He winced in mock pain. "Are you a virgin?"

"A recycled one," I said with a laugh. "I haven't had sex in a few years."

"A few years?" He coughed. "Really?"

"I got divorced and swore off men." To save myself from making another O-face, I adjusted my weight. "Then, you saved me from a thug and tricked me out of my panties."

"You're not going to camp out on my doorstep after this, are you?"

He was talking too much and fucking too little. I didn't need a lecture on how to have sex and walk away. I'd done it more times than I cared to admit. Just not recently.

"This is nothing more than the two of us having fun," I said. "Stop talking and fuck me."

"Just remember." He withdrew himself until the tip of his dick was tickling my pussy lips. "You asked for this."

After that low-level warning, he fucked me as if his continued existence depended on it.

I'd had men make sweet love to me before, and I'd undoubtedly been fucked a few times. I had never, however, been fucked like Braxton was fucking me. His savage thrusts lifted me with such force that my head hit the car's headliner.

Each inward stroke forced the tip of his dick into the soft flesh of my cervix. The subsequent jolts of euphoria that rushed through me took with them my ability to refrain from reaching climax prematurely.

The clapping sound of his hips slapping against the back of my thighs filled the car's interior. A few unplanned high-pitched squeals on my part followed, as did the occasional *Oh. My. God.*

His cologne, my perfume, and the sweet musk of sex melded together.

I had every intention of leaving a lasting impression. In fact, fucking him until he couldn't walk was my plan of action. However, a matter of minutes into our impromptu parking lot romp, and I was scratching the headliner of his two-hundred-thousand-dollar SUV with the tips of my thirty-dollar nails.

I draped my arms over his shoulders. On the verge of a sexual meltdown, I sank my fingertips into the flesh of his muscular back.

"Ohmygod," I exclaimed. "I'm..."

Before I finished my thought, my pussy tightened around his shaft. The next few strokes sent me into the sexual stratosphere. As I reached the pinnacle of climactic bliss, he continued to pound away.

An orgasm rushed through me like a tsunami overtaking a Japanese beach.

I let out a blood-curdling wail.

Overcome by the sudden surge of emotion, I blacked out momentarily. When I returned to a half-conscious state, my mind was a jumbled mess of mental jelly. He had officially fucked me senseless.

Mindless, I crawled off his lap. Sitting in my seat with shaking legs, I stared blankly at the sunshade. I raked my fingers through my hair and offered him an apologetic look. "That. Felt. Amazing."

He glanced at his lap.

I did the same.

Twitching with desire, his cock pointed at the heavens above. Before I could offer a helping hand, he peeled the condom away and began stroking himself with his right hand.

I'd never witnessed a man pleasuring himself. In awe of the sight, I watched with eager eyes. A few joyous moments and several tight-fisted strokes later, he ejaculated into the palm of his cupped left hand.

Repeatedly.

Flushed with a pang of odd sexual guilt for witnessing the act, I glanced at his face. Hoping for some type of confirmation that it was okay for me to have watched so enthusiastically, I waited for him to meet my gaze with approving eyes.

"Would you mind handing me a wipe?" he asked. "They're in the glove box."

Wondering if jacking off inside the car was a common occurrence, I opened the glove box. A package of leather interior wipes were all that was available.

I lifted the package. "One of these?"

"It's all I've got," he replied. "I keep them to wipe off the seats after my greasy-haired coworker gets out."

I handed him one. I glanced at the puddle of cum in the palm of his hand. It was a three-wipe operation.

I handed him two more. "Oh."

He cleaned up the mess and situated his slacks. After buckling his seatbelt, he looked at me and smirked. "Do you want some help with yours, or do you think you'll be alright?"

I mentally shot him a glare. Without looking, I retrieved the belt and buckled it. "I'm good."

"Yes," he said with a nod. "You sure are."

4

BRAXTON

Jacking off in my hand wasn't as satisfying as I wanted it to be. Disappointed somewhat in Anna's sexual stamina, I stared at my computer's monitor. As I recalled the highlights of my morning, Pratt stepped into my office.

The skin under his eyes was thin and dark. His hair—which was normally styled—was dry and unkempt. Wearing a look of defeat, he shuffled toward the closest chair.

"No good news?" I asked.

He poked a piece of candy in his mouth and neatly folded the wrapper before putting it in his back pocket. "Nope."

Performing surveillance on high-profile targets was one of the services I offered. Typically, I gathered information in support of someone's theory, and then provided photos and videos of the proof, at a price. Attorneys, actor's agents, and movie producers were a few of my typical clients.

My means of gathering inside information ranged from interviewing disgruntled spouses to bribing enemies, friends, and neighbors. My sources weren't always right. Some provided more accurate information than others.

Not yet convinced I'd acted on a bad tip, I searched for answers. "You were there the entire night?" I asked. "You never left once?"

"What? Left?" He looked at me like I'd punted his cat off the Vincent Thomas Bridge. "I was on assignment. You think I dipped out to Jack in the Box for a burger?"

"I'm just asking."

"Watched the place like a hawk from a little after seven last night until about thirty minutes ago."

"No movement whatsoever?" I asked. "No one came or went?"

"Nope." He lowered his backpack to the floor and took a seat by the window. "Nobody in, nobody out."

Gordon Pratt was one of the best there was. As a MARSOC Marine, the training he received in surveillance, countersurveillance, evasive driving, and hand-to-hand combat was the best the Nation had to offer. His twenty years of experience included time spent working side by side with the CIA, Navy SEALS, and the Army's elite Delta Force.

I squeezed a drop of Visine into each eye. "You look like shit."

"I'm worn the fuck out," he admitted. "Pisses me off that I hid in that tree line for twelve hours and all he did was take his dog out twice."

"You look like you haven't slept in a fucking week. Put some of this in your eyes." I tossed him the bottle of Visine. "What kind of dog?"

"I don't know." He put a drop in each eye. "I'm not a dog person. It was a little white poofy fucker with short legs."

As far as I knew, our target didn't have a dog. If he decided to get one, a "little white poofy fucker" didn't sound like something he'd pick.

"Did you get pictures?" I asked.

"Of what?"

I narrowed my gaze. "The dog."

"Sure did." He tossed me the bottle of Visine and reached for the backpack. "There wasn't much else to take pictures of, other than the neighbor chick southeast of him."

Pratt had two weaknesses that I was aware of.

Candy and beautiful women.

His addiction to lollipops and Jolly Ranchers didn't interfere with his ability to stay on task. Women, on the other hand, often did. On the rare occasion that he made a mistake, there was typically a beautiful woman involved.

I glared. "Explain to me how you could keep an eye on the objective if you were watching his neighbor?"

He pulled the camera from the bag and powered it on.

"I wasn't *watching* her," he insisted. "But I *saw* her. The sexy bitch was dressed in hooker heels, a bikini top, and a pair of cut-offs that fit her like a thong. She had tits the size of fucking cantaloupes, and she was walking a fucking leopard on a leash. Kind of tough not to see her."

He handed me the camera.

I scanned the pictures. Sure enough, the scantily dressed neighbor was quite a sight. The thirty-pound African Serval at her side was an oddity, no doubt. Even so, it wasn't enough of one to cause most men to tear their eyes away from her.

I flipped to the photo of our target walking the dog. The look on his face made one thing clear.

He lacked interest in what he was doing.

Zooming in for a closer look revealed the dog's pink collar and matching braided leather leash were fitted with what appeared to be diamonds. I held the camera at arm's length. "Look at the collar and the leash."

Pratt studied the picture. His face washed with embarrassment. "Not his dog, is it?"

Our target was an R&B artist with ties to a well-known street gang. He had been convicted of several acts of domestic violence and multiple counts of felony assault against various men. I doubted his choice of dogs would be Maltese, nor did I suspect his favorite color was pink.

"I'm guessing it's someone else's dog." I glanced at him and then shook my head. "Every time you get within eyeshot of a good-looking woman, the quality of your work goes to hell."

"I took that picture from the tree line at Bilmoor Court," he argued, hoping to save face. "It's a hundred yards from his house. Easy for you to zoom in on the fucker now and condemn me for what I couldn't see when I took that long-distance shot. With all the shit that's going on, I'm not on my A-game. Give me a break."

"What shit that's going on?"

"That Chinese virus. Fuckers are dropping like flies." He tossed his hands in the air. "We're all fucking doomed."

The virus he spoke of was extremely contagious and had proven to be rather deadly. Recently imposed travel restrictions assured the citizens it would remain contained in mainland China. For him to use fear of becoming infected as an excuse for being insubordinate was ludicrous.

"You should have zoomed in on that picture right after you took it." I gave him the camera and a look of disappointment at the same time. "That's my point. Your quality of work goes to hell when there's a woman involved."

"My quality of work goes to hell when I'm faced with a fight I can't win," he argued.

"What fight?"

"San Francisco is on lockdown," he said. "We're fucking next. Are you and I having the same conversation?"

San Francisco overreacted about *everything*. Surprised that he thought we'd be next for a lockdown, but not willing to accept it as an excuse for his shortcomings, I continued to glare.

"San Francisco is filled with a bunch of tree-hugging hippies," I mumbled. "They're on lockdown because they don't want their tofu and wheatgrass infected."

"But—"

"But nothing, Pratt. The chick with the big tits and the cat had your head elsewhere."

"You're one to talk, asshole." He shoved the camera in the bag and faced me. He raised his hands and spread his fingers wide. "I need more fingers if I'm going to count all the women you've fucked in the past year."

I raised my brows. "We're not talking about me."

He crossed his arms over his chest. "Yes, we are."

Very few men could challenge me and get away with it. Pratt was one of them. We respected one another deeply but argued and fought like brothers. At times, it was difficult for me to make a point without getting in an argument about it.

I cleared my throat. "I'm talking about how every time you've been deficient, there's a woman—"

"Jesus, Rourke. You stick your dick in every woman you meet," he said with a laugh. "How can you complain about me?"

I gave him a serious look. "Women don't have an effect on my ability to perform my job."

He coughed out a laugh. "How could they? You're the king of one-night stands. Mister pump and dump."

He was right. I hadn't had sex with a woman more than once since my divorce, nor did I have any intention of doing so. Having sex beyond a "one and done" was a recipe for disaster.

"You should try it," I said. "The lack of distractions keeps me from missing shit like the diamond-studded collar on that Maltese."

"I didn't miss the collar," he replied. "I just hadn't noticed the fucker yet."

"I'm guessing the owner of that dog is the woman we're hoping to catch him with. If we get pictures of those two together, it pays sixty grand. We need to get some wireless cameras on that place. You can take your portion of the proceeds and buy a plastic bubble to live in. That'll alleviate any concerns you've got about the virus."

"Fuck you," he replied dryly. "I'll set some cameras up this evening."

"Go back there and do it now," I insisted. "Who knows where they'll be this evening."

"You want me to go back there now?" He gave me a look. "In broad daylight?"

"You're resourceful. I'm sure you'll get something figured out."

"I'll get it done and then I'm going home to get some sleep." He started to turn away, but hesitated. "Are you coming or going?"

"Excuse me?"

"You haven't taken your jacket off." He crossed his arms. "Are you coming, or are you going?"

"I just got here."

He checked his watch. "It's noon."

"I was tied up at the police station until a few minutes ago."

He slung the bag over one shoulder. "Doing what?"

"Some shithead was trying to carjack the neighbor on my way in this morning. I grabbed the guy before he got very far. O'Malley came by and picked him up. I had to go to the station and fill out a report."

"The girl next door?" He sauntered to the edge of my desk. "The chick you thought was a realtor but ended up being the daughter of your neighbors? The one with all the hair?" He tapped his index finger against his lip as if he were thinking. "Let's see. Small waist, perky tits, and a *ferocious ass*. Her?"

"She'd be the one."

He threaded his free arm through the loose strap. He studied me for a moment, and then shook his head in disbelief. "You fucked her, didn't you?"

I grinned. "In the diner's parking lot."

His brows raised. "Any good?"

"Fan-fucking-tastic," I bragged. "Not much stamina, though."

"Single?"

"Yep."

"Probably hasn't had any dick in a while," he said. "Didn't you say her parents were from Oklahoma?"

"That's correct."

"She'd be just like those girls in Iraq that looked at us like they wanted to fucking eat us. Bet she lives in a farmhouse in the middle of no-fucking-where with a bunch of dirty-assed goats and a couple of cows. Probably not a man for miles. Her little pussy was wet the minute you saved her from the carjacker."

I coughed out a laugh. "Dirty-assed goats?"

He nodded. "I saw one up close in Afghanistan. Believe me, they're nasty little fuckers."

"I'll take your word for it."

"Anyway." He adjusted the weight of the pack. "Sounds like she was starving for some dick."

"She said it'd been two years."

His face contorted. "Since she's had any cock?"

"That's what she said."

He seemed confused. "I thought you said she was cute as fuck. Little spinner with a banging body and badass hair.

"She is."

He took a step back and scratched the side of his head with his fingertips. "Cute as fuck and she hasn't had any dick in two years?"

"That's what she said."

"You never want to be the guy that takes a chick off a dry spell." He shook his head and looked away. "You're going to have a clinger on your hands."

"She lives in Oklahoma," I replied. "She won't be clinging to me."

"After a two-year dry spell, you fucked her in the parking lot of the diner." He laughed. "She isn't going back to Oklahoma. At least not right away. She's going to spend the next few weeks banging on your door every time her twat gets that itch."

"She's going back Tuesday."

"Already got her plane ticket?"

"She's driving. I think she's planning on taking some stuff home with her. Said the drive relaxes her."

"Probably afraid of catching the virus at the airport," he said. "Smart girl."

"Not another word about that fucking virus, goddamn it."

"Fine," he snapped back. "So, this chick's leaving in five days, huh?"

"That's what she said."

"My money says she's staying. She'll have her neighbors feed her nasty little goats and she'll stay here hoping for one more chance at that dick. She'll come up with a bullshit reason for not leaving. Needs to meet with a realtor and can't get an appointment, taking some time to rethink her life's mission, need to repaint the kitchen, *something*."

If I had one weakness it was gambling, and Pratt knew it. I didn't bet on everything, only what I truly believed in or felt I could control through manipulation. Subsequently, I rarely lost a bet.

"Your money says she's staying?"

"Yep."

"How much of your money?"

He puffed his chest. "Hundred bucks."

"Make it a grand," I said.

He gave me a side-eyed look. "How good did you fuck her? Give her a little bit of forgetful dick, or did you fuck her like she was the last piece of ass on earth?"

"I beat her shallow little pussy to a pulp. Left depressions in the headliner of my car where her pretty little head hit it," I replied. "Fucked her until she couldn't see straight."

"I'll take that bet." He extended his hand. "She isn't going anywhere."

I'd made myself clear. The sex was a one-time affair. If I made the mistake of fucking her again, Pratt may be right. All I needed to do to win the bet was keep my dick in my pants for the next six days.

I shook his hand. "It's a bet."

5

ANNA

Sex with Braxton began as an itch that needed scratching. Nevertheless, in the twenty-four hours that followed since we did the dirty, I identified three reasons that assured me walking away from him wasn't going to be a simple task.

First, the fact that he saved me from being harmed—or even killed—caused me to gravitate toward him. I dismissed it as being some weird psychological issue comparable to the Stockholm Syndrome. I'd emotionally attached myself to my savior. It was probably a textbook reaction to the situation, but it wasn't something I was accustomed to.

Second, although he was breathtakingly handsome, his attractive qualities went well beyond his looks. His calm demeanor allowed me to immediately be comfortable in his presence. The willingness he possessed to intervene and go face-to-face with danger was another attractive quality. Then, there was his job, which I found fascinating.

Lastly, the size, shape, and girth of his dick ruined me from ever being satisfied by anything lesser. I hated to name something so trivial as an outstanding quality, but Braxton's cock was nothing short of prick perfection. Had it been larger, it wouldn't have worked. If it were any smaller, I would have enjoyed it, but not to the point that I'd go to drastic measures for another chance at sex with him.

Eager for one more dose of what Braxton Rourke had to offer, I'd devised a foolproof plan to get into his pants one more time.

In search of a set of sockets, I walked into the garage. Beyond the new SUV, a row of red toolboxes was situated against the wall. Seeing them sparked memories of my childhood.

My father spent his life turning ugly vehicles into gorgeous works of art. The owner of one of the Midwest's most sought-after auto body repair shops, he reconstructed wrecked cars and restored yesteryear's rusty heaps into show cars.

Until I left for college, I'd spent much of my spare time at my father's side retrieving the tools he needed to complete the job he'd been tasked with.

Socket set.

Center box, far left drawer, second from the top.

I opened the drawer. The row of chrome-plated sockets was neatly placed in the center of the foam-lined tray. I removed them and opened the drawer to the right.

The ratchets of various lengths each performed different duties. The long-handled versions provided leverage, whereas the short-handled varieties limited the amount of torque that could be applied to a fastener. Others were fitted with a swivel joint, which allowed the tool's shape to be manipulated for use in awkward places where a conventional ratchet would not fit.

Shrouded with a blanket of sadness regarding my father's untimely death yet filled with warmth from memories of spending time with him, I walked into the house with the tools I needed.

While listening to the latest COVID-19 updates on the television, I propped the frame of the couch on a stack of books, relieving all the weight from the front leg. After carefully removing the hex nuts that attached the leg to the frame, I lowered the couch onto the crippled leg. I then moved the books to the opposite end of the couch and loosened the nuts on the other leg.

Satisfied that my ploy was fault-free, I carried the tools to the garage. Upon returning, I poured a glass of wine and stared blankly at the television. I needed a few gulps of courage before I continued with my plan.

While I drank the glass of wine, the newscaster gave an update on the COVID-19 crisis. *"ABC-7 has confirmed that 143 more individuals in the state of Washington have tested positive for the COVID-19 virus, bringing the total to 1,521. The novel virus, which originated in Wuhan, China, has been described as having flulike symptoms for most of those who have contracted it. Those above the age of eighty should consider the virus to be of serious nature. We'll have the full story, including the imposed lockdown of San Francisco, at three minutes after the hour."*

The television went to a commercial. I took a healthy drink and then another. I wondered why 1,521 people being infected with a strain of the flu in Seattle, Washington caused the people in San Francisco to overreact and force people to stay in their homes.

I shrugged it off as being ridiculous.

I finished my wine. After mussing my hair and unbuttoning the top two buttons of my blouse, I used water from the faucet to cause my cheap mascara to run down my cheeks. Then, I got the nuts and washers from the living room and headed out the door.

I hoped my shoddy appearance and alcohol-laced breath would convince Braxton that I was masking the sorrow of losing my parents in alcohol. He'd then feel sorry for me, and a pity fuck would ensue.

With a tangled head of hair and mascara dripping along both sides of my face, I made my way toward Braxton's home. Hopeful that he'd easily be lured into my trap, I stumbled up his walk and onto his porch.

I rang his doorbell and took a step away from the door. Bathed in light from the home's landscape, I cradled the fasteners in the palm of my hand and waited for him to arrive.

At ten o'clock on a Thursday night, I hoped Braxton would be dressed in something other than a suit. Jeans and a wife-beater were my hope.

I'd settle for sweats and a tee shirt.

The door opened.

He was wearing black slacks and a white dress shirt. His hair was mussed. The length of his beard was a little shorter than the day we met. Now trimmed to nothing more than a layer of salt-and-pepper stubble, it revealed the outline of his strong jaw.

He raked his fingers through his hair. "What's going on?"

I suppressed the urge to tackle him in the doorway. I extended my open hand. "My couch burped these out when I sat on it. Now it just flops at one end."

He glanced at my hand and then at my face. He chuckled. "You look like hell."

I hiccupped. "Thanks."

He leaned forward and took a deeper look at my face. "Is there a problem other than the couch?"

I perceived death differently than most people. I wasn't pleased with the circumstances surrounding my parents' death, but their dying was unavoidable. Spending days upon days crying about it wasn't my way of grieving. To cause Braxton to feel sympathetic I could snivel a little bit, though.

"It's just...I don't know..." I stammered. I lowered my head and pinched my eyes shut tight. After squeezing out the remnant of a tear, I looked up. "It's just...it's hard. His tools are in the garage, but...I don't know if..." I gave a half-assed shrug. "I don't want to see the car."

He scooped the nuts and washers from my hand. "Please." He moved aside. "Come in."

I stepped inside his bright and beautifully decorated home.

"Let me grab a few tools," he said, turning away. "I'll be right back."

The open floorplan was much different than my parents', which was divided by so many partition walls that it seemed like a maze.

The floors in Braxton's home—which seemed to go on forever—were covered in gray hardwood. The walls were painted white, as was the trim. The kitchen, in plain view from where I stood, was fitted with white marble countertops and white cabinetry. Various shades of blue and gray subway tile were used for the backsplash.

I glanced around. The entire home was decorated with wonderful pieces of abstract art. One in particular—a powdery gray canvas with a lone woman in a red dress—caught my eye. A stark white umbrella was cradled over her shoulder.

I wondered if he purchased the home in the condition it was in, or if he had it remodeled to suit him. While I admired the painting, he returned.

"That's my favorite piece," he said. "Rather fitting, considering everything."

"What do you mean?" I asked.

He studied the painting. "What do you see when you look at it? Is there a story in there, somewhere?"

"I don't know," I responded. "I was trying to figure it out."

He nodded toward it. "Take a good look at it."

I gazed at the painting, seeing nothing more than a woman in a red dress standing in the rain. My appreciation of art was deep, but my ability to express it was nonexistent.

I let out a sigh. "I'm lost."

"Hidden in those shades of gray there are several people beyond her, in the street," He explained. "They're all wearing black. Their umbrellas are upright. She's wearing bright red, and her umbrella is draped over her shoulder. Although you can't see her face, you get the feeling that she's vibrant and filled with life. Excluding her, everyone in that painting is sheltered from the storm. As far as she's concerned, the weather isn't bad enough to raise her umbrella." He rubbed the side of his stubble-covered jaw with his fingertips. "Life is only as terrible as you perceive it as being."

His explanation—and the painting—were beautiful. I was now

teary-eyed for real, and for no good reason. I wiped my eyes with the knuckle of my index finger.

I admired him as he continued to look at the painting. In expressing his feelings about the artwork, he'd exposed an intellectual side of himself that I hadn't seen yet. It may have been his most attractive quality.

I reveled in his words while he appreciated the faceless girl in the red dress. Eventually, he turned to face me.

"I'm going to lower my umbrella," I said.

He flashed what could have been perceived as a smile. "I don't own one."

It was obvious that he ran into the face of the storm regardless of the forecast. I smirked at his remark. "I'm sure you don't."

He gestured toward the door with a wrench. "Let's go have a look at your couch."

Side by side—and without small talk—we meandered to my home. Emotionally crushed by his lack of expressed interest in me, I opened the door and gestured inside.

He walked past me and lowered himself to the floor. He rolled up his sleeves and surveyed the damage. "This should just take a minute."

Unwilling to accept my fate as being nothing more than a needy neighbor, I knelt at his side. I strategically positioned myself to give him an unobstructed view of my new push up bra.

He didn't so much as look in my direction.

Knowing more is always better, I unbuttoned one more button on my blouse while he was distracted.

He offered not so much as a glance.

In a last-ditch effort to gain his interest, I leaned over so far that I nearly toppled to the floor. I braced myself to keep from falling.

He stood and dusted off his sleeves. "Well, I guess that's it."

I wanted him to want me as much as I wanted him. With my face was covered in cheap mascara, my blouse unbuttoned to my navel, and my hair a mess, it wasn't going to happen.

My plan was backfiring.

I'd lured him to the home with lies and deception. It was time for me to face the facts. I looked like an idiot and he wasn't interested.

He handed me the stack of hardback books I'd left on the floor beneath the couch. "I'm guessing you were trying to stabilize the couch with these?"

"Yes," I lied, setting the books aside. "I was."

He picked up his tools and took a look around.

His strengths went well beyond his bulging biceps, big cock, and broad chest. A glass of wine and thirty minutes of small talk would be much better than a phony couch repair and an immediate departure.

Willing to accept whatever I could get, I decided to strike up some idle chat and go from there.

"This place is a lot different than yours," I said, glancing from one wall to the other. "Not as bright and open."

"Mine looked like this when I bought it," he replied. "I spent three months turning it into what it is now."

Hoping to lure him to the wine, I stepped into the hallway and turned toward the kitchen. "I can't believe you got a contractor to do all that work in three months. I called last week about having the upstairs bathroom remodeled and I was told it would be six months before they could come look at it."

"I did it myself."

I spun around. "All of it?"

"Every bit."

"Of course you did," I said with a laugh.

His eyes narrowed. "What does that mean?"

"You're like a superhero."

"Which superhero?"

"Not any of the ones who exist." I folded my arms under my chest, and then realized I was shoving what little exposed breast flesh I possessed out the top of my unbuttoned blouse. I acted like I didn't know. "You're a new one altogether."

He gave me a curious look. "What's my name?"

"I don't know," I responded. "I like *The Gray Fox*, but it's not descriptive enough and it's kind of cliché."

"The Gray Fox?" He laughed. "That's a good one."

"Captain Cockstrong," I said. "How's that? You'd wear a tight-fitting red spandex bodysuit with two overlapping C's on your chest. One end of each letter would be shaped like the head of a dick."

His brows pinched together. "Isn't cockstrong a term that's used to describe someone who is strong because of testosterone buildup due to lack of sexual activity?"

"I don't know." I shrugged. "Probably. I just liked how it sounded."

"Captain Cockstrong would achieve his superpower from abstinence," he explained. "You should probably pick something else."

His comment should have struck me as playful or cute. Instead, it struck a nerve.

I shot him a glare. "Are you promiscuous?"

He scratched his beard. "I could be described as such, yes."

My face flushed hot. Other than voluntarily providing details of my two-year hiatus from sex, we hadn't discussed our sexual activities. I now wished I hadn't said a word. Nevertheless, he'd admitted to being nothing short of a pig.

I raised my brows in false wonder. "Oh, really?"

"I told you I was ugly when it came to relationships," he replied. "I wasn't lying."

I pressed my hands to my hips. "Being ugly in a relationship has nothing to do with sexual promiscuity."

"I tried marriage once," he said, seeming to recall the experience. "I have no business in a relationship. Knowing that about myself allows me to be honest when it comes to sex. I told you it was a one-time thing between us. I didn't lie to you."

"I didn't accuse you of it," I snapped back.

He looked me up and down. "Why are you pissed off?"

"I'm not," I huffed.

"Are you sure?" he asked, looking me up and down. "Because I don't want you to be."

Wine and small talk was out of the question. Walking away before I developed feelings for him was the only answer. Anything more, and I'd only be hurt.

"I'm fine." I hurried to the door and snatched it open. "Thanks for fixing the couch. I appreciate it."

"I don't want to leave if you're mad."

"I'm not mad," I insisted.

He gave me a look of disbelief. "You're sure?"

I stepped to the side. "Positive."

He offered a shallow nod and turned away. "I'll take your word for it," he said. "Have a nice night, Anna."

I watched him saunter away. Each step he took was a reminder that he had no interest in indulging my sexual desires. When he disappeared behind the shrubbery that separated our yards, I closed the front door and locked it.

My hands balled into fists. I turned toward the kitchen. Despite the outward appearance of my clenched teeth, white knuckles, and mascara-covered face, I wasn't mad.

I was disappointed.

6

BRAXTON

Monday mornings were filled with phone calls and cryptic text messages from clients who made regretful choices over the weekend. Presented with an opportunity to make $80,000 before the sun went down, I silenced my phone and slipped it into my pocket.

"She needs to be brought to my office as promptly as practicable," Crenshaw explained. "Following her safe removal from the home, her male friend needs to be made aware that avoiding her in the future will be paramount in assuring his continued existence on this earth."

Robert Crenshaw was the attorney of choice for LA County's upper crust. Professional sports stars, musicians, actors, movie producers and celebrities of all types utilized his services.

He rarely went to trial, but when he did, he embarrassed the opposition.

The epitome of good health and sound mind, he wore his age of sixty-two years extremely well. An intimidating man in and out of the courtroom, the mere mention of his name caused the DA's office to cringe. His stature and the stern look permanently etched on his face caused everyone else to do so.

A small portion of his time was spent defending legal cases. The remainder of it was devoted to making problems disappear long before his clients were charged with a crime.

Facing the desk, Pratt stood in the far corner of Crenshaw's office, attempting to peel the wrapper off a miniature sucker he'd received from a bank teller.

Seated in a chair at the opposite side of the office, I mulled over the proposed assignment.

Pratt pulled the sucker past his lips with a *pop!* "This is the same girl we picked up three or four years ago? Over and over?" He looked at the lollipop like he'd never seen one before. After a thorough inspection, he poked the blue candy sphere back into his mouth. "The producer's daughter? Weinberg, or whatever his name is?"

Crenshaw diverted his attention from the stack of paperwork he held. "That is correct. Mica Weinberg."

"She's got to be, what, twenty-one years old?" I asked.

"Twenty-two," Crenshaw replied, meeting my gaze. He seemed annoyed that I'd asked. "Why?"

The last time I'd seen Weinberg's daughter she was seventeen years old.

The first time we found her, a San Diego Chargers VIP aftergame party had turned into a week-long session of her abusing drugs, screwing half the football team, and allowing them to record the events in a video. We removed her, the recordings, and her father's wrecked Bentley from the estate.

Upon learning her age, we were both shocked. Lip injections, breast enhancement surgery, and an endless high-end wardrobe allowed her to pass for being much older.

At the time, keeping her whereabouts out of the news was her father's main concern.

Three weeks later, we found her in the bed of an up-and-coming recording artist, naked. Her clothes, purse, and Maserati were nowhere to be found.

Three months later, a matter of weeks before her high school graduation, she'd disappeared again. Topless and sprawled out beside the pool of a professional basketball player's Torrey Pines mansion, she seemed to be having the time of her life.

"The last time you had us pick her up, she was a senior in high school," I explained. "Now, she's an adult. She can do whatever she pleases. Weinberg might not like it, but he doesn't have any say in the matter."

Crenshaw set the paperwork aside and sharpened his gaze. "He certainly does have a say in the matter. He's her father. He's concerned with her coming in contact with someone who may be infected."

"With what?" I asked.

"COVID-19, of course," he replied.

Pratt glanced in my direction and raised his brows. I felt like laughing but refrained. I shifted my attention to Crenshaw. "COVID-19, of course."

"Are we in agreement?" he asked.

"To what extent are we to encourage the boyfriend to keep his distance?" I asked.

Crenshaw locked eyes with me. "Whatever length is necessary."

"Make it a hundred grand," I said. "If this guy lives in Calabasas, he's not some low-level thug. This won't be a walk in the park. It's going to take some planning."

He shifted his gaze to Pratt.

Pratt pulled the sucker from his mouth. "It'll be a bitch. Surveillance. Half a day of recon. One man extracts the girl while two or three others secure the residence and its occupants. Then, there's the boyfriend. I don't know the guy, but my guess is if he's in some Calabasas mansion, he's wrapped up in something illegal. Probably drugs. With dope, there's always guns. The dope and guns mix means he'll be crazy and armed. It's not a good combination. He's going to be pissed that we're taking his flavor of the month. Violence and torture will be the only way to—"

"Stop!" Crenshaw raised his hand as if offended by Pratt's

theories. "I don't want to hear the details." He looked at me. "Fine. Return her to my office without harm. One hundred thousand."

I stood. I tugged the wrinkles from the sleeves of my jacket. "I'll be in touch."

Calabasas was home to many who saw inner Los Angeles as overcrowded and violent. The city contained an eclectic mixture of properties. Modular homes in a mobile home park sold for $250,000, while golf community mansions were listed for $25,000,000 or more. Situated in a neighborhood on a hill, the boyfriend's residence was a secluded home valued at $12,000,000.

The large trees and lush landscape filling the half-acre lot gave the owner a sense of separation from the remote neighbors. The dense foliage provided us reassurance that our actions weren't going to end up recorded by a neighbor—and then appear on the six o'clock news.

Pleased that there wasn't a gate to contend with, I eased my way up the palm tree-lined brick driveway. I came to a stop at the front of the sprawling Mediterranean residence no differently than if I owned the place.

Pratt methodically screwed the silencer to the end of his pistol's barrel. He shoved the weapon into the holster hidden inside his name-emblazoned work coat. He reached for his utility belt. "I'll follow your lead."

I exited the vehicle and looked the place over. The landscape—and the home's exterior—were meticulously maintained. I caught Pratt's gaze and turned toward the house. Clutching an aluminum clipboard in his left hand, he accompanied me to the front door.

As I searched for the doorbell, the door opened. A lean twenty-something Latina female stood in the opening.

Loose-fitting gray sweats hung low on her shapely hips. A ribbed white tank clung to her unsupported breasts. Upon seeing us, she raked her fingers through the sides of her curly shoulder-length brown hair.

"Good afternoon." Wearing an ever so slight smile, she alternated glances between us. "How can I help you?"

She had no discernable accent and spoke with humble authority. I wondered if she was one of the boyfriend's many female companions.

I reached into my jacket and produced a business card. The official-looking ADT Security cards had proven useful on many previous similar occasions.

"We're with ADT Security," I said, handing her the card. "Can we speak with the owner of the home?"

She studied the card. Upon satisfying herself that it was legitimate, she met my gaze with a smile. "I'm Sophia Santos," she said. "The homeowner."

The home was listed as being owned by Samuel Santos. Instead of challenging her, I nodded in agreement.

"We've had a series of problems with the security systems in the area that were installed between 2005 and 2015," I explained. "Sadly, the motherboard isn't allowing the system to communicate with the main switchboard during an intrusion. We're in the neighborhood this morning hoping to check the sequence numbers of all applicable systems. If it's in need of replacement, we'll get it scheduled for first thing next week with the repair division. May we come in? It should only take a few minutes."

She stepped aside. "Absolutely."

I removed two protective Tyvek booties and slipped them over my shoes. Pratt did the same.

"That isn't necessary." She gestured toward the living room. "Come in."

We followed her inside the expansive home. Other than furnishings, it appeared no differently than it did in the photos from the home's previous real estate listing we'd reviewed thirty minutes prior.

The open floorplan allowed the rear of the home to be viewed from where we stood. A group of scantily clad women—one of which I recognized as Weinberg's daughter—were poolside, drinking margaritas and lounging in the sun.

Mica being surrounded by women who were giggling at each other's stories was far different than being pumped full of drugs by a sex-crazed member of the Sinaloa Cartel. Luring her away from the pool party without raising eyebrows wasn't going to be a simple task.

Before I did anything, I needed to find out where the true homeowner was, and what his ties to Mica were.

"We have a few documents that will need to be signed after completing the survey," I explained. "The system is registered to Samuel Santos. If it won't be too much trouble, we'd like to get him to sign the work order once we're finished."

"Sam's my brother," she replied. "He's upstairs."

Pratt tapped his index finger against the clipboard. "Let's get him to sign this while Jake is checking the main panel."

"Sure," Sophia said. She turned toward the staircase. "Follow me."

The last place Pratt needed to be was upstairs with the braless Brazilian beauty. While they laughed and joked their way up the stairs, I turned toward the garage. "I'll check the serial number on the panel."

Getting Mica away from the pool without someone recording the incident on their phone would be a challenge. I walked toward the garage, surveying each room for security cameras as I passed. Upon reaching the panel, I opened the cover and mulled over potential scenarios to lure Mica into the home.

Two minutes later, Sophia's screams caused my sphincter to pucker.

"Jake!" Pratt bellowed. "Get up here!"

If I learned one thing in my thirty years in the Marine Corps, it was to expect the unexpected. Even so, when I reached the room where Pratt was located, I stared in disbelief.

Sophia and Samuel were seated on the floor between the desk and where I stood. Their wrists and ankles were bound with tie straps, and their mouths were covered with tape.

Samuel, a lean man with olive-colored skin, was wearing dark gray slacks and a pressed white shirt that was splattered with fresh blood stains. The source appeared to be a two-inch gash beneath his left eye, on the upper portion of his cheek.

I scanned the room. Obviously used as an office or study, there were matching bookshelves on two opposing walls. Each were filled with hardbound books from top to bottom. Situated in front of a picturesque window, a large wooden desk was free of clutter. In one corner, there was a two-inch stack of neatly situated paperwork. In the center, a cell phone. Those two items were all that littered the surface.

I looked at Pratt. Clutching his pistol in his right hand, he shook his head in clear disbelief of the situation.

I shifted my gaze from Pratt to the bound siblings. "What the fuck happened, Jared?"

He holstered his pistol. "I told dumbfuck that we were going to be taking Mica. He didn't seem to give a fuck. His sister, on the other hand, started screaming like I was pulling off her fingernails with a pair of pliers. She wouldn't shut up, so I smacked her in the throat. He got all pissed off because I hit her. Fucker charged at me like a raging bull. I had to bust him in the face before he spider monkeyed me."

Our option pool was shallow when we arrived. It seemed all but non-existent now. Having Samuel lure Mica in from the pool party was the only scenario that originally came to mind. If she saw him with a two-inch gash on his cheek, it would only be a matter of minutes before everyone at the pool had their cell phones out, filming the event as it unfolded. In Samuel's absence, getting Mica away from the pool without arching the eyebrows of her scantily clad poolside friends would be difficult, if even possible.

Frustrated, I shot Pratt a glare. "What's your plan for getting her away from the pool?"

Like a scolded dog, his gaze fell to the floor. He scratched the sides of his head for a moment before looking up. "Not sure."

Regardless of the manner in which we coerced Mica away from the pool, Samuel needed to be made aware that her departure would be permanent. I stepped in front of him and crossed my arms over my chest.

"We're taking Mica Weinberg with us," I said in a stern tone. "Under no circumstances will she be permitted to return to this residence. Regardless of the reasoning behind it, if she's allowed into this home at any time in the future, my friend Jared will come back. If you speak to the police about our visit, he'll come back. If he comes back, neither of you will live to tell the story of what happened. Is that understood?"

His eyes darted to his sister. Mine followed. After the two of them shared an awkward look, she met my gaze. Her brown eyes were filled with worry.

She nodded.

Somewhat confused as to why she was acknowledging my request instead of her brother, I alternated glances between Samuel and Sophia. They both returned worried looks. Sophia's won the award for the most theatrical presentation.

I shifted my eyes from her to Pratt. "What the fuck's going on here?"

He chuckled. "Looks like Sophia and Mica are bumping uglies."

I glanced at Sophia and raised my brows. "Are you intimate with Mica?"

Her eyes shot to her brother.

"Don't look at him," I said in a demanding tone. "I asked you a question."

With some hesitation, she nodded.

I didn't care which one of them was in a relationship with Mica.

All that mattered was that they understood the repercussions associated with continuing the relationship.

"In the future, if she calls, you won't answer," I explained. "If she sends you a text, don't respond. In fact, blocking her number would be in your best interest."

Repeating myself was a pet peeve. Nevertheless, making sure Sophia fully understood the severity of the punishment for any continued relationship involving Mica was critical. "Just to make sure you fully understand, I'll repeat what I've already told your brother. We're taking Mica with us. Under no circumstances will she be permitted to return. Regardless of the reasoning behind it, if you let her in this home, Jared will come back here. If you talk to the cops about our visit, he'll come back. If he comes back, he'll likely kill you, your brother, and anyone else that's here. Is that understood?"

She nodded again.

I was taught to never raise my hand to a woman. After seeing the damage first-hand that a woman was willing to inflict on a US Marine, I realized in matters of my work that both sexes must receive equal treatment. Ghosts of my past often prevented me from physically coercing women to comply with our desires. Through the course of completing a mission, Pratt had no qualms treating a woman no differently than a man.

I fixed my eyes on Sophia and sharpened my gaze. "I'm going to take the tape off your mouth. If you do anything other than speak softly, you'll regret it," I warned. "Understood?"

She gave an eager nod.

I pulled the tape away from her mouth with a yank. "Where's your cell phone?"

"Downstairs," she said, her voice cracking as she spoke. "In the...I think it's in the kitchen."

"Describe it."

"It's an iPhone 10," she replied. "It has a gold jeweled case."

Assuming she had pictures and video footage of Mica, securing her phone and eliminating all necessary data would be an essential step in assuring neither Mica nor her father would be compromised—or blackmailed—in the future.

I motioned toward the door with my eyes. "Go get the phone, Jared."

He returned in a moment with Sophia's bedazzled iPhone. He tossed it to me no differently than if he was throwing me a piece of his beloved candy.

I cut the strap from Sophia's wrists and handed her the phone. "Unlock it and delete your cloud storage," I demanded. "Is it backed up to your laptop?"

She shook her head. "No."

I narrowed my gaze. "If it is—"

"It's not," she insisted, nearly coming to tears. "I swear."

Being located by the police "pinging" a stolen cell phone led to the downfall of many low-level criminals. Removing the battery was the only way to assure a phone couldn't be traced. Performing the task with any phone other than the iPhone was simple.

Apple's phones were sealed with adhesive, making their disassembly nothing short of impossible without proper tools. I had a specially designed kit that would dislodge the screen—allowing removal of the battery—in a matter of minutes.

I looked at Pratt. "Grab the iPhone kit."

I watched Sophia delete the saved data from her cloud. When she was done, I held out my hand. She extended hers, offering me the phone, and then hesitated. "Will I get it back?"

"Afraid not," I said.

I tucked her phone into my inner jacket pocket and reached for my wallet. I removed two thousand dollars in cash and tossed it on the desk behind her.

"There's two thousand bucks." The 100-dollar bills fluttered onto the desk's surface like dry leaves. "You can each buy a new one."

Tool kit in hand, Pratt hustled into the room. The first thing he noticed was the money. He nodded toward the desk. "What's with the cash?"

"I'm paying her for her phone."

"Fuck her," he said. "She screamed."

"You probably startled her."

"She could have got us busted."

"He scared me," Sophia offered.

Pratt's eyes darted in her direction. "Who the fuck asked you?" He looked at me. "Why's the tape off her mouth?"

"I had to ask her questions," I responded.

He gave me a look. "You done?"

"I suppose."

He removed the roll of duct tape from his utility belt and tore off a six-inch strip. After stretching it over Sophia's mouth he glared at me. "Last thing we need is for her to start screaming again. Or spitting the virus on us." He glanced at his watch. "We've been here five minutes too long as it is. We need to get."

"Enough about that fucking virus." I tossed him the phone. "Here. Get to work."

I grabbed the other phone from the desk and gave it to Samuel. "Same thing for you. Delete your cloud storage."

He complied with my demands without question. I gave Pratt the phone. After splitting the phone cases and removing both batteries, he pocketed the phones.

"What now?" he asked.

In my opinion, we had only one option. Sophia was going to have to lure Mica away from the pool.

"She's going to get Mica to come up here," I responded. "Alone."

"I don't like it," Pratt responded. "She could pull some stupid shit." He gestured to her with his eyes. "She's not above it, she already proved it."

"Got a better idea?" I asked.

"What about the Olympic soccer chick? Do it like that?"

It wasn't a bad idea at all. Disappointed that I hadn't thought of it, I gave Pratt a reassuring look.

"I like it," I said. "One of us will need to stay in here." I gestured to the doorway. "Grab the masks. Let's get it done."

Two years prior, we were faced with the necessity to extract a client from a Brentwood house party. After a few hours of surveillance and much consideration, we opted to raid the residence wearing Halloween masks. Since then, we'd kept the masks in our arsenal of tools.

Pratt returned with two masks. He tossed the Brian Cranston "Heisenberg" mask to me. He quickly donned the realistic-looking Jennifer Anniston mask and adjusted the eyeholes into place.

"Be back in a minute," he said in a muffled tone.

In a few moments, the sound of women screaming caused Sophia to wince. Illegible demands from Pratt followed. More screaming. A muffled conversation. The sliding door slammed closed. The whimpering from the pool area fell silent.

"Let's go, Jake," Pratt shouted from below.

I pulled on the mask and gave the room's two occupants a nod. "Don't forget what I said. You don't want him to come back here, believe me."

I bounded down the steps two at a time and met Pratt at the vehicle. He opened the back door and tossed a bulging pillowcase inside. Wearing an orange bikini and sandals, Mica stood at his side with an annoyed look on her face. A neon green leather bag was draped over one shoulder. Her bikini top was barely large enough to cover the nipples of her DD-cup breasts. The bottom was wedged between her butt cheeks, leaving ninety-nine percent of her youthful ass exposed. Half-naked and obviously annoyed, she had no apparent idea what was going on. The look on her face made it clear she didn't care to hear any details of why she was being dragged away from the home.

Wondering if being kidnapped was on her wish list, I took off my mask. Upon recognizing me, she smirked.

"I thought I was being kidnapped for ransom," she said, seeming disappointed. "I should have known I couldn't be so lucky. He'll never let me grow up." She looked at Pratt and then at me. "How much is he paying you?"

Trying to maintain a professional posture, I cleared my throat. "That's confidential."

She cocked her hip. "I'll give you more." She eyed me up and down before I could respond. "A lot more."

"Sorry," I replied. "We've got an agreement."

Pratt guided her into the back of the vehicle and climbed in at her side. I took the driver's seat and locked the doors.

"Are you taking me to that creepy attorney?" she asked. "To his office?"

I glanced at her reflection in the rearview mirror. "That's the plan."

"Oh, hell no," she snapped back. "Take me to your house. Or some random 7-Eleven. Have my dad pick me up somewhere or meet you, or whatever. Anything. That attorney's a fucking creep."

"Why do you say that?"

"Because," she replied. "He's gross."

"Our instructions were to deliver you to his—"

"He creeps me out," she whined.

"Sorry," I replied.

"He wants you to take me there so he can stare at my tits and make suggestive comments about sex," she complained. "He's nasty."

Her boobs were clearly intended to be the focal point of her sparse wardrobe. I had no idea how she expected someone to look elsewhere.

"Nasty or not," I replied. "He's the one who hired us."

"He. Tries. To. Fuck. Me," she interjected snidely. "He always rubbing his dick when he talks to me. If I go in there wearing this, he'll probably try to rape me. Do you want that to happen?" She glared at me through the rearview mirror. "Are you into that kind of crap?"

Despite his instructions to do so, taking her to Crenshaw's office now seemed like a terrible idea. Being creepy in a twenty-year-old's eyes was one thing. Forcing oneself upon them sexually was another. While I mulled over my options, Mica continued.

"Take me to your house," she said, appearing perturbed that I'd consider anything else. "Or just take me to my dad's."

Pratt rolled down the window and tossed the pillowcase and its contents onto the side of the road. "You can drop her off at my house," he said, fighting not to laugh. "I'll look after her."

I adjusted the rearview mirror and shot Pratt a glare. If she went with him, he'd be fucking her before I backed out of the driveway.

In my opinion, I had only one option. "I'll take you home with me," I said. "You'll be safe there."

"Safe?" She smirked. "Too bad I can't say the same about you."

7

ANNA

Giselle Rinke worked for one of LA's most prestigious realtors. Beyond her naturally pouty lips and oversized breasts, she was tall, blonde, and irresistibly sultry. She may have been a real estate agent by trade, but she could easily pass for a movie star.

While she and I walked through my parents' home, I told the tale of the parking lot fling with a silver-haired hunk who earned a living rubbing elbows with Hollywood's upper crust. Although I hadn't mentioned Braxton specifically, I'd thrown out a few names of people he'd met and described his line of work in detail.

Having seen all there was to see, we walked back to the starting point, the living room. She lowered herself into the loveseat and crossed her legs.

"His name isn't Braxton Rourke, is it?" she asked.

I was halfway to the couch. I stopped in my tracks. "This just got awkward." I looked at her. "You know him?"

"Everyone knows Braxton." She flattened her skirt against her thighs before looking up. "He's a local legend, of sorts."

Hoping to seem disinterested in discussing the matter further, I took a seat and scanned the living room. "I guess you can use that as a selling point for this home."

She laughed. "You want me to tell potential buyers that the homeowner had sex with Braxton Rourke?"

"No." I tilted my head toward the front door. "You can tell them that he lives next door. If he's a local legend, that could be enough to get them to make an offer."

"He lives next door?" she asked, obviously surprised by my announcement.

"He does."

Her eyes shot wide. She fidgeted in her seat. "Seriously?"

She was far too excited. My stomach flip-flopped at the thought of her and Braxton doing the dirty.

"You two haven't—" I wagged my finger toward the inside of her tanned thighs. "You didn't—"

"Oh. No. I'm just—" She cleared her throat. "A few years ago, I saw him on TV escorting Selena Gomez at the music awards. I couldn't help but notice that he had a very confident presence. I've been intrigued by him ever since. That's all."

Despite what she said, her face was flush with excitement. I wasn't convinced she was completely disinterested in Braxton.

"Intrigued," I said under my breath. "Yeah. He's intriguing, that's for sure."

"It's quite a little bonus that he's your neighbor," she said. "Did he come over and introduce himself? Is that how you met?"

"No. I was backing out of the driveway and a guy tried to steal my car. Braxton was driving by when it happened. He grabbed the guy and called the cops. While the police were processing the paperwork, we went to breakfast. I've already told you the rest of the story."

"Someone tried to steal your car?" Her face contorted. "Here?"

Having Braxton Rourke for a neighbor may have been good selling feature. The potential of having a car stolen out of the driveway wasn't.

"Yeah," I said dismissively. "It was some guy just passing through. I was backing out of the driveway with my window down. I must have looked like easy prey."

"Oh my God!" she exclaimed. "That wasn't a theft. It was a carjacking."

"Is one worse than the other?" I asked. "I guess I didn't realize there was a difference."

"He tried to take the car while you were in it, right?"

"That was his plan."

"It's a good thing you weren't hurt." She plucked a few pieces of fuzz from her skirt and then looked up. "At what point did Braxton show up?"

I envisioned her slinking her way to Braxton's house after I went back to Oklahoma. Following each showing of the home, she'd take her ample cleavage and full lips with her and sashay next door. Given her level of expressed interest, it was bound to happen.

Considering Braxton's promiscuity, he'd grant her sexual wish, but only once.

With slight reservation, I gave a few more details regarding the day in question. Elaborating enough to satisfy her wasn't going to hurt matters. There was nothing I could say to make her any more interested in Braxton than she already was.

"I was backing out of the driveway, and this tattooed guy leaned inside my car window. He was yelling at me to get out of the car," I explained. "The next thing I knew, someone yanked him away. Then, Braxton came into view and asked me to open my trunk—"

"Open your trunk?" She seemed perplexed. "Why?"

"He wanted to throw the guy in there to contain him."

She shook her head in disbelief. "That's got to be the craziest thing I've ever heard."

I laughed at the thought of it all. "It all happened pretty fast. It didn't seem odd at the time. Not really. He smacked the guy, choked him until he was passed out, and then zip-tied his hands and feet." I paused and considered what I'd said. "Now that I'm talking about it? Yeah, it seems kind of weird."

"He locked the guy in your trunk, and then the police showed up?" she asked.

"Yeah. The cops quickly recognized the guy. He'd just been released from prison. The officer in charge talked like the three-strikes law was going to make sure he was locked up for a long time."

"Hopefully he'll make a plea deal and you won't have to testify in court."

Testifying hadn't crossed my mind. I didn't like the thought of staying in California, going into a courtroom, or seeing the tattooed thug ever again. I swallowed the foul taste that came with the realization that at least two of those three things may happen.

"I hope he makes a plea deal, too," I admitted.

"So." Her brows raised. "Where do you and Braxton stand now?"

"What do you mean?"

"Are you two seeing each other?"

I let out a muted laugh. "No."

She seemed amused by my response. "Sore subject?"

"He's not interested in a relationship or anything that resembles a relationship," I replied. "I'm going to have to be satisfied with 'one and done' for once."

"One and done?" She gave me a side-eyed look. "Is that what you want? One and done?"

It wasn't at all what I wanted, but I wasn't the one making the decisions. Braxton was. I knew little about him, but I was sure there was no way on earth I could make him do something he didn't want to do.

"No, it's not," I admitted. "I'm not the one making the decisions, though."

She arched one of her perfectly plucked brows. "You could be."

I leaned forward. "How so?"

"Men want everyone to think they're in charge of things," she said. "They're not. We are."

The one with the pussy has the power. I'd heard the phrase before. The claim was myth, not fact. Although I'd had the pussy in all my relationships, I'd never had the power. The one with the dick was the decision maker. Always.

"I don't think Braxton will be too receptive to me suggesting we have sex again. I kind of tried that already." I exhaled until my shoulders slumped in defeat. "It backfired."

"Giving a man the opportunity to get laid is like offering a dog a steak," she explained. "No matter how disciplined he is, when no one's looking he'll take the offer."

"You're suggesting I get Braxton alone and offer him sex?"

"If you want more than a one and done with him, that's my suggestion."

It sounded like she knew what she was talking about. I mulled over the idea. In a moment, I quickly came to my senses.

"Two and done doesn't sound much better than one and done," I complained.

"Having him agree to sex is only half of it," she explained. "The other half—the key half—is how you do it."

"How I do what?"

"The sex."

She was talking in cryptic circles. Most of what she was saying—although interesting—made little sense.

"Can you elaborate?" I asked.

"Let's say you get him alone and offer him sex. He agrees. You hike up your skirt. He pulls his pants down to his thighs and gives it to you in the kitchen. That would probably secure you a 'two and done' position."

My curiosity vanished. I looked at her like she was nuts. "I'm confused. I'm not any more interested in a 'two and done' than I am a 'one and done.'"

"My point was that you can't just have sex with him." Her gaze hardened. "You've got to fuck him like you're trying to kill him."

"Kill him?" It sounded too good to be true. "I'm going to fuck him to death?"

"No, you'll just fuck him like you're *trying* to kill him," she clarified. She nonchalantly checked the clasp on her Cartier watch. "It's called a hate fuck. It's the only answer."

I choked on my spit. "Hate fuck?"

She stood. "Have you ever been frustrated enough to throw a utensil? Kick a door? Punch your fist deep into a pillow?"

I felt like I was watching a late-night informercial about acne cleansers. *Have you ever had to cancel a date? Felt embarrassed about going out in public? Given up on cleansers because they simply didn't work?*

I stood. "Yes, yes, and yes."

"Channel your frustration into fucking him." She reached into her purse. "You can either have basic sex and end it or you can fuck him like you're mad at him and secure your place in his life. It's sad that a man's life revolves around sex, but it does." She pulled out a business card and gave it a quick look. "They're all pigs."

We agreed on one thing, at least. Men were pigs. I reached for the card. "I like your way of thinking."

She pulled away. "I'll take the listing on the home, but only if you agree to keep me apprised of your progress."

"Do you really think this will work?"

"I know it will work." She smirked. "It's how I got my husband. It sounds like he and Braxton are—well, were—a lot alike."

"You're married?"

"Very much so."

I gestured toward her hand. "You don't wear a ring."

"It's better for business if I don't. More proof that men are pigs."

"I'll keep you informed," I said, reaching for the card. "But I have my doubts about this mission's success."

"My husband was a single thirty-five-year-old multi-millionaire who had no interest in being in a relationship. We met one night at a restaurant, of all places. We had an instant connection. He left the two men he was meeting with and took me out for drinks. The attraction was undeniable, so I agreed to sex. In the weeks that followed, I couldn't get him to do so much as answer my calls. Then, I saw him at a showing of a high-end estate. Based on the advice of a coworker, I fucked him like I was trying to kill him. The next day, my phone lit up like a Christmas tree."

"It was that easy?"

"I ghosted him for a week or two, afterward." She grinned slyly. "Men want what they can't have."

"Well," I said, pocketing the card. "I guess it's time for a hate fuck."

I waited for Braxton to return from work. Upon seeing his SUV drive past, my heart raced at the thought of implementing Giselle's plan.

With my fourth glass of liquid courage cradled in my hand, I nervously paced the living room. Eager to see him—but not wanted to seem so—I sipped my wine and wondered how long I should wait before I meandered to his door.

If I waited too long, he might leave. It wasn't uncommon for him to come and go throughout the evening and well into the night. If I went too soon, it would make it seem like I was staring through the window waiting for him to return.

Although my drunken face was plastered to the glass as he drove past, I didn't want him to realize it. I hoped to portray myself as someone who cared little about what happened between us, even if that wasn't necessarily the case.

I finished my drink and contemplated pouring another. After a lengthy mental battle, I set the glass in the sink and meandered to the bathroom. I checked myself in the mirror. The pants suit I was wearing was unflattering. I changed into a pair of micro-shorts that I'd mistakenly purchased from a local clothing store. I could never wear them in Oklahoma. They were only suitable for tweens, prostitutes, and 1970's roller-disco queens.

They were perfect for what I intended to do. I could rush to Braxton's home, go inside, and then parade around in front of him for fifteen minutes. The brief presentation would convince him sex was a great idea. My "no strings" offer that followed would push him over the decision-making edge.

I would then fuck him like I hated him, all the while celebrating in the fact that he'd spend the rest of his life regretting his decision to do the dick 'n dump.

Filled with drunken certainty that the plan was foolproof, I sashayed to his door as if I were walking along the runway of a French fashion show. Once within earshot of his home, I heard commotion. Footsteps. Elevated voices, one of which was female.

Fuck, fuck, fuck!

Getting him alone was step one to a successful hate fuck.

I rang the doorbell.

The arguing stopped. It started again.

I rang the doorbell. The arguing stopped.

The door opened.

Dressed in a dark tailored suit that accentuated everything about him, Braxton gave me a thorough once-over. Twenty feet beyond him, a leggy twenty-something stood in the kitchen. Wearing nothing but a tangerine-colored bikini, she was gorgeous in a European kind of way. Her tan legs went on for miles, coming together to form the shapely ass of a gymnast. Her most eye-grabbing feature, however, were her big round boobs.

She leaned to the side and looked me over.

I shot her a "he's mine, not yours" glare.

"Good afternoon," Braxton said.

A look of disdain was etched on his face. There was no denying my arrival caught him by complete surprise. He seemed nervous. Frustrated maybe. Interested in fucking me?

Not. At. All.

He looked just like Bruce Miller on the afternoon I caught him with Karen Carter. Bruce and I had been an on-and-off couple throughout our senior year in high school. I'd paid him an unscheduled visit at one of the times when we were officially together, only to have him answer the door looking like he'd swallowed a rotten oyster. I later found out that Karen was hiding in the bedroom closet, naked.

"Just thought I'd stop by and bid you farewell," I said, cocking my hip unapologetically. "I'm leaving tomorrow."

It was a complete and utter lie. I wasn't going anywhere. For the sake of luring him away from the tween porn star, lies, however, were a must.

He glanced at my ass. "Did you put the house up for sale?"

I arched my back. "I did."

He took another peek at my lower region and then looked up. He seemed confused. "Are you okay?"

"I'm fine, why?"

His brows pinched together. "You look like you're uncomfortable."

I was hoping for irresistible.

Drunk, disappointed, and forced to take in an eyeful of Braxton's next victim, I wasn't pulling it off very well. As I considered my options for a smooth recovery, the long-legged gymnast stepped behind Braxton and pressed her massive mounds against his back.

A hint of patchouli oil wafted past me.

I surveyed her from head to toe. She was undeniably flawless. And young. Her golden skin was smooth and wrinkle-free. The beautiful highlights woven through her hair appeared to be natural. She had long lean legs, a tight round ass, flat stomach, big tits, skinny arms and a gorgeous face.

I hadn't been young since before she was born. I had short legs, wrinkles, and lunch lady arms. My boobs were miniscule, and my hair was a natural curly disaster.

I was hoping to convince mister one and done to agree to a round two. The skinny whore, on the other hand, was a shoo-in for round one. Her prep time would be non-existent. She was already nearly naked.

My self-confidence escaped me like air from a whoopie cushion. I was clearly outmatched by the big-boobed youngster. I felt foolish for believing I could lure Braxton into a pity fuck. He was obviously a player, and I had merely been played. Irritated with myself for allowing him to play me, I forced the corner of my mouth to twist into a smirk.

"Uncomfortable?" I asked in rhetoric. "No, not at all. It's just—"

Despite my attempts to squash my frustration, it morphed to anger. I contemplated turning and walking away. I gave each of them a quick glance while they waited for me to finish speaking.

Braxton's look of slight concern remained. The post-teenage porn star ogled me with curious eyes.

If he had the gall to parade the blonde tramp in front of me like a trophy, I needed to depart with a bang.

A loud one.

"I wanted to come by and thank you for screwing me in the diner's parking lot the other day," I said in a whisper loud enough that the buxom nymph was sure to hear. "It's been a long time since I had sex in a car. Thanks, it was fun."

The porn star's eyes shot wide. Braxton swallowed so heavily I could hear it. Satisfied that I'd done all the damage that I was capable of doing, I turned around and walked away.

On my way home, I exhaled a breath of frustration. Giselle's hate fuck plan was a bust.

Being used—and knowing it—was painful. The only way to feel better about myself was to get as far away from Braxton Rourke as I could.

It was for the better, anyway. Sooner or later someone was bound to migrate from Washington state to California. The possibility of them being infected with the virus was minimal, but it was a possibility.

To err on the safe side of things, I needed to be long gone whenever it happened.

And that's just what I intended to do.

Be long gone.

8

BRAXTON

"You fucked her in the parking lot?" Mica eyed me from head to toe. "Her? Seriously?"

I closed the door. "What we did or didn't do is none of your business."

"You'll hit that, but you're telling me no?" She laughed dryly. "Tell me how that makes sense."

It didn't make sense. Mica wanted to fuck. Granted, she offered herself to anyone who was willing to reciprocate, but she had offered, nevertheless. Saying "no" wasn't as easy as one might think. There was a long list of reasons I shouldn't fuck her, and I knew each and every one of them. With each breath that I took, however, the list seemed to get smaller and smaller.

Faced with the aggravation of knowing Anna was disappointed in me—and that Mica was going to spend the rest of the afternoon parading around my home half-naked—I brushed my way past Mica and into the kitchen.

"It doesn't need to make sense to you," I said. "But it makes perfect sense to me. That's all that matters."

"We're all going to be dead in a month, anyway," she said. "You just as well die happy."

I looked her up and down. "What in the fuck are you talking about?"

"The virus," she replied. "San Francisco order people to stay at—"

"I'm tired of hearing about that fucking virus," I snarled. "We're not having sex, virus or no virus."

Her bottom lip jutted out.

I should have let her leave with Pratt. They could have discussed the end of the world, became convinced it was imminent, and then fucked each other's brains out.

I poured a glass of scotch, neat, and paused. The last thing she needed was a shot of liquor. I set the bottle aside. As I sipped the scotch, she continued to display her pouty-lipped expression, hoping to coerce me into feeling sorry enough for her to fuck her. I had news for her: there wasn't a woman on earth who could manipulate me into fucking her once my mind was made up.

I took a sip of scotch. Mica's legs went on for miles. I dragged my eyes up her lean frame. While not a God-given feature, her boobs were incredible. I finished what remained of my drink in one gulp. With my gaze fixed on the bulging mounds of flesh, I blindly poured the glass full.

I wondered what her father paid for her tits. I sipped the scotch. However much it was, they were worth it.

I realized halfway through my second glass of whiskey that I wasn't physically aroused. Mentally, I was a devout admirer of the big-boobed coed. Physically, it appeared she did nothing for me.

I was as limp as a wet noodle.

Frustrated with my anatomy's lack of interest, I imagined her lowering herself to her knees and begging me to stuff my cock in her mouth.

My dick didn't so much as twitch.

Although fucking Mica was out of the question, I needed to know if I'd somehow become impotent. Normally, thinking about sex aroused me.

Assuming my subconscious mind was elsewhere, I decided to give the verbal path a try. Talking about it always brought my dick to full attention.

"You think you want to fuck, huh?" I asked over the rim of my glass.

She hopped onto the kitchen island. Her endless legs dangled over the edge. She wagged her knees back and forth in an obvious effort to entice me. "I know I do."

I gave her a flippant look. "You're young enough to be my daughter."

She squeezed her breasts together with the inside of her biceps. Her tanned flesh bulged out of the skimpy top.

Seeming surprised at her accomplishment, she smirked. "I'll call you daddy if that's what you want."

Despite her efforts—and the wayward sexual conversation—my limp dick remained completely disinterested.

I downed the scotch and set the glass aside. "I'll be back in a minute."

I pounded the back of my clenched fist against Anna's door. After a short wait, it opened.

Dressed in a pair of sweatpants and a wrinkled tee shirt, Anna stood just inside the doorway. Her curly hair was gathered into a tangled mess that sat atop her head. Cradling a nearly empty glass of wine in her hand, she looked me up and down.

"Well, that didn't take you long," she said upon meeting my gaze. "What happened?" She gulped what remained of the wine. "Did she have a curfew?"

"She's a client."

She wiped the corner of her mouth with the heel of her palm. "Catering to half-naked teens now?"

"She's twenty-two," I retorted.

She coughed a dry laugh. "In dog years, maybe."

I had no desire to bicker with her about Mica. Determining if I had erectile disfunction was my only concern. Instead of beating around the bush, I decided to get right to it. Knowing a verbal exchange would suffice, that's the direction I traveled.

I gave her a quick look and then met her glassy-eyed glare. "I want you to suck my cock."

My dick twitched at the thought of Anna complying with the request. It wasn't much, but it was a start.

"Fuck you," she said, eyeing me as she spoke. "Suck *my* cock."

My gaze narrowed. "You don't have a—"

The door slammed shut.

Amused by her apparent jealousy—and her feisty mood—I rang the doorbell. Following a lengthy wait, it opened.

Eager to determine if the twitch was a fluke, I decided to start with an apology and go from there. After a few more sexually suggestive comments, I'd know for sure if I was broken or merely subconsciously uninterested in Mica.

"Listen," I began. "I'm sorry I started off like that. It's just...I was trying to—"

"Take off your pants." She gestured toward my crotch with a freshly filled glass of wine. "Get your big cock out."

Like a rocket, my dick shot from its flaccid state. Thrilled that everything seemed to be in working order—but unwilling to disrobe at her command—I met her drunken gaze with a stern glare. "I'm not whipping out my—"

The door swung closed with a *thump!*

Slightly irritated—but thoroughly amused—I knocked on the door.

It opened.

Clutching the doorknob in one hand and her wine glass in the other, Anna took a drink. She lowered the glass, sloshing wine at her feet in the process. "I've got little use for you other than sex." She stepped to the side and gestured toward the living room. "You can either come in and get busy or go back to your teenage bikini model."

"I can't—"

"Can't come in, or can't go back to the twenty-two-year-old?"

I pressed my palm against the door to prevent her from slamming it shut in my face. "Can't come in."

"Why?"

"I'm not going to leave her over there by herself."

"Afraid she needs help posting selfies to Instagram?" she asked in a sarcastic tone.

"She's a client," I said. "And she's alone in my home."

"Why'd you come here?" she asked.

I wasn't willing to admit I had an erectile disfunction, even if it appeared to only be applicable to Mica. Explaining the "I want you to suck my cock" declaration I'd made wasn't going to be easy.

"I wanted to antagonize you," I said, although it wasn't true. "I'm sorry. It was uncalled for."

"You're a prick."

"Actually, I'm not as bad as it might—"

"You weren't that good, anyway," she said under her breath. She pushed against the door. "Forget it."

She was much stronger than I expected. I braced the edge of the door with my foot and then looked right at her. "Excuse me!?"

She gave me a flippant look. "Forget it." She gulped her wine. "I'll finger myself. It'll be just as satisfying."

"Just as satisfying as what?"

"As satisfying as sex." She gave me a quick once-over. "With you, at least."

"Drunk or not," I warned. "You need to watch your tone."

She peered down her nose at me. "Or what?"

I edged my way inside. I faced her and crossed my arms over my chest. "Or else."

As if thoroughly entertained by my remark, she chuckled. "Now that you're in here, I'm going to fuck you." She stepped around me and kicked her bare foot against the door. "My way."

The door slammed closed.

She wasn't going to do anything of the sort. Nevertheless, my attention was piqued by her remark. I followed her with my eyes as she walked in front of me.

"Your way?" I asked.

"We had sex in the parking lot your way." She shifted the wine glass from her right hand to her left. "Now, it's my turn."

She was so close I could taste the sweetness of the wine on her breath. Her alcohol-induced courage was cute. No differently than Mica, she wasn't going to coerce me into having sex. I was far too strong-willed to succumb to her drunken advances.

Besides. I had a $1,000 bet on the line.

"You're not getting a *turn*," I insisted. "We agreed it was a one-time thing."

Without warning, she grabbed my cock, which was as stiff as a stone. "I changed my mind." She squeezed the shaft firmly. "You might not be interested, but *he* sure is."

I glanced at her hand. "What the fuck do you think you're doing?"

With my cock gripped firmly in her hand, she lowered herself to her knees. Before I had a chance to object, my slacks were unzipped.

She stroked my cock with her free hand. "My way."

I desperately wanted Anna to suck my cock, but knew I had to fight the urge. I swallowed hard, preparing to object to her intentions. At the instant my lips parted, hers did the same.

Paralyzed by desire, I gawked as she slid her mouth along the rigid shaft.

Just like that, I'd been hornswoggled into a blowjob by my drunken neighbor. It was a first, but technically it wasn't sex. Provided I went no further with Anna, I'd win the bet with Pratt, and continue my pattern of "one time only" when it came to sex.

Still cradling the glass of wine loosely in her left hand, she withdrew her mouth until her lips rested around the rim of the swollen head.

Anna was an adorable woman. Seeing my cock in her mouth was driving me insane with sexual desire. I didn't want her to stop but allowing her to continue would likely lead me along a sexual path I wasn't prepared to travel upon.

Following a short pause—during which time I contemplated pulling away—she engulfed half my cock in one gulp.

I sucked a choppy breath. "Jesus fucking—" I stumbled backward until my flattened palms came to rest against the door. "Christ."

On her knees, she followed me every step of the way, never allowing my dick to spring free of the warm confines of her mouth.

I watched with wide eyes as she continued her open-mouthed assault, eagerly taking my dick into her throat at a pace so rapid I feared I wouldn't last much longer than a matter of minutes.

Her saliva covered the length of my shaft. Seeing it glisten as she withdrew her mouth was a huge turn-on.

I closed my eyes.

Slurping sounds bounced from one interior wall to the other.

I tried desperately to block them out but failed. It was no use. I opened my eyes and eagerly watched as she continued to suck my cock like doing so was going to save someone's life.

I was no newcomer to blowjobs. I had never, however, been so aroused in my life.

Anna wasn't completing a task, she was performing art.

Seconds before I was sure to ejaculate in her mouth, she pulled away. Grinning a sly smile of accomplishment, she met my downward gaze.

I wanted to throw a fit. To demand that she complete the task she started. Still hypnotized by her oral ability at the moment, I was incapable of expressing my opinion. While I collected my thoughts, she did a quick about-face and pushed her sweats past her knees.

They fell in a crumpled wad at her feet.

With a swift motion of her right foot, she kicked them aside.

My eyes darted to her naked lower half. Her narrow waist flared out into a wide set of hips, forming an ass like none I'd ever seen. As I stared in admiration of the heart-shaped wonder, she spread her feet shoulder width apart.

Her outstretched fingers gripped her ass cheeks. She bent at the waist until her forehead was inches from touching the hardwood floor. Her forearms tensed as she spread herself wide.

Her pussy opened like a flower.

My mind screamed *no*, but my mouth gave no opposition whatsoever.

Incapable of doing nothing but complying with her unspoken wish, I fumbled to unbuckle my belt. Before I'd completed the task, she guided the tip of my swollen cock between her upper thighs.

I lowered the waist of my slacks to just above my knees.

Still bent over at a ninety-degree angle, she pushed her weight against me. Her tight pussy slowly swallowed my rigid shaft until the entire length disappeared completely.

If her pussy were any smaller, sex between the two of us would be impossible. By the grace of God, all the pieces fell into place, leaving the two of us feeling like we were having sex for the first time each time we committed the act.

"Damn that feels good," she announced.

I hated admitting it, but it felt heavenly.

"Fuck yes, it does," I agreed.

Prepared to fuck her like she owed me money, I reached for her waist. As my hands came in contact with her smooth skin, she started bucking her hips like a mad woman.

With the pace of a jackhammer and the predictable rhythm of a well-written song, her ass came crashing against my thighs. The unmistakable sound of skin slapping skin filled the entryway.

Pressed firmly against the door, I had no option but to allow her to continue. I wasn't accustomed to being on the receiving end of a woman's sexual onslaught, but I wasn't about to complain. It felt amazing.

Her twerking and bucking continued, never slowing in pace or losing authority. She was fucking me *her way* and I was enjoying every stroke.

A series of grunts and moans that couldn't be confused as being anything but expressed sexual pleasure escaped each of us, overshadowing the sound of bare skin against bare skin.

The clap, clap, clapping of her hips against my thighs. Her tight pussy squeezing the length of my shaft with each stroke she took. The erotic moans...

Everything melded together.

Within a matter of minutes, I felt myself being sucked toward a climactic conclusion.

"Your. Cock. Feels. So. Good," she said in perfect timing with the movement of her hips.

A *bang!* at the door caused my heart to nearly leap from my chest. Instantaneously, the door swung open, causing me to lose my balance.

With my slacks around my ankles and my cock pointing skyward, I stumbled through the opening, only to land against a half-clad Mica Weinberg.

She glanced at Anna, and then at my quickly shrinking hard-on.

"What. The fuck," she gasped in clear disgust.

"What the fuck is right," I snapped. "What the fuck are you doing here?"

"What the fuck are *you* doing here?" she retorted. "You're supposed to be—"

I reached for my belt with one hand and gestured toward my house with the other. "Get your ass in the house."

"Fuck you," she spat.

She turned away and began parading across Anna's yard, in the opposite direction of my home.

"God damn it Mica," I complained, buckling my belt. "Get your ass back here."

"Fuck her," Anna declared. "Let that inconsiderate bitch go."

Although it was only momentarily, I'd forgotten about Anna. I glanced at her, and then at the quickly disappearing Mica.

"I'm sorry," I said, meeting Anna's fiery-eyed glare. "I've got to—"

The door swung closed with a *bang!*

There were two directions I could go. One would net me $100,000, and one would end with me likely losing a $1,000 bet.

Although I was torn, I turned toward Mica and took off running.

9

ANNA

Sitting at the kitchen table, I sipped my coffee during one of the lulls between the throbs of my pounding headache. Furious about the previous night's impromptu home invasion, I waited anxiously for Giselle to bring the contract for the home listing. After signing it, I could spend a few days preparing the home, and then be on my way back to Oklahoma. Within a week, I'd be free of Braxton Rourke—and his odd sexual issues—forever.

My phone pinged. I swept the tip of my index finger across the screen. It was a message from Giselle.

Have you seen the news?

I picked up the phone and typed my response.

No. Why?

Her response was immediate.

Turn it on. Channel 7

I reduced the sound to the lowest setting, activated the closed captioning, and turned on the news. I watched in complete shock as the words swept across the screen beneath a mask-wearing newscaster's face.

In an effort to contain the virus, Governor Gavin Newsom has ordered California's nearly 40 million residents to stay at home. In effect immediately and until further notice, the residents of the state are to "shelter in place", and not to leave their homes except for essential purposes.

Essential purposes are defined as getting groceries, obtaining prescriptions, and receiving healthcare. Commuting to jobs that have been deemed essential will also be allowed. All non-essential businesses are to be closed immediately and will remain closed until further notice. With the exception of deliveries, all restaurants are to remain closed to the public. Bars will remain closed to the public. Violators of this order will be charged criminally, leaving the residents no alternative but to...

I called Giselle. As soon as she answered, I let out a heavy sigh. "Oh my God. This is insane."

"Washington and New York did the same thing earlier this morning," she said. "They're saying it's going to be nationwide in a matter of days. The infected count in Washington is doubling every day. They're up to 5,000 infections now, and it's killing people at a much higher rate than what they claimed in China. They said in the news conference that China lied intentionally. Something about trying to protect trade."

"Where does...what...are you still," I stammered. "Are you still going to list the house? Can you?"

"Realtors aren't *essential*," she replied. "All things considered I don't think it's in either of our best interest to list it now. It will just sit on the market until this is all over. It's anyone's guess how long this will last. If other states follow suit, maybe it'll be over in a month. If they don't, and the virus continues to spread, maybe it will take two or three."

"Two or three months?" I shrieked. "*Months*?"

"They said that's a possibility."

"People are supposed to go three months without work?" I tried to wrap my mind around the thought. "The nation will go broke."

"The stock market crashed already," she said. "As soon as the governor of New York made the announcement it fell nearly two thousand points. When our governor did the same, it fell another two thousand."

My heart sank. The amount of people who were destined to lose money was in the tens of millions. If things didn't change soon, it would be hundreds of millions. I stared at the television in disbelief that things could change so drastically in an instant.

"Are you going to be okay?" she asked.

"Financially," I replied. "I'll be fine."

"If nothing else, you can get to know that neighbor of yours."

Being confined to a home next door to Braxton was appalling.

I cringed at the thought. "I know enough about him to know staying away is the only answer."

"Did something happen?"

"The hate fuck." I exhaled a breath of frustration. "It didn't work."

"Are you sure?"

"Quite," I replied. "Why?"

"It takes time."

"Well," I said with a laugh. "It looks like time is on my side."

She chuckled. "I'll be in touch. Let me know if there's anything I can do to help."

"Thank you."

"Be safe."

"Same to you," I said. "Again, thanks."

I hung up the call and pushed the phone to the center of the table. I glanced at the television. The news segment continued, warning viewers of spreading the virus from one person to another.

To slow the rate of infection, the Center of Disease Control is urging people to practice what is described as social distancing. Maintaining a six-foot distance between other people, while in public, is crucial to slow the spread of COVID-19.

Residents of the state should wear protective masks or respirators, if possible, when outdoors. Publicly accessed grocery carts, fuel pumps, and other hard surfaces should be handled with gloves or sanitized before touching with bare hands. Proper hand washing is critical, as is sanitizing one's hands after touching anything in public.

If a resident is having groceries delivered by one of the many companies who offer such services, they should be cleaned and disinfected prior to...

I lowered my head into my hands. What was happening was incomprehensible.

For the next several hours I wandered throughout the home, taking inventory of what I had. Short of wine, there wasn't enough groceries in the home to feed a mouse.

There was no hand sanitizer, Lysol, or any other bacteria-killing cleanser. Although there was a reasonable supply of toilet paper, I'd need more if the order to stay at home was extended beyond a month.

I downloaded the *Instacart* application on my phone. After placing a quick order for what I felt was essential, I tried to embrace the idea of being locked in a home that I didn't want to be in, which, consequently, was next door to a man who I'd quickly grown to despise.

For an entire month.

It dawned on me that he, too, would be locked in his home. There was one upside, though.

We'd be in separate homes.

10

BRAXTON

I couldn't fucking believe it. In addition to dodging thousands of bullets, I'd managed to live through the threat of sarin gas, anthrax, and the countless chemical weapons that we exposed ourselves to throughout my tenure as a US Marine. Having survived those real-life threats, I was now being forced to stay home and safeguard myself from a disease that had symptoms mimicking the seasonal flu.

The governor of California was an utter and complete idiot.

Although my research on the matter was far from thorough, the information was readily available, and the consensus was obvious. It was apparent that the deaths associated with the common flu were far in excess of the deaths associated with COVID-19.

Men over the age of eighty with underlying health issues were those who should be concerned. A middle-aged male in perfect health wasn't a candidate for complications. Frustrated beyond comprehension, I picked up my phone and called Pratt.

He answered on the first ring. "Pratt's soon-to-be sanitary supply warehouse, how can I help you?"

"Sanitary supplies," I said with a laugh. "I'm guessing you saw the governor's press conference?"

"Hate to say I told you so," he sang in a sarcastic tone. "But I told you so."

"Fuck you, Pratt."

"Mark my words," he said. "This shit's going to sweep across the nation like a plague. The Chinese were lying about their death count, who's at risk, and the long-term complications associated with it. Now our government knows the truth about China's lies, and they're running scared because the only statistics they have available aren't worth a shit. They're saying, 'Stay at home, everything will be fine in 30 days.' It won't be fine in 30 days. I doubt it'll be fine ever again. This one's going to be a game changer, Brother."

Pratt was a conspiracy theorist. I was a realist. While he clung to theories, possibilities, and the most far-fetched of notions, I embraced nothing but facts and statistics.

I glanced at the open website on my laptop. "80,000 people were infected in China and there were 3,000 deaths, *total*. Keep in mind they have a population of 1.4 *billion* and that they all live on fucking top of one another like canned sardines." I grabbed my phone and did some quick math. "That's roughly fifty people infected per million. At that rate, the United States will see about..." I pressed the keys on my phone's calculator. "Applying China's math, the USA will see 16,400 infected, and 660 deaths. Hell, 30,000 people died last year from the flu. This is a political ploy if I've ever seen one. They didn't get him impeached, so they're going to do whatever they must to get him out of office."

"Brother, we'll see 660 deaths a day once this gets going," Pratt warned. "This isn't about politics."

"You're an idiot."

"I'll be a healthy idiot," he said with a laugh. "I'm going to get a 100,000-volt cattle prod and carry it with me when I go get groceries. If anyone gets within six feet of me, I'll shove the end of it against their neck and shock them so hard they'll piss down their leg. Anti-social distancing is what I'm going to practice."

Knowing Pratt, he was serious. It was just like him to do something drastic while trying to protect his odd system beliefs.

"If you shock someone with a stock prod, you'll end up getting arrested," I said.

"I might be arrested, but I'll be alive and uninfected."

"You think you'll be able to maintain a safe distance in the county jail?" I asked. "Do you think they're practicing social distancing in there?"

"Hadn't given that much thought."

In my opinion, no one had given any of it much thought. That was the problem. No thinking, and too much knee-jerk reacting.

"What the fuck are you going to do?" I asked. "Big picture? Cower in fear?"

"Seriously?"

"Yes," I said. "I'm being serious."

"Stay home, practice good hygiene, and maintain a safe distance from anyone I have to encounter. It's only fair to everyone else."

"What the fuck does that mean? Fair to everyone else?"

"I could be a carrier. Hell, one man can get this shit and not know it, and the next gets it and dies. If I'm out running around, I could be carrying it from place to place, infecting hundreds. Maybe thousands. It's my responsibility to be responsible."

"Are you fucking serious?"

"I might be wrong," he said in a sarcastic tone. "But I don't think being a low-level thug qualifies as an essential business. Why don't you call the governor's office and ask 'em what they think? Tell 'em we kidnap people, stage murders, and manipulate evidence for whoever pays us the most. See what they say. Hell, who knows? Maybe we are essential. I'll warn ya, though. If you get within six feet of me, I'm shocking your big dumb ass."

"He can't force businesses to close," I argued. "That's on the cusp of communism."

"Call it what you want," he said. "But it's already done. He signed an executive order under a state of emergency. Groups of more than ten people, anywhere, aren't allowed. Restaurants are closed, bars are closed, hell, after tonight you won't even be able to go to Best Buy and get a big screen TV. If it's not food or drugs they're closing at midnight tonight. Oh, and they cancelled the entire NBA season. Baseball, too."

"This is fucking ridiculous," I snarled.

"If you don't pay attention to this, you'll be saying that from your grave."

"I'm healthy," I argued. "I don't have anything to worry about."

"Kid in Washington died, and he was 32. Left a wife and two little kids wondering what the hell they did wrong."

"He probably had lungs that were burned out from smoking meth. Either that, or he died from something totally unrelated, and they claimed it was this shit, just to put the scare in us."

"Man can't win an argument with you, Rourke," he complained. "That's for sure."

"There's nothing to argue about," I said. "Like I said. Statistics. That's all I'm interested in talking about."

"Put this down in your statistics. I'm going to get toilet paper before everyone runs out."

"Why the fuck would we run out of toilet paper?" I pulled the phone away from my ear and glared at it. "Is diarrhea a symptom?"

"You don't get it, Brother. I'm going for crapper paper. Call me in a couple of hours," he said. "We need to brainstorm on how to make money during this deal. What the next big moneymaker's going to be. I'm thinking sewing machines."

"Well," I said with a laugh. "It sure as fuck isn't going to be toilet paper."

11

ANNA

It had been nine days since the stay at home order was given. During that time, things changed.

In fact, *everything* changed.

Nationally, there was no available supply of toilet paper, paper towels, Clorox wipes, rubbing alcohol, and hand sanitizer. Stores had more bare shelves than stocked ones. Essentials like bread, milk, meat and cheese were often unavailable. A few of the independent grain alcohol distributors had shut down manufacturing of their craft vodka and were now bottling hand sanitizer.

The World Health Organization declared a pandemic. The president blamed the media, the media blamed the president, and the American people blamed each other.

Fights broke out at gas stations, stores, and in food lines over people not practicing social distancing measures. Videos were posted to social media showing women in fist fights over toilet paper. An elderly woman was kicked to death in New York City for sneezing on someone. A Chinese man was beaten for being Chinese.

The entire nation was up in arms, and over half the states were shut down from any activities, short of what was deemed essential by their respective governor. The stock market had set a new record for a one-day loss, unemployment was at an all-time high, and the ICU's in New York City's hospitals were nearly filled, all from COVID-19 related admissions.

Hospitals in many of the highly infected states feared they'd run out of the ventilators required to keep the critically ill patients alive. Some hospitals had already spent their supply of Personnel Protective Equipment and were now forced to fabricate their own masks or reuse the ones they had.

Those dying from COVID-19 weren't able to be seen by the living family members because of the contagious nature of the disease. In fact, family members were prohibited from so much as visiting a hospital, let alone seeing the dying patients.

Most were saying goodbye to their loved ones via video conference calls like Skype, Zoom, and Facebook Messenger. My nights were spent watching CNN in a drunken stupor, crying at the COVID-19 death stories as they were unveiled.

Initially, those who were listed as vulnerable were eighty years old with compromised health. It soon changed to include anyone over sixty with compromised health. Two days later, it was anyone fifty or older, regardless of their condition.

Now, it was anyone. Period.

Women. Children. Men. Young. Old. Healthy. We were all at risk.

It seemed every day something changed. The symptoms. The prognosis. The statistics. The vulnerable.

One thing that remained unchanged was Braxton. He continued to come and go at will, driving past my home no less than 3 or 4 times a day.

I had no idea where he was going, but I doubted what he was doing was essential.

It frustrated me that he was zooming up and down the street while I was stuck at home watching the news as if my life depended on it. As frustrating as the information was, it seemed I couldn't stop watching CNN.

From when I got up to when I went to bed, the news played. If I wasn't watching it, I was on my laptop, checking the daily statistics of each state, the nation, and the other countries who had a high rate of infection.

The statistics and the stories seemed to be my life blood.

But it wasn't healthy. I was drinking more than I ever had, eating an unhealthy amount of food, and wasn't active at all.

At whatever point in time they lifted the stay at home order, I'd have a pickled liver, be grossly overweight, and physically out of shape. One way or another, I was destined to die. If COVID-19 didn't get me, my failing liver would.

I thought about dying more often than I ever had. Although I was able to accept the death of my parents, I couldn't find a way to accept my own. Maybe it was because I was young, and I felt that I hadn't lived a full life. At least not yet.

I sipped my morning mimosa while watching the news. A 36-year-old DJ in Florida contracted the virus and died soon thereafter. He was in good health, had no underlying conditions, and wasn't considered a person at tremendous risk.

The DJ's wife and young daughter were being interviewed. Although I was already one glass beyond my self-imposed mimosa limit for the morning, I opened my third bottle of champagne, and poured another. The wife explained how her husband couldn't get tested because he didn't fit the criteria. How he became ill, had difficulties breathing, and still couldn't get tested.

Within a few days he became so ill that he wasn't able to stand or walk. She drove him to the emergency room. The hospital then tested him, found that he was infected, and immediately admitted him.

With the hospital on lockdown, his wife was not allowed to come inside.

Two days later, he was dead.

She never got to say, "I love you" or "goodbye."

The daughter told stories about her father dancing in a ballet competition with her. In closing the segment, the newscaster explained that the deceased had worked a week prior to his illness as a DJ at a local bar. The venue was filled with college youth on spring break. Although no one knew for certain, it was expected the he contracted the virus then.

My eyes welled with tears. It was more than I could take.

Witnessing the family express how the events unfolded gave confirmation to the severity of the disease, the necessity of the stay at home order, and the importance of social distancing and proper hygiene.

While I wallowed in sorrow, the familiar drone of Braxton's SUV caused me to look up. Pissed off about the dead DJ, disappointed with Braxton in general, and filled with mimosa-induced courage, I rushed to the window just in time to see him get out of the vehicle.

He was wearing a pair of dark washed blue jeans, a black tee-shirt that clung to him like a coat of paint, and leather dress shoes. It was the only time I'd seen him wearing something other than a suit, and it was the first time I'd caught a glimpse of his tattooed biceps.

In a tattoo fueled swoon, I sank into the sofa, nearly spilling my mimosa in the process. Following a quick recovery, I took a drink of the sweet nectar and stole another glance at my promiscuous neighbor.

Without thinking, I rapped my knuckles against the glass.

In the midst of unlocking the front door, he glanced over his shoulder.

I didn't know what else to do, so I flipped him the bird.

He shook his head as if disgusted with my antics and walked inside.

We hadn't spoken since the hate fuck debacle. I'd never been so embarrassed—or pissed off—in my life. I wondered what Braxton thought about the incident, and why he hadn't taken time to apologize, check on me, or at least say *something*—even if it wasn't related to the underdressed twenty-two-year-old's home invasion.

I finished my mimosa and crawled off the couch.

The news flashed to the head of the CDC, who was supposed to give an update on the rapidly growing rate of infection.

Normally they gave updates in the late afternoon.

I glanced at my watch. It was four o'clock. Shocked at how the day had managed to escape me, I glanced around the living room.

Magazines that I'd had delivered with my grocery orders—most of which couldn't keep my interest for longer than ten minutes—were scattered about the floor like steppingstones. A weeks' worth of dirty champagne and wine glasses covered every inch of available table space. A dirty pair of sweats was draped over the back of an oversized chair.

The living room looked like an underaged house party ten minutes after the cops showed up.

I lifted my arm and sniffed my arm pit.

I smelled like a wet goat.

My life had come unraveled at the seams. In the foreseeable future, I doubted things would get much better. Frustrated with the situation—and with myself—I finished my drink, picked up the living room, and took a shower.

Upon returning to the living room, I peered through the window, toward the salmon-colored Mediterranean home across the street.

Short of the two additional cars parked in front of the home, everything looked the same.

I opened the front door and poked my head outside. An eerie silence enveloped me. The noise from the freeway was absent. In fact, the typical noise from traffic—in general—was non-existent.

The only sound was that of me, breathing. I peered to the left.

Nothing.

I peered to the right. Two doors down from the Mediterranean home, an elderly woman was pruning one of her bushes. The ground around her was peppered with the trimmings from her afternoon's work.

She was tall for a woman and had a petite build. Her curly hair was cut short. The frosty white color gave hint from afar that she was high on the list of people who were "at risk." Realizing that fact made me sad.

Wearing a pair of bright red pants and a lemon-colored short sleeved top, she looked like she was dressed for a night out with her husband.

I waved, but she was preoccupied with her work.

I wondered if she was single or married. Why wasn't her husband outside with her? Had he contracted the virus? Was he sick? Had he died? Did she get to say she loved him before he drew his last breath?

I watched and waited, hoping to catch her attention.

She set the shears aside and gathered her trimmings in a bag. She took a step back and put her hands on her hips. Seeming satisfied with her work, she picked up the shears and turned toward the driveway.

I waved. Then, I waved again.

She was halfway up the drive, looking the other direction.

"Hi!" I shouted.

She glanced around. Upon seeing me, she smiled and waved.

"I'm Anna," I said. "How are you doing this afternoon?"

"Just fine, thank you," she replied. "I'm Margaret. Marge."

"Nice to meet you, Marge."

She set everything down before turning to face me completely. "Likewise."

"Crazy, isn't it?"

She cupped her palm beside her right ear. "Pardon?"

"This is crazy," I shouted. "Isn't it?"

"Yes, it sure is," she said. "Reminds me of what happened with polio, in 1952. I was 11 at the time. Scared to death, to say the least. A few years later they had a vaccine. We all let out a sigh of relief."

I walked to the middle of the drive. "They're saying it might be 18 months before they have one for this."

She looked up one side of the street, and then the other. "Hopefully, we'll all still be here when the time comes."

"I sure hope so," I replied. "Are you staying home?"

She shuffled to the end of her driveway. "I don't have a choice. My asthma's terrible. I doubt I'd last a week if I got it."

"I'm not taking chances, either," I said. "I'm staying here until this is over."

"Were they your parents?" she asked, nodding in my direction. "The former owners?"

"Yes," I replied. "They were."

She lowered her head. "I'm sorry."

"Thank you," I said, nearly choking on my reply.

"When this is all over," she said. "You'll have to come for dinner."

I'd been alone, eating Little Debbie's snacks, Cheetos, and sliced Swiss cheese for the past 9 days. Human interaction sounded like a wonderful idea, especially if there was a homecooked meal involved.

"I'll look forward to it," I said with a smile.

"I better go in." She gestured toward the door. "It's almost time for dinner."

I hated to ask but I had to know. I cleared my throat. "Are you married?"

She didn't immediately reply. I wished I would have asked differently, or not bothered to ask at all.

"I'm widowed," she replied after a moment of thought. "It's been three years. He was two inches shorter than me and seven years older. He was always happy, but he got feisty if he didn't eat at five. I'm maintaining the tradition."

"What was his name?" I asked.

She smiled. "Raymond."

"I won't keep you from your dinner," I said. "Nice to meet you, Marge."

"Maybe see you again tomorrow?" She reached for her things. "I'll be out here about four o'clock. I am every day."

My heart filled with warmth. "I'll see you tomorrow."

"I look forward to it."

12

BRAXTON

I talked to my father every Sunday. When deployed, I either spoke to him via satellite phone or in the form of a letter. One way or another we communicated once a week, in person if possible. He was much more than a father.

An onlooker wouldn't know it from listening to us argue, but he was and had always been my best friend.

Following my military career, our Sunday time together was quite predictable. Like clockwork, he meandered to the front porch with a cooler full of beer just after noon. He sat there until sundown, drinking beer with me, his neighbor, and whoever else might show up. The group discussed whatever subjects my father chose to speak of, most of which were entertaining to say the least.

Typically, he chose issues that he knew would get a rise out of whoever it was he was antagonizing. For the foreseeable future, that person would be me.

The neighbor, a former member of an outlaw motorcycle club, was a close friend of ours. Over the years my father had provided advice, watched the young man mature, and eventually attended his wedding.

Much to my father's chagrin, every member of the neighbor's now defunct motorcycle club was in San Diego spending their "shelter in place" time together at a former member's beach house. Although my father was invited, he reluctantly declined. In his eyes, the possibility of infection was far too great.

The change in his Sunday routine, the lockdown of the entire state, and the fear of infection had him on edge.

I pulled into the driveway and shut off the engine. He was sitting on his porch of his two-bedroom ranch home drinking a beer, alone. Upon seeing me he raised his bottle of beer in toast of my arrival.

His face was long, and his trademark snow-white crew cut was in bad need of a trim.

I pushed the car door open and stepped into the warm mid-day sunshine. "How's it going, Old Man?"

"Slow and steady," he replied. "Did you stop anywhere?"

"No. I did not."

Wearing a look of uncertainty, he sipped his beer. "Are you sure?"

"I'm not like you," I replied. "I don't forget shit. I'm sure. No stops."

He tilted the neck of his beer bottle toward me. "Is that suit fresh, or is it some recycled shit from yesterday?"

"My clothes are clean."

"You didn't answer my question."

I cleared my throat. "Today's the first day I've worn these clothes since they were dry cleaned."

"Leave the shoes in the drive," he demanded. "They said that shit can live on the soles for a goddamned week. I don't need you tracking COVID-19 dust all over my clean porch."

Pratt warned me on a daily basis of all things COVID-19 related. According to him, I needed to disrobe at the door and walk straight to the shower upon returning home. Infectious shoe bottoms was a new one, though.

"A week on my shoe bottoms?" I laughed. "That's bullshit."

"Leave 'em in the drive, Son."

A former Marine and a Vietnam War veteran, my father was cantankerous, opinionated, and argumentative. Winning an argument against him, however, was impossible. Although I disagreed with his opinion about my shoes, I knew not to express my opinion in the form of defiance.

I kicked them off at the edge of the drive. "How's that?"

He stood and looked me over. "Other than those ugly socks, I suppose you're fine."

I glanced at my feet. "What's wrong with the socks?"

"Your suit's black," he said. "Ought to be wearing black socks. Those blue fuckers stand out like a turd floating in a punch bowl."

"Go to hell."

He shrugged and took his seat. "They look like shit."

Unwilling to be lured into a discussion about fashion with an old man who wore khaki pants and a white tee shirt regardless of his surroundings, I meandered across the yard and stepped onto the porch. He sat in the first of four chairs that were evenly spaced along the length of the covered deck. A beer cooler was situated beside him.

He removed a bottle of beer and blindly tossed it into the air. "Heads up, Dipshit"

I caught the bottle and twisted off the cap. I flipped it into his lap. "Thanks, Old Man."

He dropped the beer cap into a half-filled gallon jar that sat beside his chair. "Kid sent me a text message," he said, referring to the missing neighbor. "Said him and the crew are living it up. Goose is cooking fresh seafood and steaks and they're having parties on the roof. Sounds like they're not bothered by this much."

I lowered myself into the chair beside him. "I think everyone's about as bothered as they'll allow themselves to be."

"It doesn't bother me much, other than fucking up my Sunday routine." He pulled the cooler from beside his chair and pushed it in front of him. He propped his feet onto it. "Retired life has its benefits, I suppose."

"I suppose."

"Speaking of benefits." He glanced in my direction. "How's that curly-headed neighbor of yours?"

A week prior, I'd explained the situation with Mica, and how she'd barged in on Anna and me during sex. I'd previously shared the parking lot sex story with him as well. He assumed, based solely on the fact that we'd had sex twice, that I was interested in her beyond sex.

"Haven't spoken to her since the last time I was here," I said.

"It's been, what? Two weeks?"

"Since she and I talked?" I shrugged. "Twelve days, give or take."

"Twelve isn't a 'give or take' number, Son. Twelve's a definite."

I scowled. "What?"

"You can't say, '*Twelve* days, give or take.' That's like saying 'roughly thirteen.'"

I glared. "What in the hell are you talking about?"

"You said, 'twelve days, give or take.' That makes you look stupid. Twelve's not a 'give or take' number. You can say 'ten, give or take', or you could say 'twenty, give or take.' Not twelve. That's like saying 'nine, give or take' or 'three, give or take.' You sound like a damned fool. What the hell's wrong with you?"

"It's been exactly twelve fucking days since I spoke with her, Old Man," I said snidely. "Twelve. Exactly twelve. No more, no less. How's that?"

"That's better," he said. "Why'd you add the *give or take* part?"

I couldn't win with him. I let out a sigh of frustration. "I don't know."

He looked me over dramatically. "You sure you're not infected? Seems like your brain's pickled. It happens with adults when they get a high fever. Turns their brains to mush."

"Fuck you," I said jokingly.

He took a long drink of beer. When he lowered the bottle, he grinned. "Speaking of fucking, I'm guessing you fucked that neighbor gal for the last time. Screwed thar deal up like all the others."

He'd never see me in a relationship, and we both knew it. I was the only one who accepted it as being reality. He was right about one thing. I had fucked Anna for the last time. Knowing my opinion of women, I was curious as to why he mentioned it.

"Why do you say that?" I asked.

"Been thinking about that since last Sunday when you brought it up. By my guess, she's angrier than a sack of wet cats about now. I can't say that I blame her. If someone opened the door on me when I was goin' at it, I'd be mad, too. Not as mad as if my partner took off running down the street afterward." He gave me a dismissive look. "That was a fool's move, Son."

"We weren't partners."

He rested his forearms against his knees and turned his head to the side. "What were you?" He arched one of his wiry gray brows. "Lovers?"

"No."

"That's what I thought. If you're not lovers, then you were partners." He sipped his beer. "You were fucking, so you were one or the other."

"We weren't *fucking*. We fucked. I painted my kitchen. It doesn't make me a painter. We weren't partners. I'm not going to argue about it."

"Well, you didn't just poke your cock through a hole in the wall and have some random stranger comply with your sexual desires. You went to your neighbor's house, who, might I remind you, you had already been intimate with. One thing led to another, and—"

"I was there, Old Man. I know what happened."

"The two of you were sexual partners," he said sternly. He chuckled a dry laugh. "Now, she's moved on to bigger and better things. Just like all the others."

"She hasn't moved on to anything or anyone."

"I thought you hadn't spoken to her?"

"I haven't. She hasn't gone anywhere since the stay at home order was given. If she hasn't left, she hasn't moved on."

His brows pinched together. "How the hell would you know what she's doing unless you're being a *creepy neighbor*?"

"I'm attentive."

"When I was being attentive with that dipshit that lives across the street, you said I was a creepy neighbor."

I chuckled. "You were sitting inside with a pair of binoculars, peering across the street through the corner of the window with the drapes pulled aside."

"Well, I couldn't have seen through the damned things," he said. "I had to pull 'em aside."

"You know what I mean, Old Man."

"Sounds to me like you're just as creepy as me," he scoffed.

"She gets groceries delivered every other day," I explained. "She never leaves. There's nothing creepy about noticing that. Hell, it's hard not to notice. I'm home most of the day."

"Most of the day?" He seemed surprised. "Where the hell are you going, other than coming here?"

"Pratt and I have a few business ventures we're trying out."

His posture straightened. "Business venture?" He faced me and scowled. "What in the fuck needs to be done while we're knee deep in a pandemic? You don't need money."

"Settle down, Old Man." I set my empty beer bottle beside my chair and raised my open hand. "Everything will be just fine."

He glared at me for a moment before tossing me another beer. "How can you be so sure? If you're coming in contact with people, you could be a carrier of this disease. From what they said, you might not even—"

"They're full of shit, Pop. Believe me. This is no different than the common flu. I don't want to argue about it."

"Neither do I." He sipped his beer. He looked at the bottle like something was wrong with it. "This fucker tastes funny. In fact, it tastes like nothing. They say that's a sign of the virus. Taste buds go to hell."

"Everything's a sign of the virus." I rolled my eyes. "They want everyone to think they're infected. If their numbers of infected citizens go up, it validates everything to the general population. At least the everyone that's buying into this shit."

"Still think it's a government conspiracy, huh?" He asked in a sarcastic tone. "You still trying to sell that story?"

"You don't have to agree with me, but this is a political move. I'm telling you. It is."

He gave me a look. "The Center for Disease Control, the World Health Organization, and every hospital in the free world that's got an ICU filled with dying souls are all in on it together, huh?"

I raised my index finger in protest. "I said I'm not going to argue about it."

"Neither am I. I'll just go on the record as saying if you make me sick from your travels, I'll smack you in the head with a hammer."

"You're going to hit me with a hammer?"

"Yep. Right between the running lights," he said with a nod. "For being an idiot."

"Whatever, Old Man. This'll be over as soon as they get the economy on the downturn. That's all they're after."

"Let's change the subject back to the curly-headed gal next door."

"No."

"We can talk corona or curls, you pick."

I didn't want to talk about either subject. I peered at the home across the street. Normally, there was activity in and out all day. There was no indication of human life, whatsoever. Frustrated with the entire situation, I stared blankly at the front door.

"I'll take your silence as a no vote." He finished his beer and grabbed another. "There's a possibility that the curly-headed gal is still interested. She's just waiting for you to apologize."

"Apologize?" I shot him a glare. "For what?"

"For taking off after the producer's daughter."

"What else was I supposed to do? That was my reputation—and a hundred grand—running down the street."

"I'm not saying what you did is wrong. I'm saying you need to apologize."

"If I didn't do anything wrong, why would I apologize?"

"Because, that's what it takes to keep a woman happy. I was married to your mother for 50 years. During that time, I apologized more times than I can count. For the sake of this conversation, let's call that number..." He sipped his beer for a moment. "18,000 times. Of those 18,000 times—"

"What?" I glared. "18,000?!"

He nodded. "Once a day for 50 years. That's probably accurate. Anyway, of those 18,000, maybe a dozen of them were heartfelt apologies."

"A dozen out of 18,000?"

"That's just a guess, but I'm saying it's pretty damned accurate."

"Why'd you apologize the other 17,988 times?"

"Because that's what it took to keep her happy. When a woman loves a man, and he does something that she takes exception to, it ignites a fire within her that can't be extinguished by anything other than an apology."

"*When a woman loves a man*," I said. "That theory doesn't apply to me."

"It's not a *theory*," he said in a snide tone. "It's a fact, and it applies, believe me."

"How so?"

"You poked your dick in her, that's how so. You can't go poking your cock in a woman—especially your neighbor—and expect that she's not going to develop feelings. Screwing a single woman is like feeding a stray cat a bowl of milk. They'll keep coming back until the milk's gone. Your milk will never be gone, because you live next door."

"I'm not interested in her beyond what's already happened."

"Maybe you ought to be."

"She's hot-headed."

He raised his hand to his chin and pondered my response before meeting my gaze. "Might be part Italian," he said straight-faced. "Italian gals are like Mexicans. They've got tempers like drunken sailors."

"She's not Italian."

"How can you be sure?"

"Her name's Anna Wilson."

He looked at me like I was an idiot. "What the hell does that mean?"

"Ever met an Italian named Wilson?"

"Her mother's maiden name might have been Spaghetti or Rigatoni, or something." He finished his beer and grabbed another from the cooler. "You never know."

"Can we give this a rest?" I asked.

"Not much else to talk about," he said. "Talking about the virus pisses you off."

"There's plenty to talk about," I argued.

"Let's talk about the Rourke legacy. You're my only child, and it'll die with you if you don't get busy and have some kids. Whether it happens in my lifetime or after I'm long gone, it needs to happen."

I spit beer across the porch. "I'm not having kids with my neighbor."

"She's the only one I can think of since your ex-wife that you've had sex with more than once." He grinned a cheesy smile. "She sounds like a prime candidate. You said she owns her own car dealership, so she's got—"

"She tricked me," I replied. "The second time. I wasn't planning on—"

He burst out into a laughing fit. "She duped you into having sex?"

"Pretty much."

"Nobody's ever tricked you into anything. Not even once," he argued. "Give that some serious thought before you try to argue it."

I couldn't argue it.

He was absolutely right.

13

ANNA

Elbow deep in a bag of Chex Mix and halfway finished with my second bottle of champagne, I watched intently as the governor gave a televised statement as to why ninety percent the state's many golf courses were closed.

I hoped that one day I would be able to get out of bed and *not* watch the news. I desperately needed to find a way to move forward with living my life—even if I had to make changes while I was still sheltering in place.

I had an unhealthy obsession with knowing what was happening regarding everything that was COVID-19 related.

There had to be a way to find a balance. At the moment, nothing in my life was balanced. I was living a life of extremes. Overdrinking, gorging myself with junk food, and sleeping less than I had since college wasn't healthy, and I knew it.

Change, however, was not coming easily.

I stared blankly at the television after the press conference was over, wondering what the next news highlight was going to be. They hadn't updated the death total for the United States yet, nor had they shared the new total for infected residents in the state of California.

I wondered how things could ever get back to normal. They were now saying that a second infectious wave would hit the United States in 8 or 9 months. According to the CDC, the vaccine for COVID-19 wouldn't be available for use on humans for another 18 months. By that time, it was probable that they would need another vaccine, altogether.

I feared my life would continue the same pattern of deterioration until I was in so deep that I could never dig my way out. Like the dirty dishwater draining from the kitchen sink after a holiday family feast, the Cheetos, empty champagne bottles, and my tired sunken eyes would eventually be sucked into downwardly spiraling vortex. I'd, of course, go right along with them, never to be seen again.

All that would be required to set the event in motion was for someone to pull the plug.

I needed to develop a new routine. A schedule that included exercise, eating properly, and keeping my mind occupied with work would be a good start. For now, my only chance at a normal slice of life would be my daily meetings with Marge. Not that shouting halfway up the block at a stranger was normal.

Maybe it was the *new* normal.

Nearly comatose from my early morning news intake, I finished the bag of Cheetos and washed it down with the bottle of champagne. While I considered getting up from the sunken couch cushion, my phone pinged.

I had no idea where it was.

Following a frantic 10-minute long search, I found it in the kitchen amidst the previous night's Milano cookie wrappers and a weeks' worth of empty orange juice cartons.

A message from Braxton illuminated the screen. Beyond frustrated with him, but eager to see what he had to say, I tapped the text with the tip of my finger and opened it.

Sorry about how things unfolded the other night. I'd like

to extend an olive branch. No games. No BS. Only a heartfelt apology. Let me know.

I quickly typed my response. Before I pressed *send*, I read the message to make sure I didn't sound like an asshole.

I'm not opposed to an in-person heartfelt apology, but I'll only accept it after you've been home for 14 days. I can't take any chances on being infected. I doubt you'll be up for that, considering that you come and go like nothing's going on. lmk

I changed "lmk" to "let me know" and pressed *send*.

Satisfied that I'd made my point about my beliefs regarding his lack of compliance with the stay at home order, I clutched my phone and paced the floor. After an hour passed with no reply, I took a shower.

The next two hours passed at the pace of a foreign language documentary.

I checked my watch every five minutes, for an hour. Then, every ten minutes or so for the following hour.

The remaining thirty minutes passed one moment at a time, with me staring mindlessly at my phone as the seconds ticked away. Finally, four o'clock arrived.

Well, almost.

To prevent myself from going completely bonkers, I stepped outside at ten minutes before the hour.

I walked to the middle of the drive and peered across the street. Marge was down on her hands and knees, digging beside an Agave. Dressed in a pair of lime green pants and a short sleeved white blouse, she looked better than she did the day before.

I was dressed in sweatpants, an old tee shirt, and a pair of flip-flops. My sweats were clean, but it was obvious that I needed to step up my late afternoon outfit game if I was going to compete with Marge.

"Good afternoon," I shouted.

She glanced over her shoulder. Upon seeing me, she stood. "Good afternoon." She gestured toward the cactus with the small shovel she held. "I was just killing some time. This agave needed some attention."

"This place is so weird," I said. "Nobody has grass in their yards. Only rocks and cactus."

"Grass won't grow," she said with a laugh. "It needs rain." She gazed up at the cloudless sky. "It never rains here."

"My mother said this place is the land of drought and dreams."

She smiled. "In other words, sunshine and happiness."

Although it was late afternoon, the sun felt brutal. I shielded my eyes from it and peered at Marge. "How long have you been out here?"

She looked at her watch. "Oh, I don't know." She removed her gloves and tucked them into her armpit. "Maybe an hour."

I felt cheated. It was an hour that I could have had some resemblance of normalcy in my life. Talking to someone—anyone—was the only thing that was going to keep me sane throughout the pandemic.

I was convinced of it.

"An hour?" I tried to hide my disappointment. "Oh. I've been..." I paused, not knowing whether to reveal the entire truth of what I did with my time or give an abbreviated not-so-true version. I decided the truth wasn't anything I wanted to share. "I've been picking up the house," I said, smiling as I spoke. "The afternoon almost got away from me. It was just by a stroke of luck that I happened to notice what time it was."

"It seems that time stands still anymore." She walked to the end of her yard and stepped into the edge of the street. "It's not that I did all that much before any of this started, but now all I do is watch the news. I can't stop."

I was relieved that I wasn't alone.

"I can't, either," I admitted. "Everything they say is frustrating, but I'm fascinated with it at the same time."

"I don't think I'm fascinated too awful much." She lowered herself to the curb and sat down. "I feel like I need to know everything they know. I'm afraid they don't know too much, though. At least not yet. They sure seem to contradict themselves a lot."

"I don't think they know, either," I said in agreement. "One day it's this, the next day it's that."

She gazed in my direction, not seeming to focus on much of anything. I wondered if she heard me. I walked across my yard, paused, and then sauntered the width of Braxton's lot. I sat down at the near edge of his drive. Instead of being two hundred feet apart, we were now within talking distance.

"I like your outfit," I said.

"Thank you." She smiled and nodded in my direction. "Yours looks comfortable."

"Thanks."

"Do you have family here?"

"No," I replied. "My parents came here on a whim after my father retired. We lived in Oklahoma."

"You're married? Or, no?"

"No."

"Do you work? Back home?"

"I own a car dealership," I replied in a pride-filled tone. "It's a small one, but it's all mine. I really like it."

"That sounds like fun. Was your father a car guy? Raymond was." She grinned. "Corvettes."

"My father loved cars. He rebuilt them. He owned a body shop. He loved to make old cars look new again. *Better than new*. That's what he always said."

She smiled. "That's fascinating."

"I always thought so."

She nodded toward Braxton's home, which was right behind me. "Have you met him yet? Braxton?"

I didn't know what to say, so I said very little.

I forced a smile. "I have."

"He's easy on the eyes, isn't he?"

I laughed just a little. "He is."

"He works with the movie stars. Did he tell you that?"

"He mentioned it."

The corners of her mouth curled up. "I'd sure like to see him end up with someone nice. A nice loyal woman."

I almost laughed out loud at the irony of her statement. I didn't want to say anything to change her opinion of Braxton, so I refrained from making snide comments about loyalty.

"I think he's married to his work," I said, giving Braxton the benefit of the doubt. "He probably doesn't have time for a woman in his life."

She inched along the curb, stopping when she reached her driveway. "Did he tell you about that awful woman he was married to?" she asked. "It's no wonder he hasn't remarried."

I didn't know about Braxton's ex-wife, but I sure wanted to. I glanced over my shoulder, toward his front door. After seeing no movement inside the home, I looked at Marge.

"No," I said. "Well, not anything specific. Why?"

"While he was away in the war, she got pregnant." She glanced at his home and then at me. "It wasn't his," she whispered. "She was having an affair."

"Oh. My Gosh," I gasped. "His wife got pregnant and it wasn't his?"

"She was quite the trollop. They argued about it each time he came home. He was over there for years and years, you know? When Raymond was away, in Korea, we wrote letters back and forth. That was enough, but I loved Raymond with all my heart. I don't think a woman can do those things if she truly loves a man, do you?"

Braxton's lack of willingness to commit made a little more sense. "No," I replied. "I don't."

She checked her watch and then looked up. "Did he tell you about his brother?"

He hadn't mentioned any siblings. I shook my head. "I guess not."

"When Mister Rourke was in his military training, his brother died. An overdose. I suppose no one will ever know for sure if it was an accident or intentional, but it sounds like it might have been intentional. I can't imagine how he continued after losing his only sibling and then his wife. He was committed to protecting this nation, that's for sure." She brushed the dirt from her gloves and then looked up. "He's got more war medals than my Raymond. They compared them one day after dinner."

"Medals?"

"From the war," she said. "Mister Rourke's quite the decorated veteran. That's what brought him and Raymond so close. Them both being veterans, and all. Raymond in Korea, and Braxton in the Middle East. That's what they call it, isn't it? The war in the Middle East?"

My opinion of Braxton hadn't changed, but I couldn't help but feel compassionate toward him for the losses he endured.

"I think so," I replied.

"Do you have any siblings?" she asked.

"No, I don't. Do you?"

"Two. Mary's three years younger than me, and Mark is two years younger than Mary—according to him. It's actually a little more than a year, but he says it's two. Mary's in Santa Monica, and Mark is down south, in Escondido. Raymond and I weren't ever graced with children, though." Her face grew long. "It wasn't in our cards, I guess."

It was sad to hear that she didn't have children. To mask my sorrow for her not having children, I expressed tremendous joy in her siblings. "So, your brother and sister are in California? Or no?"

She laughed a little. "I forgot that you're not from here.

Escondido's two hours south if there's no traffic, and Santa Monica's twenty minutes away, on the coast."

"Oh. That's nice that they're close."

"It is." She checked her watch. "We don't see each other as much as we should, but we talk often. When you get older, you'll realize the value in having someone to talk to."

"I realize it now," I said. "*Right now.*"

"This is nice," she said with a smile.

"Is it dinnertime?" I asked.

She brushed off the thighs of her pants. "It is."

"See you tomorrow?"

"I'll look forward to it."

"Okay. Me, too."

"You should write Braxton a note and fold it into a paper airplane." She made a motion with her hand as if throwing something. "Throw it on his porch. You don't want to get too close to him, he's still coming and going like he's on a mission."

"I might do that," I said.

"Let me know if you do," she said with a smile. "In case you can't tell, I'm kind of a gossip."

"Whatever you've said stays with me," I said. "I can assure you of that."

She chuckled. "I wish I could say the same."

14

BRAXTON

I paced the kitchen floor. "Well, how many do we have left?"

"Twenty-three," Pratt replied. "Guy wants fifty. I can ship him the twenty-three, but I was thinking if we're not going to be able to get any more, I might want to make a new ad and raise the price of the last bunch of 'em. I could tell him we're sold out, and then raise the price. What do you think?"

"Twenty-three?" I asked. "That's all we've got left? I thought we had about eighty of them yesterday when I left."

"Guy in New Jersey bought fifty last night," he said. "He's opening some kind of support shop, making masks for the hospitals up there. Setting up a production shop, basically."

"Sell him the machines at the price on the ad. If they're listed for that price, we're already committed."

In anticipation of a protective mask shortage—and the necessity to make an equivalent by hand—Pratt and I had purchased every inexpensive sewing machine we could get our hands on. We started with over 500 of them and were down to 23, in roughly two weeks. At $175 markup on each $90 machine, we'd made nearly $90,000 in profit.

"Get your ass over here when you can," he said. "I need to get a couple of wooden crates made of some sort."

"Ship the machines individually."

"We'll get a break on freight if they're packaged together in a crate."

"We figured individual shipping, just ship them separately. It'll be less hassle to haul them to UPS."

"Less hassle, but more in shipping costs," he argued. "More shipping cost means less money in our pockets."

"I've got to get down to San Diego, I don't have time to run and meet you right now."

"What's in San Diego?"

"Hap. He's of the opinion that he's sick. This is the third time. His taste buds weren't working. His equilibrium was off. Now, he says he feels flush. It's a new symptom every day."

"Why doesn't he go get checked out?"

"He doesn't want to go to the hospital if there's nothing wrong. So far, there's been nothing wrong. All I need to do is go have a beer with him and tell him he's fine."

"Were you there on Sunday?"

"Just like always."

"Was he okay when you were there?" he asked.

"He was."

"He just wants some company. He's fine."

Pratt was right but arguing with my father was impossible. I needed to see him, reassure him he was fine, and have lunch with him.

"I'm sure you're right," I said. "I need to satisfy him, though. Ship the machines individually."

"Tell the old prick I said hi. Oh, and tell him he cost us about $500 in profit."

"I'll let him know."

I turned the lock and pushed open the door. "What the fuck are you doing, Old Man?"

The living room was empty. I glanced toward the kitchen. "Where you at, Old Man?"

His Cadillac was beneath the awning when I pulled into the driveway, so I knew he hadn't gone anywhere.

Unless someone gave him a ride.

"Old Man?!" I shouted, making my way into the hallway. "You fall asleep?"

I hoped that he didn't get one of the men from the VFW to take him to the doctor. Short of my father, none of them could see well enough to tell a traffic signal's color until they were in the middle of the intersection.

I pushed open his bedroom door. "You fall asleep, Old—"

My heart stopped. He was in a pile on the floor beside his unmade bed, wearing nothing but a pair of boxer shorts.

"God damn it, Hap," I rushed across the room. "Don't you dare die on me."

I knelt at his side and felt for a pulse. Although it was faint, he had one. His skin was hot to the touch and pale in color.

I hoisted him over my shoulder. As I rushed toward the door, I dialed 911 on my cell phone.

"911, what's your emergency?"

"My father's unconscious and he's got a high fever. Where's the closest hospital?" I huffed.

"Has he been exposed to anyone who's tested positive—"

"Where's the closest fucking hospital?!" I bellowed. "I haven't got time for your bullshit."

"Sir, I'll need you to answer a few—"

"I'm at 648 Wichita Avenue and I'm loading him in my car now. Where's the closest hospital?"

I opened the back door of my SUV. My phone clattered across the drive. I slid Hap onto the seat, situated him, and shut the back door.

After retrieving my phone, I got into the driver's seat and started the engine. I pressed the navigation button on the steering wheel and spoke into the car's interior. "Drive to the nearest hospital."

The vehicle's navigation system responded. *"Drive to the nearest hospital, is that correct?"*

"Yes."

"Driving to Scripps Mercy Hospital, 4077 5th Avenue, San Diego, California. Please turn right on Wichita Avenue."

I backed out of the driveway, shifted into gear, and stomped the gas pedal. The supercharged V-8 engine shot the SUV down the street like a rocket.

"Stay with me, Old Man," I said, searching for his reflection in the rearview mirror. "We'll be there before you know it. This fucker's a lot faster than the old Cadillac of yours, that's for sure."

The vehicles phone rang.

I pressed the steering control and answered it. "Rourke."

"This is the 911 operator. We were cut off."

"I'm taking him to Scripps Mercy on 5th. Tell them I'm en route. Ten minutes. Less than ten. If someone tries to pull me over, I'm not stopping."

"Is the person in question male or female?"

"Male."

"Age?"

"Seventy-five."

"Does he have a pulse?"

"Yes, it's faint."

"Any known health issues or concerns?"

"None."

"Allergies?"

"None."

"Has he been exposed to anyone who has tested positive for COVID-19?"

"He hasn't been exposed to anyone. He's been home, alone, for two weeks."

"Your name?"

"Rourke. Romeo, Oscar, Uniform, Romeo, Kilo, Echo."

"Hold please..."

A faint voice could still be heard. *"This is SD County Sherriff dispatch, I have one en route, ETA 11:13, high fever, faint pulse, no known exposure to COVID-19."*

The voice became more prominent. *"Rourke, Scripps is asking that you reroute to—"*

"Reroute? I'm not rerouting to anywhere." Luckily the freeway was nearly empty. Traveling at 120 miles an hour, I changed lanes to keep from hitting an Amazon delivery truck. "I'm goddamned near there, right now."

"Sir, the hospital's ICU is nearly at capacity with COVID-19 patients. If he hasn't had exposure to anyone with COVID-19, they're asking—"

I pressed the button on the steering wheel to hang up the call. "Go fuck yourself."

I drifted from the fast lane to the exit lane, still traveling in excess of 120 miles an hour.

"Rourke, are you still with me?"

"I told you to go fuck yourself," I snarled. I pressed the button again. "Go fuck yourself."

"Mister Rourke, Mercy is asking that you redirect to—"

"I'm not going anywhere else, asshole." The hospital was just off the Cabrillo Freeway, within eyesight. "I can see the hospital," I declared. "Have them outside at the emergency room entrance."

"Hold please..."

I heard mumbling, and then he returned. *"They'll be beneath the awning with a stretcher. You won't be able to enter the facility, Mister Rourke. It's on lockdown."*

I took the Washington Street exit at over 100 miles an hour, and then immediately took a right on 5th. The hospital was 300 yards away.

"He's not a fucking dog," I said, pointing the front of the vehicle toward the hospital's entrance. I stomped the gas pedal. "I'm not dropping him off."

"Sir, visitors are prohibited from—"

"I'm not a fucking visitor," I snapped. "I'm the only family this man has."

I careened over the curb and screeched to a stop beneath the emergency room awning, right beside where two men wearing hazmat suits and full Personal Protective Equipment stood.

Between them was a stretcher.

I rolled down the window. "He's in the back."

They loaded him onto the gurney and began taking his vitals. As one of the two men wheeled him into the hospital, the other pointed an electronic thermometer at my forehead.

"Stand still," he said.

"I'm going with him," I argued.

"You're not going anywhere until I take your temperature," he said. He paused, looked at the device's screen, and then gave me a nod. "Ninety-eight-point-eight."

I burst through the door and rushed toward the man who was wheeling my father down the corridor.

Two armed guards stepped in front of me. Both were wearing respirators. "Sorry," one of them said. "No one is allowed beyond—"

"That's my father," I barked, pointing toward the rapidly disappearing gurney. "I'm going where he goes."

"I'm sorry, Sir," the second one stated. "No one is allowed beyond the lobby."

I had news for him. Neither of them was big enough to stop me. Armed or not, they weren't going to intimidate me into leaving my father.

I cleared my throat. "Maybe you didn't hear me. That's my father."

"Sir," he said, raising the tone of his voice an octave. "If you venture beyond the lobby you will be arrested." He placed his hand beside his weapon. "This hospital is on lockdown. For your, and for everyone else's protection."

I glanced at his hand. I met his cold gaze. "You've got to be fucking kidding me. My protection?"

"Believe me," he responded. "It's for your own safety. We've got the entire ICU filled with infected."

I noticed the crown of an anchor peeking from beneath his shirt sleeve. I nodded toward it. "Military?"

He gave a curt nod. "Marines."

"I was with the two-seven," I said. "Twenty years."

"Ooh-rah," he said. "The three-nine."

"Semper fi, do or die." I glanced over each shoulder, and then stepped in front of him. "Tell me something, would you?"

"Sure."

"Between two Marines." I leaned close to him. "This is just you and me talking. Is this shit real?"

He seemed puzzled. "What shit's that?"

"This COVID-19 bullshit," I said. "It's bullshit, right?"

His eyes responded long before he opened his mouth. He nodded his head. "This hospital is nearly at capacity, all from COVID-19. They're losing 3-4 patients a day from respiratory failure. Patients are going from healthy to critical overnight. Young, old, healthy, unhealthy. It doesn't matter. This disease doesn't discriminate. It's as real as it gets."

I glanced the length of the corridor. My father was gone. With him went my certainty that all would be well.

I lowered myself into the nearest chair and did something I hadn't done since the war.

I began to pray.

15

ANNA

Day one.

The exhaust note from Braxton's SUV caught my attention. It was almost six o'clock. He'd been gone since just before noon. I peered outside just in time to catch a glimpse of him carrying a brown paper bag through his front door.

I wondered what he'd done all day. I doubted any of it was essential.

It frustrated me that he took time to send me a message, but never bothered to reply after I responded. It was painfully obvious his offer to apologize lacked sincerity. In Marge's eyes he was a saint. In reality he was an inconsiderate self-centered prick.

With my phone paired to the television's surround sound, I scrolled through my playlist. Upon finding Lady Gaga's *I'll Never Love Again*, I pressed *play*.

Listening to the song on loop, I contemplated sending Braxton another message. I needed to tell him that he was an utter and complete asshole. While I mentally formulated the tongue lashing, a one sentence message popped up on my phone.

Can you come to your front door? I'm at mine.

I walked to the front door and opened it.

Braxton stood in his doorway with his arms dangling at his sides like strings. Wearing a stark white tank top, dark washed jeans, and a pair of dress socks, he appeared out of place. His attire wasn't the only thing that was different. His face wore a distressed look.

It seemed as though he'd been defeated.

"What's going on?" I asked.

"This is day one," he deadpanned.

"Excuse me?"

"Day one," he said. "Of fourteen."

"Oh. You *did* get my text message," I said in as sarcastic of a tone as I could muster. "I didn't think it went through, not having heard back from you and all. I thought maybe the cell towers were overloaded with people streaming Netflix on their iPhones."

"I tested positive," he said flatly.

My stomach turned. In my haste to hate fuck him, we didn't bother to use a condom. The last thing I needed in my life was an STD.

"For what?" I blurted.

He swallowed hard. I prayed it was something an antibiotic could cure. I didn't want a lifelong reminder of the poor decisions I'd made when it came to sex.

"COVID-19," he replied. "Presumptive positive, anyway. I'll know for sure in a day or two,"

My heart sank into the pit of my stomach. "What!?" I gasped. "How?"

I knew how. He'd been running around like there was nothing to worry about. I had to ask, nevertheless. No matter how he contracted it, I wouldn't wish the disease on anyone. The thought of losing him, no matter how much of a prick he could be, was heartbreaking.

He raised his hand and took a bite of a sandwich. I wondered if he had it in his pocket, because I hadn't even realized he was holding it.

"My father is on a respirator fighting for his life in Mercy Hospital," he said over the mouthful of food. "He's been in contact with no one, other than me. I touched him, carried him to the car, and we've shared cooking utensils in the last few days. They gave me some chicken-shit test. They said it's inaccurate. They're assuming I'm positive. The results from the real test won't be until day after tomorrow, at best."

I felt sick. I needed to say something reassuring, but I didn't know what I could share that might make him feel any better.

I put on a false smile. "I saw this morning that a man in Iraq survived, and he was 103 years old. Then, there was this woman in Spain that was 101. She went home yesterday. How old is your father?"

"Seventy-five."

"Pffft," I waved my hand in his direction. "If he's anything like you, he'll be just fine. Wait and see."

"They won't let me see him." He lifted the sandwich, looked at it, and then lowered it without taking a bite. "I can't even get into the hospital."

"Probably for the best," I said. "They're trying to contain the spread."

He nodded, repeatedly. Almost mindlessly. When his head stopped bobbing, he looked up. "I'm sorry."

"For what?"

"Being inconsiderate. For constantly coming and going while the rest of the state is on lockdown. For not believing this pandemic was real. For leaving the other night when Mica came. I guess I'm apologizing for being a prick."

I hated to rub salt into an open wound, but I wasn't going to accept his apology if it wasn't heartfelt. As things stood, I wasn't sure if he was sincere or not. Having Braxton disappoint me again wasn't going to do me any good whatsoever. If I accepted his apology without an explanation, I would potentially set myself up for being hurt again.

"I'm not going to accept your apology just because you're feeling sorry for yourself," I said. "If you truly mean it, I mean *truly* mean it, I'll consider it."

"It wasn't easy for me to offer an apology to you in the first place," he explained. "It's not something I do very often. When you sent that text message asking for fourteen days, it pissed me off. All along, I thought this disease was nothing but bullshit. I know now that it's not. You were right, I was wrong. As far as I can tell, my father got infected from me. I don't know how else he could have contracted it, honestly. Me being inconsiderate has risked his life. By requesting fourteen days from me, all you were trying to do was protect yours."

"Apology accepted," I said.

He looked at the sandwich. Seeming disgusted, he blindly tossed it over his shoulder, into his house. He wiped his hand on the thigh of his jeans. "Want to start over?"

I stared in disbelief. "Whaaa?"

"Start over," he said. "At the beginning." He folded his arms over his chest. "Do you want to?"

"Where's the beginning of this mess?"

He seemed surprised at my response. "Mess? You think this has been a—"

"Don't act like it's been anything but a mess."

"Alright. I'll give you that," he said. "Fine, it has been a mess. To make it better, let's roll the clock back to where I tossed that guy in your trunk. We'll act like everything after that never happened. How's that sound?"

"Pretty good." I hoped to remain emotionless. I grinned a giddy smile, instead. "Hi. I'm Anna Wilson."

"Name's Rourke," he said. "Braxton Rourke. Nice to meet you."

"Do you ever smile, Rourke, Braxton Rourke?"

"I've been known to from time to time," he replied. "When the mood strikes me."

I lifted my tee shirt to my chin, exposing my very naked boobs for him to ogle. I hadn't worn a bra since the entire COVID-19 thing started. I hoped at some point my lack of lingerie would come in handy. It seemed my prayers had been answered.

At least one of them, anyway.

"Damn." He wagged his brows. "Is that standard procedure when you meet a man?"

"Not for all of them," I replied. "Only the cute ones."

He choked on a laugh. "I'm cute?"

In his jeans, tee shirt, and socks he was adorable. I offered him a smile of reassurance. "Yes, you are."

He may have blushed a little. It was hard to tell, because his beard hadn't been trimmed in a few days.

He smiled. "Thanks."

"I'm sorry about your father."

"So am I."

"I'll say a prayer for him." I pointed at the sky. "I'm in tight with the man upstairs."

He winced. "I'm not sure where I stand with him. If I was forced to guess, I'd say I'm pretty low on the totem pole. Wouldn't hurt to have someone else asking for favors, that's for sure."

"Consider it done."

He pointed behind his shoulder with his thumb. "I'm going to go pick that drive-thru sandwich up off the floor and make something else to eat. Do this again, sometime?"

"Sure."

"I'll have my people get with your people and set something up."

"I'll look forward to it," I said. "It was sure nice to meet you, Rourke, Braxton Rourke."

"Likewise."

16

BRAXTON

Day two.

I paced the floor like a nervous cat. My father's lungs were failing. His only hope for survival was the respirator that was doing the breathing for him. The hospital couldn't give me any information beyond "we're doing all we can", no matter how frequently I called or who I talked to.

What little time I wasn't pacing the floor, I was sitting at the kitchen island on my laptop, reading practices, procedures, and professional opinions of how to stop the disease from attacking the respiratory system of its victims.

There wasn't anything that had been proven. Not yet. There were only theories based on opinions. Nothing—not one procedure—was backed with facts or statistics.

Filled with frustration, I questioned the existence of God. How could a compassionate and caring God allow anything so deadly and unpredictable to encompass the globe? Why did he allow the world's most intelligent minds to scratch their heads in wonder, clueless of what to do to treat the novel virus?

I took my temperature every thirty minutes, only to find that nothing had changed. The disease may have been highly contagious, but it wasn't predictable.

I wanted to trade places with my father. I'd give anything to be fighting for my own life and allow him to healthily pace the kitchen floor, worried. He'd lived through one of the deadliest wars the United States had ever seen. For a virus to take his life without warning or reason seemed unfair.

Pratt called repeatedly, but I didn't answer. To hear "I told you so" or "I warned you" would only worsen matters. I needed to find a way to dig myself out of the state of depression I was in, not fall deeper into it. Pratt was going to have to wait.

Mindlessly, I marched through the living room and did an about-face when I reached the northern wall. I headed toward the kitchen. Upon reaching the sink, I turned around and started over, again. At the rate I was going, I'd have a path worn into the finish of the hardwood flooring in no time.

Midway through my 1,374th lap for the day, a knock at my door startled me out of the hypnotic state I'd slipped into.

I glanced at the security monitor on the kitchen countertop. In the upper right-hand pane, there was an image of Anna running across my yard. I laughed to myself. I meandered to the front door and opened it.

She'd placed an open-top box directly in front of the door. A folded sheet of paper sat atop several filled Ziploc bags, a bottle of wine, a bottle of canola oil, and a small box sealed with Amazon Prime tape. I picked up the box and gazed toward Anna's door.

She stood in the threshold of the doorway. Her frumpy sweats and oversized tee shirt had been traded for a form-fitting turquoise dress and pumps. Her hair was pulled close to her head and braided tightly.

She looked remarkable.

"Read the note, and then call me," she said with a smile. "We're having dinner together."

She closed the door.

I carried everything inside and placed the box on the kitchen island. I unfolded the note and read Anna's neatly written offering.

Braxton,

Let's make our own new normal, together. We'll start with Italian Wednesday (Taco Tuesday is so overrated).

We'll be having chicken parmesan, a tomato-mozzarella salad, and cabernet sauvignon. Everything you'll need is in the box. Well, almost everything.

Please shower and get dressed as if we were going out. I refuse to eat Italian unless I'm dressed for the occasion.

When you're ready to get started, call me. We'll cook it together. Make it quick, I'm starving.

Your friend,

Anna

I couldn't help but smile. The only part of the entire thing that bothered me was the way she signed the hand-written note. I don't know how I could have expected her to sign it in any other manner. It troubled me, nevertheless.

As Anna requested, I showered, got dressed, and returned to the kitchen. After separating the contents of the box out onto the countertop, I was mildly confused. One of the items seemed out of place.

I called Anna, hoping for clarification.

"How do you feel?" she asked upon answering.

"Fine."

"Any fever?"

"No. Nothing."

"Good," she said. "Are you ready to get started?"

"I think so," I replied. "I've one question, though."

"What is it?"

"What part does the tripod play?"

"That's going to come in handy," she said. "Believe me."

I lifted the small box and looked it over. "What am I going to do with it?"

"Your phone's an Android, isn't it?"

"Yeah, it's a Samsung."

"A new one?"

"I got it last year."

"Inside the Google options icon, there's Google Drive, Google Photos, Gmail, and a little movie camera symbol that says 'Duo.' When we get off this phone call, you're going to attach your phone to the tripod, situate it to point at you, and then you're going to call me on the Google Duo app. It'll let us do a video call."

"Sounds good," I replied.

"My phone is on the tripod right now," she said. "Get yours all hooked up and then message me using the app. Okay?"

"Will do."

I unboxed the tripod, attached the phone cradle mechanism, and adjusted the height to where I thought it should be. When I was satisfied, I called Anna using Google's Duo application.

When she answered, her face covered the entire screen, and a toothy smile covered her face. A small window in the lower corner contained a real-time video image of me.

She backed away from the camera and waved. "Hi."

"This works pretty well," I admitted. "The picture is great, and the sound is clearer than the phone."

"I like your choice of clothes," she said. "Is that shirt purple?"

I thought a suit would be too much and knew a tee shirt would be too little. I decided to wear my favorite button-down shirt with jeans and a nice pair of shoes.

"It's somewhere between pink and purple," I said. "It's perfect Italian Wednesday."

"Agreed. Are you ready?"

"I suppose."

"Roll up your sleeves," she said. "I don't want you to get chicken on your cuffs."

I didn't want chicken on my shirt, either. I did as she asked and rolled up the sleeves.

She wagged her finger toward the camera. "Do you have a rolling pin?"

"I do not."

She frowned. "A meat mallet?"

"A what?"

"It's like a hammer, but it's probably square. The face of it is covered with little spikey things." She made a striking motion with her clenched fist. "You tenderize meat with it."

"No kitchen hammers." I shrugged one shoulder. "Sorry."

She scowled. "You have a skillet, don't you?"

"I do."

"A cookie sheet?"

"More or less." I laughed. "It's kind of a long story. Abbreviated version is this: Pratt used it to change the oil on his Harley. It's kind of bent up, but it works just fine."

She scowled. "Who?"

"Pratt. He's a coworker and friend."

"I should have sent utensils." She scratched the side of her head. "Do you have a big hammer?"

"I've got a rubber mallet in the garage."

"Perfect," she said excitedly. "Go get it."

I returned in a moment with a rubber mallet. I presented it to the camera as if it were for sale. "One rubber mallet."

"Okay," she said. "We're going to leave the chicken in the plastic bag, place it on the countertop, and beat it to twice its size with that hammer. First, you're going to preheat the oven to 350. After you've done that, come back."

I turned the oven on and returned into the view of the camera.

"Watch me," she said, coming so close to the camera that she filled the entire screen with her face. "Okay?"

"Okay."

She backed away from the camera and panned it toward the

countertop. She raised a rolling pin, grinned slyly, and then commenced to beat the absolute shit out of a plastic wrap covered chicken breast.

"You. Pound. The. Meat. Like. It's. Your. Most. Regretful. Ex," she said, pounding the rolling pin against the meat with each spoken word. "Whoever. Screwed. You. Over. The. Most. Becomes. The. Meat."

When she was done, the meat was just as she'd described—nearly twice its original size.

She faced the camera. "Do that to your meat."

I left the chicken in the large Ziploc bag, situated it in the center of the island, and imagined it was my ex-wife.

An anger fueled tirade with the mallet ensued. When I came to my senses, I set the hammer aside and looked at the chicken. It was nearly see-through.

I looked at the camera. "How's that?"

She laughed. "Wow. Your meat's huge. Your chicken meat, not your...never mind. I'm stopping talking now."

I was as satisfied as I'd been in a long, long time. Something about preparing an impromptu meal with Anna was therapeutic. Beating the shit out of the chicken was an added bonus.

"I'm actually enjoying this," I said.

"Me, too." She smiled a cheesy grin. "Are you ready to continue?"

"Sure."

"Put the two eggs in a bowl and beat them with a fork. Not like you beat the chicken. Beat, as in, whip. You've scrambled eggs before, haven't you?"

"I have."

"Do that to them," she said. "Then, get three plates. Dump the flour-spice mixture on one of them, the breadcrumb mixture on the other, and leave the third one clean."

I gathered the things she'd asked me to. She guided me through the process of coating the chicken in the flour mixture, the beaten eggs, and the breadcrumbs. I then transferred the chicken breast to the plate.

"We're going to fry that in a skillet at medium high heat for about two minutes a side, and then we're going to cook it in the oven," she explained. "While it's cooking in the oven, we're going to prepare the salad. Get your skillet and grab the little bottle of oil, okay?"

With Anna's guidance, I fried the chicken, coated it in the sauce she provided, and then placed the two slices of mozzarella cheese on top.

My past experience with cooking included hamburgers, steaks on the grille, a variety of eggs, and sandwiches. Feeling like an accomplished chef, I placed the rather attractive creation on the mangled cookie sheet and slid it into the oven.

"I feel like I could do this on my own the next time," I said proudly. "Hell, it was easy."

"The next step is this..." She pressed her hands into the flour mixture. She presented them to the camera. She then made two white handprints against the otherwise spotless midriff of her dress. She smiled. "Now, it's your turn."

"Why would I do that?" I asked.

"Because," she replied. "It's fun."

I had nothing to lose. I reluctantly covered my favorite purple-pink shirt in flour handprints, laughing the entire time. It was the first time in as long as I could remember that I had laughed out loud.

I patted my hands against my shirt, repeatedly. When I stopped, I was covered in flour. So was the island, the floor, and the barstools.

"Are you done?" she asked, trying to catch her breath from laughing, too. "Holy cow. You're a mess."

"Done? I think so," I replied. I looked at the mess I'd made. "I needed that."

"Wash your hands," she said. "That flour had raw chicken in it. You don't want to live through the coronavirus and then get salmonella."

After washing our hands, we prepared the mozzarella and tomato salad. When the salad was finished, I removed the chicken from the oven.

With a glass of wine and a plate filled with food, I sat at the table and situated the camera in front of me.

"I was raised in the bible belt," she said. "When I was a kid, we prayed before we ate. It's been a while, but do you care if I say a prayer? Before we eat?"

Like most people I knew, I prayed when I saw no other alternative. Not having prayed in nearly a decade, I'd now said a dozen prayers in two days. Allowing Anna to say a prayer wasn't going to hurt matters one bit.

"Go right ahead," I said.

"What's your father's name?"

"Hap."

"Bow your head," she said.

I closed my eyes and lowered my head.

"Heavenly father, we come before you on this day to ask your blessing on this food. We also ask that you consider placing your healing hands on Hap Rourke—and on anyone else that's been stricken by this awful disease—because recovery, at least for some, has been difficult. Lastly, we'd like to ask that you give us the gifts of understanding and of acceptance, because sometimes, understanding your will is difficult. That leaves accepting it equally as difficult. We humbly ask these things in your name, Amen."

Amen.

Anna had provided just what I needed at the exact time I needed it. During the preparation of the meal, I had failed to feel guilty, wallow in self-pity, or openly worry about my father's condition.

I opened my eyes and looked at the phone. A smiling Anna looked back at me. She raised her wine glass.

"To being alone, together," she said.

I lifted my glass. "To being alone together."

"Cheers." She clanked her glass against her phone, knocking it askew in the process. After seeing several different views of her kitchen floor and a few seconds of total darkness, she righted the camera and pointed it in the proper direction.

"Sorry," she said. "This is going to take some getting used to."

"Yes," I said in complete agreement. "It sure is."

17

ANNA

Day 4

Braxton received word from the hospital that he was, in fact, positive for COVID-19. Even so, he hadn't shown any signs of infection, whatsoever. He had no fever, no difficulty breathing, nor did he have a headache or sore throat. According to him, he felt no differently than he did on any given other day.

He may not have felt differently, but there was no doubt that things had changed. Life was different. The new normal was worlds apart from what either of us was accustomed to.

I had no complaints. My afternoons, from 4:00 until 5:00 were spent with Marge. I could have easily talked to Braxton all day but settled for a couple short video calls. I knew smothering him wasn't in my—or his—best interest, so I kept our time on the phone low in volume and high in quality.

I was surprised to see that he was wearing a black tee shirt when he answered my late morning call.

"Good morning." He glanced at his watch. "I guess it's still morning."

"For another hour," I said. "Any word on your father?"

"He's stable." He looked away and shook his head. "That's all I'm getting. It's frustrating, but it's going to have to be enough. Everything I've read says 10-14 days to rid yourself of the disease. I'll keep my fingers crossed."

There was no assurance that the infected recovered over the course of a 10-14-day timeframe. Some took longer. The 14-day period was the window of time that the disease was contagious. Beyond that, the infected could remain sick, but they could not pass the disease to others.

I kept my opinions to myself and put on a reassuring smile. "I'll continue to pray."

"As will I."

Braxton looked remarkably well for having the virus. He stood as proof that the disease affected everyone differently.

"What about you?" I asked. "No fever?"

"No anything," he replied. "I started coughing last night, but it's inconsistent. I feel like I have a hair caught in my throat or something."

"Does that happen often?"

"A dozen times a day." He shrugged. "I don't know. After I cough once, it's over."

"No, I meant having a hair caught in your throat. Is that a common thing?"

"You're funny, Anna."

I smiled. "I try." I raised my notepad and pen. "I have a notepad and a pen."

He moved close to the camera in hope of seeing what I had written on it. "Am I supposed to applaud?"

I quickly placed the pad on the table, out of the camera's view. "You can if you like."

"What are all the notes?" he asked. "Recipes?"

"If you'll be quiet for a minute, I'll explain it."

He leaned away from the camera. "I'll let you have the floor. For now."

"You're familiar with Jimmy Fallon, and, what's the other guy, Kimmel? Jimmy Kimmel??"

"I know who they are."

"You're aware they have talk shows? That they get guests in front of a studio audience and talk about things?"

He looked at me like I'd offended him. "Do you think I'm an idiot, Anna?"

"I'm just asking a question."

"Yes, I'm aware that late night talk shows exist. Furthermore, I'm familiar with the show's architecture."

"We're using big words today, are we?"

"Which one threw you off?" he asked. "*Aware*, *familiar*, or *exist*?"

"Architecture," I replied. "I was surprised to see it used in that context."

"Architecture." He raised his index finger. "The complexity of design."

I flipped the camera the bird. "I know what it means, Mister Rourke. I was setting the stage for a joke."

He grinned. "And I derailed your train."

"If you prefer, the train will travel along the tracks of seriousness."

"I have no preference."

"If you're aware of the show's architecture," I said in a mocking tone. "This should be an effortless ride for you. Climb aboard."

His brows raised slightly. He seemed far from excited about matters. "You're going to ask me questions?"

"You're smarter than you look."

He flipped me the bird.

"Are you ready?" I asked.

"I suppose," he murmured.

I glanced at my notepad and then at the camera. "Excluding any aircraft or motorized automobiles of any sort, if you had to choose one mode of transportation to utilize for the remainder of your life, what would be your choice?"

"Only one?" he asked.

I tapped my pen against my lip. "Yes, only one."

"A skateboard."

"A skateboard?!" I arched a brow in opposition to his response. "Mister Rourke, that would make simple tasks like getting groceries nearly impossible. There are no wrong answers here, but I've got to ask. Of all the modes available, why a skateboard?"

"First, call me Braxton." He situated himself in his chair until he was comfortable. "In response to your question, riding a skateboard is similar to surfing. It provides a feeling of freedom that can only be obtained through a handful of transportation options. It's my first choice and that's my final answer."

Braxton wasn't a typical man, and he wasn't going to give typical responses. Although I'd prepared a line of questioning assuming what his answers were going to be, I decided to ad-lib the remainder of the interview.

I tossed my notepad into the air. As it fluttered to the floor, I continued. "You mentioned a feeling of freedom being found while riding a skateboard. Do value your freedom?"

"Yes, I do," he replied. "In fact, I value it enough that I fought in a war to preserve it for every citizen of this country."

"I'm sure the viewers appreciate the sacrifices you've made in that regard," I said. "I know I do."

He gave a slight nod. "Thank you."

"You've recently tested positive for COVID-19," I stated. "What do you have to say to the people of the nation regarding the stay at home order?"

"Travel exposes us to the disease. With exposure comes risk of infection. Becoming infected isn't the same for everyone. It's like being blindfolded and diving into a pool of water without any knowledge of the water's depth. For some, the pool is ten feet deep. For others, it's six inches deep. If we can stay at home—just for now—why take the risk?"

"Interesting analogy," I said. "Thank you."

"Absolutely."

"Back to something you said a moment ago. You're a war veteran. When most of us think of combat, things like death, destruction, and other atrocities associated with war come to mind. In hope of changing the viewer's outlook on war in general, can you share your fondest memory of your time in combat?"

"Sure." His gaze fell out of the camera's view. He exhaled a long, slow breath. After a moment, he looked up. "Can you give me a moment to put everything together?"

"Absolutely," I replied. "We can come back to this question if you'd like."

"Let's do that."

I thought the question might persuade him to recall one good thing from a sea of what was bad. In doing so, I hoped he'd see that current matters weren't as bleak as they seemed to be. I now felt like a heel for asking.

I did my best to mask my disappointment with myself. "Moving on," I said with a smile. "Your life's biggest regret, Braxton. What is it?"

"I don't have any regrets."

"Not one?"

"Nope."

"A car you didn't buy?" I asked. "An investment you didn't make? A wave you failed to ride? Nothing?"

"Nope."

I scowled. "I find that hard to believe."

"My actions and decisions, be them good or be them bad, have formed me into the man I am today. To harbor regrets is to wish I could go back and change something. To make changes to my life would potentially alter the man I am. That's not something I'm comfortable doing."

"So, you're completely satisfied that there's no room for improvement when it comes to the life of Braxton Rourke?"

"I didn't say that," he replied. "I have faults. I'm not willing, however, to make changes to the person I am."

"Your response leads right into the next question." I twirled my pen between my fingers while studying the look on his whiskered face. "It's common knowledge that you're a promiscuous man. You've admitted it. I have two questions along that line. One, how has the lockdown challenged your promiscuity? And two, what are you doing to keep that licentious boat afloat during this time of trouble?"

He glared.

I leaned away from the camera and crossed my arms. "Would you like me to repeat the question?"

"Licentious?" he said. "Really?"

"Licentious." I raised my index finger and cleared my throat. "Lustful or shameless," I said in a low man-like voice. "I thought we agreed it's big word day?"

"I know what the motherfucker means," he snarled.

"Let's try to keep the expletives to a bare minimum, shall we?"

"Sure," he said snidely. "I'll refrain from saying things like fuck and cocksucker."

I smiled. "Thank you."

He rolled his eyes. "Although I may be described as promiscuous, I'm not an addict when it comes to sex. Therefore, the lockdown hasn't caused any problems in my sexual life. It's—"

"Are you're saying that you can abstain from having sex?"

His brows pinched together. "Absolutely."

"For what length of time?"

"I don't know," he replied. "A month?"

"A month?" I coughed. "I'm sure many in our audience would view a month without sex as standard relationship protocol. A normal breather between lovemaking sessions, if you will."

He stared blankly at the camera. "A one-month dry spell is considered a *breather*?"

"For some?" I shrugged. "Sure."

"I disagree. Let's take a look at you for instance. You once went two years without sex. By my guess, you were pissed off at the male population in general. That wasn't a breather."

My face went flush. I'd forgotten that I shared that tidbit of information with him. My line of questioning was now off-course, and I'd become the butt of the joke. I was ready to end the interview and start talking about what we should order from Grubhub for lunch.

Discussing our favorite sushi sounded much better than delving into the reasons behind my 2-year hiatus from sex. I exhaled a breath of frustration and began to tell the condensed version.

"I wasn't angry at the male population, in general," I explained. "Just one of them, really. The subsequent 'dry spell' wasn't a breather. It was a conscious decision I made *not* to have sex. My body, my decision."

He twirled his index finger in a circular motion. "Moving on..."

It must not have been the answer he was hoping for. Based on his reluctance to attack me when he had an open door, I decided to continue with the interview.

"Starting the clock on your nineteenth birthday, what's the longest period of time you've ever gone without masturbating?" I asked.

His face quickly filled the screen. "Say again?"

"Self-administered sexual gratification," I said. "Masturbation. Pulling the proverbial pud. What's the longest period of time you've gone without doing it?"

He leaned away from the camera. A serious look covered his face. "Thirteen weeks, I suppose."

"Your response came without much thought," I replied. "Is that a common period of abstinence for you?"

"That period of time was during basic training for the Marine Corps. It's an easy one for me to remember."

"What would an average period of abstinence be?"

"From masturbating?"

"Yes, we're still on that subject."

"9-1/2 hours," he said flatly.

"Nine point five?" I chuckled. "That's an interesting number. Care to elaborate?"

"Usually I do it before bed, and then again before I start my day. That's two times during a period of 19 hours a day that I'm awake. As I can't do it while sleeping, I'd say the average must come from the waking hours. 19 waking hours divided by 2 sessions equates to a nine- and one-half hour average."

"You only sleep for 5 hours a night?"

"I never sleep more than 5 hours."

"Why?"

"It's all that's needed."

"And then you wake up and whack off?" I asked, laughing. "Like clockwork?"

"Yes. When I wake up and before I go to bed," he replied. "What's your average?"

"Sleep, or my average period of abstinence?"

"Abstinence. We're still on that subject," he replied mockingly.

"My average is going to hell." I let out a sigh. "I've been too distracted, lately."

"When is the last time you masturbated?" he asked.

"Truth or a lie?"

He chuckled. "The studio audience prefers the truth."

"Let's see." I twisted my mouth to the side and glanced at the time. "I'd say, roughly 43 minutes ago."

"Is an eleven o'clock diddle pretty common?"

I laughed. "Diddle?"

"That's what it's called when women do it."

"What's it called when men do it?" I asked.

"Whacking off," he replied as if he were answering a question on *Jeopardy!*

"In response to your question," I said. "The time of day isn't important for me. I'm partial to events. Showering, for instance. I do the dirty little diddle when I shower."

"Before or after you wash yourself?"

"During," I replied. "It's like an intermission. Have you ever been to a hockey game?"

"I have."

"Then you know the importance of the intermission. That's the way a shower is for me. I need a little break between washing my body and washing my hair."

"It gets pretty boring, otherwise?"

"The diddle breaks up the monotony of showering."

"Is it an 'every time you shower' type of affair?" he asked.

"That's affirmative."

"How many times a day do you shower?"

"Normally, at least once." I laughed at the thought of how filthy I'd become a week prior. "A week ago? Once a week, maybe."

His face contorted. "Once a week?"

"I was going through an adjustment period. A confinement meltdown."

"No shower, no diddle?" he asked. "Is that the rule."

"That is correct. Dirtiness deprived me of the diddle."

"Is showering the only time you do the diddle?"

"No, no, no, no, no." I shook my head in protest. "Not at all."

"How often do you partake?"

"Whenever the opportunity presents itself."

He rested his chin in the web of his hand and rubbed his stubble with his thumb and forefinger. "What qualifies as an opportunity?"

"Generally speaking? Five or ten minutes of solitude. I've done it at a stoplight and in the drive-thru at Taco Bell, once. There was a van from the old folk's home in front of me, so the line was moving really slowly."

"What gets your mind headed in the right direction? Are you a partaker of porn?"

"No, no, no," I said. "A memory, the right song, or the smell of certain colognes set me off. Often, the slightest suggestive comment is enough. It doesn't take much, as long as I'm not in a funk."

He lowered his hand. "Interesting."

"What's your weirdest story?"

"In general, or masturbating?" he asked.

"Let's go with masturbating."

"The combat jack."

I stared. "The com-what?"

"The combat jack," he replied. "It's jacking off while in combat."

"Wait...how can—" I waited for him to laugh or say he was joking, but he stared back at me stone-faced. "When you're in combat?" I asked. "Like, at war?"

"Right in the middle of it," he replied. "We had contests. To see who could be the most creative. One of the guys did it while he was firing his machinegun."

I couldn't come close to reaching climax unless I was completely relaxed. Getting the job done while bullets whizzed past would be impossible.

"That's just weird," I said. "I need music and serenity. If there's a horn honking in the distance I've got to throw in the towel."

"You said you did it at a traffic light," he argued. "And at a Taco Bell drive-thru."

"I had the stereo playing and my eyes were closed."

He looked at me like I was nuts. "You close your eyes?"

"Always," I replied. "You don't?"

He laughed. "Nope. I like to watch myself ejaculate." He smirked. "The cum shoots out of the tip of my dick like a rocket. It's really something to see."

I swallowed a ball of desire as it climbed up my throat. "I think this interview's over."

"You were right." He laughed. "It doesn't take much, does it?"

With the right man, it didn't.

As much as I wanted Braxton to be nothing more than a friend, he continued to inch his way closer to my heart each time we saw each other.

Even if it was through the lens of a cell phone's camera.

Marge was on the top step of a three-foot step ladder, washing her windows. The day's attire was a pair of bluish green pants that came to mid-calf, and a royal blue top. I would have never thought to put them together, but they looked remarkable.

I stepped into the street and shook my head. "You're going to fall if you're not careful."

"I've been washing these windows like this for longer than I care to admit," she said over her shoulder. "I'm just about done."

"You're making me nervous."

She wiped the window with the towel she held, laughing all the while. "Well, you're making me nervous."

I cringed as she swayed back and forth, rubbing like her life depended on it. "Sorry."

She leaned her head from side to side, looking for streaks. When she found them, she wiped the glass vigorously until they were gone.

She took one last look at the window, and then began her journey down the ladder. "Have you ever struggled with something you wanted to say but couldn't decide if there was enough value in mentioning it to go ahead and mention it?"

"I suppose."

She leaned the ladder against the side of the house and draped her rag over the top rung. She walked to the curb and then turned and came up the street almost even with where I stood, but across the street.

She brushed the wrinkles from her top. "I can't decide whether or not to bring something up. There's a part of me wants to mention it, but the part of me that's reserved tells me to keep my mouth shut." She looked up. "The part of me that's reserved is a small part."

I shrugged. "I say mention it."

She smiled. "Alright, I will." She nodded toward Braxton's house, which was right behind me. "The other night you were standing on your porch talking to Braxton, and you pulled your shirt over your head. It looked to me like something that was deliberately flirtatious. Has there been progress made since we last spoke of him?"

My face went flush. "Uhhm. You saw that, huh?"

"Honey, I think the entire neighborhood saw it."

"I was trying to cheer him up."

"Did it work?" she asked.

I was so embarrassed. "he seemed to enjoy it, yes."

"Well, I suppose that's all that matters." She touched the sides of her snow-white curls as if to make sure they were still there. "Are you two seeing one another now?"

"I wouldn't say that, no."

Her brows raised. "What would you say then?"

"Well, we had a virtual dinner the other night. It was fun. We did it over our telephones on a video call. Have you even seen one of those?"

"I have them with my sister all the time."

"Well, we cooked dinner together on a video chat. Then, we ate together. We've been doing something together each day over video chat."

"Sounds like you two are sweet on one another."

"He's nice," I said. "Or, maybe I should say he can be nice."

"Men are like watermelons," she said. "It's what's inside that counts."

I laughed. "I like that."

"Braxton's a good man on the inside. He's just got a really tough rind that you've got to get through. He gave someone his heart and they didn't take care of it, remember?"

"I remember."

"Give him every reason in the world to believe you'll never hurt him. That's all you can do. I guess you could flash him from time to time." She giggled. "That wouldn't hurt matters."

"I don't know where we stand right now," I said. "We're really just friends."

Her face scrunched up. "Honey. This is Marge you're talking to.

When you talk about him your eyes light up like a Fourth of July fireworks display. You can tell that old busybody, Fred, that lives north of you whatever you want. You should stick with telling me the truth."

"I like him, but I don't know if he likes me," I said. "In the same way, that is."

"Give him time, and he'll come around," she said.

"I hope you're right."

"I'm sure of it," she said with a smile. "Because you're an easy one to like."

18

BRAXTON

Day 6

When I was deployed, there was one thing that helped me escape the reality of war. The exercise—although for only for a few hours at a time—was crucial to maintaining my sanity. Keeping a level head allowed me to remain in combat for roughly a decade without ever losing touch with my true self.

When my unit finally left the Middle East, many of my fellow Marines were already suffering from Post-Traumatic Stress Disorder. Once removed from the war, their minds were incapable of processing the atrocities they had been exposed to. Sadly, they would likely live the remainder of their lives fighting a new battle.

With themselves.

Fortunately, I was one of the few who would recall every battle, each loss of life, and all the combat-related mistakes I felt I'd made without allowing those things to become controlling of my mind or my life.

The difference, I was convinced, was how I spent my idle time while at war.

What was my saving grace?

Reading.

When the war was over, I cast my books aside. Over the years, I wondered if I associated reading with the war, and therefore chose not to risk resurrecting those memories by cracking the cover of a book.

Feeling I needed a means of escape once again, I was willing to determine if the risk of opening a book was worth the reward of peace of mind.

I joined Amazon Prime and ordered two copies of my three favorites, Mark Haddon's *The Curious Incident of the Dog in the Night-Time*, Nicole Krauss' *The History of Love*, and Frank McCourt's *Angela's Ashes*.

I anxiously waited all day for them to arrive. Disappointed somewhat with their midafternoon arrival, I unpackaged the books and looked them over. I removed one set for myself. After disinfecting the other three books, I placed them in the box with gloved hands, and then added a hand-written note. I carried the box to Anna's door and rang the doorbell.

I walked to the middle of her yard, paused, and faced her door.

It swung open. Waves of caramel-colored curls cascaded over her shoulders. She was wearing a cotton mask over her mouth. Dressed in khaki shorts, a sleeveless leopard-print silk top and leather sandals, she looked adorable.

"I like your outfit," I said. "You look cute."

"Thank you," she replied, her voice muffled slightly from the mask. "I like yours, too."

I was wearing a pair of sweatpants, a ribbed tank top, and house slippers. Normally, I reserved such outfits for my Sunday morning cups of coffee in my kitchen. Now, things were different. There were only three days to be concerned with. Today, tomorrow, and yesterday.

"I'm going for the relaxed look," I said.

"You accomplished it well," she said. "I like it when you dress nice, but that looks pretty awesome, too." She nodded toward my hands. "What's with the gloves?"

"I disinfected everything with Lysol, including the box," I replied. "Then, I washed my hands, put on gloves, and carried it to your door. There's no such thing as being too safe."

"Thank you." She glanced at the box. "What's in there?"

"Books. There's three of them. Decide which one you want to start with. Let me know what you decide. We'll read five or six chapters, and then discuss it."

"Like a book club. Sounds fun," she said. "I haven't read a book in forever."

I nodded toward the box. "Those are my three favorites."

She picked up the box and peered inside. Seeming giddy with excitement, she looked up. "Give me a few minutes to decide, and then I'll give you a call."

"Okay."

I'd read *Angela's Ashes* twice, cover to cover. The winner of the Pulitzer Prize the year after it was published, the book was proof that there's always someone whose struggle is worse than your own. The tale is told from the perspective of the Irish American author, Frank McCourt. He grew up in the early 1900's, living in poverty with his mother, father, and six siblings. During his childhood, his sister and twin brothers died from various causes. His mother was manically depressed over the loss of her children but somehow managed to maintain her keen sense of humor. His father was an alcoholic who loved to tell Irish folk stories.

I'd probably read *The Curious Incident of the Dog in the Night-Time* a dozen times. The book's narrator, a teenage boy who was a mathematical genius with a behavioral disorder, had an entertaining voice. Although written by a man in his forties, the book seemed to have been written by the 15-year-old boy. I found each page of the story as interesting as the next.

The History of Love, one of Nicole Krauss' many novels, spanned the lifetime of an 80-year-old man, Leo Gursky. Following the

German invasion of Poland, Leo and his then girlfriend are separated, leaving her to raise Leo's child in the United States without his immediate knowledge of being a father. It was a story woven with many pieces of yarn, each thread being a story in itself. I'd read the book more times than I could count. Every reading provided another morsel of the author's intention.

I wondered which book Anna would choose. My father had carefully selected each of the stories, shipping them overseas when I was deployed. Ready to get started, I sauntered home and sat down at the kitchen table.

I thumbed through the books for thirty minutes or so before Anna called. Eager to find out which of the three books she had chosen, I answered the phone filled with nervous excitement.

"Did you decide?" I asked.

"These are really interesting choices," she said.

"Have you read any of them yet?"

"Not yet."

"Good. Which one are you thinking?"

"This is cute," she said with a laugh. "You sound really excited."

"I haven't been this enthusiastic about something in a long time," I admitted. "The last time I read a book was when I was overseas."

I was excited for many reasons. I wanted to share the books with Anna more than anything, but I also hoped that reading could take me away from the reality of my life. A life in which my father was hospitalized, sickened by a disease that had no known cure.

"Well?" I asked, fanning the books out in front of me. "Which one?"

"I'm going to suggest we start with the one about the dog," she replied. "It sounds fun."

"*The Curious Incident of the Dog in the Night-Time.* That's probably my most favorite of them all."

"How are we going to do this?" she asked.

"I was going to suggest we read five chapters or something like that, and then discuss what we'd read. The author in that book only used prime numbers for the chapters. So, it starts with 2, and then goes to 3, and then 5, 7, 11, 13, 17, 19, 23, etcetera, etcetera. I guess we could read 2 through 23. The chapters are really short. We can play it by ear after that."

"Do you want me to call you when I'm done?"

I grinned at the thought. "Sure."

"Okay. Dog book, it is. I'll call you when I get done with chapter 23."

I reached for the book. "Okay."

"Talk to you in a bit."

I hung up the phone and opened the book to chapter 2. It seemed that no time had passed and I was finished. Instead of re-reading the previous chapters, I read ahead.

I laughed at the antics of the book's teenage narrator, Christopher. When I began chapter 41, my phone rang. Anxious to find out what Anna thought of the book, I nearly knocked the phone on the floor when I scrambled to reach for it.

"It's official," she said. "I'm in love."

My heart faltered. "With?"

"Christopher. And this book. Oh my gosh, this is wonderful. It's like a murder mystery."

"It is a murder mystery, written by a 15-year-old."

"I love it," she said. "Let's discuss the first few chapters, and then I need to get back to reading."

"So, what do you think so far?" I asked. "Sounds like you're enjoying it."

"I find it interesting that Christopher doesn't understand how people's facial expressions correlate to their moods, but he can name every country in the world. It's really cute how he talks to the reader just like he'd be talking to you if you were sitting across from him in the living room."

"His voice is remarkable, isn't it?"

"I'm enjoying it," she said. "Immensely. I like how he said there will be no jokes in the book, because jokes require using words that have dual meanings, and words with dual meanings make him uncomfortable. And that he made little charts to explain how prime numbers are determined. It's a really well put together story. It's so cute."

"Who killed the dog?" I asked.

"I have no idea!" she blurted. "That's part of what's so exciting about it. I know it wasn't Christopher, because I think it would be impossible for him to tell a lie. I also don't think he could stab a dog with a pitchfork. A pitchfork and a gardenfork are the same thing, aren't they?"

"I think so."

"It was also kind of funny that the police made him remove his shoelaces and all the stuff from his pockets when they arrested him, so he couldn't hang himself or attack one of them with his pocketknife. The way he describes things is so no-nonsense. I'd like to have a friend like him because you'd know what you were getting. No bullshit, only the facts. He'd tell you up front how things were going to be, and that's the way they'd be. I love it."

"How would you like to proceed?"

"Are you kidding me?" she asked excitedly. "I want to read the book. All of it. Call me when you're done."

"Okay." I laughed. The laugher started a coughing fit. Before I knew it, I was out of breath.

"Are you alright?" she asked.

"I'm..." I coughed until the fit finally subsided. "I'm fine."

"You sound awful.

"Thanks."

"No fever?"

"No, just a nasty cough."

"Do you feel pressure on your lungs?"

I did, but it wasn't terrible. Not worth worrying her over, that was for sure. It was nothing more than a tight chest and a cough.

"No," I replied. "Not yet, anyway."

"They say it creeps up on you. You go from feeling like you've got a chest cold to having full-blown pneumonia in an instant. I want you to call me if it gets worse."

"I will."

"I mean it."

"If this turns into more than a cough, you'll be the first to know," I assured her.

"Okay," she said. "If that's all it is, let's stop talking about it and get busy reading."

"Sounds good to me." I stifled an oncoming cough. "Let's get to it."

"Call me when you're done."

There was an annoying tickle in my throat. I needed to end our call, or I was going to end up in another coughing fit.

I tried to keep from drawing a breath. "We'll talk then."

"I meant what I said," she said. "About the cough."

"I heard you," I replied. "We'll talk later. When we're done with the book."

As soon as I hung up the phone, the coughing started. It didn't end until I was too exhausted to continue.

A wave of body aches surged through me, repeatedly.

The high fever and accompanying chills were next.

19

ANNA

Day 7

I finished the book a little after midnight. I enjoyed it so much that I reread at least half of it, immediately. I eventually fell asleep at about 4 am. When I awoke five hours later, I felt like I'd been cheated out of half my day.

Feeling invigorated by my resurrected love of reading, I sprung from my bed and checked my phone. There were no messages or missed calls. Assuming that Braxton stayed up all night reading no differently than I did, I dismissed the fact that he had not called.

I ate breakfast, showered, and picked my outfit for the day. Braxton and Marge's consistent presence in my day-to-day life had changed my outlook on everything from the food I ate to the clothes I wore.

The friendship Braxton and I now shared was playful, expectation free, and without the problems associated with a sexual relationship. I looked forward to the time I shared with him as much as I did my afternoons with Marge.

At 11:00, after hearing nothing from Braxton, I sent him a text message confirming I had finished the book.

The next hour seemed to drag on forever. Braxton didn't contact me, leaving me wondering if his cough worsened, or if he had grown sicker as the night progressed.

I tried calling, but there was no answer. I recalled what Braxton said during my makeshift interview about his sleeping habits. He claimed he never slept more than 5 hours a night. He shouldn't be sleeping.

I began to wonder if he'd grown sicker, or if he needed help.

I called again. And then, again.

I debated whether or not to beat on his door. By the time 1 o'clock arrived, that's exactly what I did.

Donning a facemask, rubber gloves, and a package of Clorox wipes, I sterilized Braxton's door. Then, I pounded on it with all my might. I paused. The sound of a distant truck on the highway was the only sound to be heard. I tried the handle.

Locked.

I pounded and pounded, calling Braxton's name as I pummeled the door with my knuckles, fist, and foot. Continued silence. It was time to call the police. I fumbled to retrieve my phone with my sweaty hands slathered in rubber.

Someone unlocked the door.

I took a few steps back and waited for it to open.

The door opened, slowly. Braxton was leaning against it to keep from falling over. It appeared he was wearing the same outfit as the day before, but with one difference. His clothes were drenched in sweat.

My heart sank into my stomach.

"Oh my God," I gasped. "What's wrong? Are you okay?"

He shook his head. "I ache."

His voice sounded like he had eaten sand for breakfast and washed it down with salty crackers. He looked like recycled death.

"Do I need to call an ambulance?" I asked.

"It's not as bad as it looks," he muttered.

"You look like death."

"I feel worse."

He struggled to catch his breath between responses. His raspy breathing was impossible to hide. He was sicker than he wanted to admit. I needed to convince him to let me call an ambulance.

"Do you have a fever?"

He nodded. "103 last time I checked."

"Chest pain?"

"Pressure," he said. "Not pain."

"You need to go to the hospital." I raised my phone in the air. "I'll call an—"

"No." He drew a labored breath. "I'll be fine. The hospitals need the room for people like my father. I don't need their help. Not yet."

It was difficult to admit, but Braxton was right. The hospitals were overflowing with critically ill patients who were much sicker than he was. Considering his notoriety, they'd probably admit him, nevertheless. Then, they may turn away a patient who needed the bed much worse than he did. I'd seen several cases on the news where institutions had turned away patients due to overcrowding only to have them die at home a day or two later.

He swayed back and forth, nearly too weak to stand. I fought against my selfish desires.

"If you'll do this my way, I won't call an ambulance." I took a step in his direction. "If you won't, I'll call one right now and tell them who you are and demand that they take you in."

He raised his right hand. "Don't come any closer."

"Will you do it my way?"

"Depends."

"You're going to go to bed, drink plenty of liquids, and take as much Vitamin C as you can swallow. Then, you're going make sure your phone is plugged in. You're going to call me and leave the phone on speaker—from now until you're better. No exceptions. I want to be able to hear you. At all times."

"What if—" He coughed until he was breathless. "—what if the hospital calls?"

"Disconnect the call to me and answer it."

"Okay."

"Are we in agreement?"

He nodded.

"Do you have Vitamin C?"

"Yes."

"Plenty of it?"

He nodded.

"Bottled water?"

He nodded.

"Do you need anything?"

He shook his head. "Thank you."

I wanted to lead him to his bed and tuck him in. The disease was far too contagious for me to get within six feet of him. "I mean it, Braxton."

He glanced at his feet. "I'm going to get a key and drop it here. In an hour or so, come sterilize it. Keep it on your keyring. Only use it if you absolutely have to."

The thought of needing it caused my throat to tighten. I swallowed against it. "Okay."

"I'll call you as soon as I get to bed."

I nodded. "Okay."

If there was a hell—and I was convinced there was—Braxton was living in it. He sounded like his next breath was sure to be his last. He looked worse.

I stood in the middle of the yard with my face obstructed by a rudimentary mask I ordered on Amazon, my hands covered with rubber gloves, and a can of Lysol clenched in my left fist.

I wondered what had become of the world I once knew, and if it would ever return to normal.

I sat in silence and listened to the rhythm of Braxton's breathing.

He drew a moisture saturated breath. A long pause followed. The sound of him exhaling resembled a distant freight train's horn. Following another pause, he drew a gurgling breath. He often sounded as if he were choking. The process, as grueling as it was to listen to, continued in a predictable fashion.

I told myself if it worsened, I'd call an ambulance.

My phone's alarm buzzing startled the hell out of me. I quickly cancelled it, hoping the vibrating sound didn't wake Braxton from his sleep.

Thankfully, his labored breathing continued.

I hadn't told Marge about Braxton's condition, or that he'd tested positive for the virus. I didn't want to alarm her, nor did I want her to worry about contracting the virus.

I slipped the phone into my pocket and fitted the earbuds into my ears. A final adjustment to my hair camouflaged the fact that I'd be paying attention to something in addition to my conversation with Marge. I didn't want her to think she'd become any less important to me. If anything, I felt closer to her with each passing day.

Since the beginning of our afternoon gatherings, we had inched closer and closer to one another. Now, we were having our afternoon meetings no more than 30 feet apart.

With my earbuds and phone out of view, I ventured to the end of Braxton's driveway. Marge was on her hands and knees, plucking small pieces of debris out of her rock garden.

"Good afternoon," I said.

She looked up. She set her plastic bag of trash aside and sauntered to the closest edge of the neighbor's driveway. "Good afternoon, Anna."

I moved to the far edge of Braxton's drive. We were only twenty feet apart. "How was the pot roast last night?" I asked.

"It was wonderful," she replied. "I used the leftovers for lunch today, and it was remarkable. It's funny. I can't fathom putting mustard on pot roast, only ketchup. But, when I make a sandwich out of the roast, I want mustard on it."

"I'm the same way with a meatloaf sandwich," I said. "Ketchup on it when I eat it hot, but I put mustard on a meatloaf sandwich."

"Why is that, do you suppose?" she asked.

I shrugged. "That's how my mother always served it to me. Maybe that's it."

She considered my response for a moment, and then smiled. "My mother always served the three of us leftover roast beef sandwiches on white bread with butter. We didn't get a choice, that's how she made them. I don't know that we always had mustard, I can't recall."

"I can't imagine life without mustard."

"Mayonnaise has got to be one of my favorites. That, and wine." She laughed. "Not together, of course."

"You like wine?" I asked.

"I drink it every night. Always have. Not in excess, of course. At least not always. I prefer the sweet wines."

"I drink it quite often, too," I admitted.

"They say it's good for you." She lowered herself to the curb. "In moderation, of course."

The predictable sound of Braxton's breathing became hypnotic.

Marge's outfit, as always, was awesome. The orange pants and a blue short-sleeved shirt she'd chosen were adorable. I realized I'd yet to see her wear the same thing twice. She took pride in how she presented herself, and I looked forward to seeing her clothing choices each afternoon.

I wanted to be like Marge in forty years. She was part of a generation that was nearly extinct. She came from an era that was easy to admire and difficult to duplicate.

I realized that there were many like her who wouldn't live through the pandemic. People who were set in their daily routines of eating at five o'clock, watching Wheel of Fortune before bed, and eating toast with their cup of coffee when they woke up.

Men and women who had played their part in forming the country into a great place to call home. People who had made their contribution to the younger generations who lived amongst them.

People who had lived nearly a full lifetime but weren't quite ready to depart this earth, and now simply hoped to exhale and enjoy the last leg of their journey. Many had already been deprived.

Countless more were destined to.

Braxton's cough brought me out of my dreamlike state. I smiled. "I know I sound like a broken record, but I love your outfit."

"Thank you. I got this on sale at Neiman Marcus." She swept her palms across the thighs of her pants. "I buy a lot of my clothes there. Did you see where this is going to cause them to declare bankruptcy? I sure hate to see it. They've been around since 1907."

"That's sad."

She shook her head. "The entire thing is sad. They said on the news last night that of those tested, 10% were infected. The more people they tested, the more positive cases they found. They said 36% of those infected have died, and that 88% of the patients in New York that required a ventilator didn't make it. It's just awful. All of it."

I'd all but stopped watching the news, I couldn't take it any longer. Absorbing Marge's statistics nearly brought me to my knees. The bottom line, according to the numbers, was that if you contracted the disease, regardless of your physical condition, there was a distinct possibility that you may die.

Braxton coughed. He fought to catch his breath. It sounded like he was blowing bubbles in a jar of mayonnaise.

I tensed from head to toe.

He drew a gurgling breath. He coughed. A few choppy breaths followed. The room fell silent for a few seconds before he settled into his routine.

I exhaled a breath of relief.

"Are you okay?" Marge asked. "You seem, I don't know. Preoccupied. Worried, maybe."

I put on a false smile. "I'm fine," I said with a dismissive wave of my hand. "I've just. I've got a friend who is...he's uhhm." I swallowed heavily. "He's ill."

She gasped. "With the virus?"

I wasn't sure what to say. If I told her the truth, she might overreact. If I lied to her, I wouldn't be much of a friend. I struggled with what to say for a moment as I watched the look on her face morph from content to worried.

At the instant I began to tell her an abbreviated version of the truth, Braxton coughed again. I paused. His coughing fit lasted much longer than normal. Eventually, he relaxed into his labored routine of breathing.

I sighed. "It's Braxton," I said, gesturing behind me. "He's...he's sick."

I waited for her to gasp, make some distance between us, or explain that it wasn't in her best interest to continue meeting with me until he was either diagnosed, or better.

She searched my face for clues as to what was wrong. "Does he have—"

"He..." I murmured. "He uhhm..."

I couldn't say it. I bit against my quivering bottom lip and nodded. Tears rolled down my cheeks. Marge took a step in my direction.

"Oh, Honey," she said. "I'm so sorry."

"Marge, no," I blubbered, taking a step back. "You shouldn't. We're supposed to stay six feet apart. You can't—"

"Honey, there's a lot of things I can't do." She took me into her arms and pulled me against her chest. "But standing here watching my friend come unraveled in front of me isn't one of them."

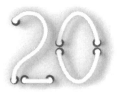

20

BRAXTON

Day unknown

The blast from Ketner's shotgun tore the locking mechanism from the doorframe. Standing free of the trafficway to the right side of the door, Ketner planted the heel of his left boot against the bottom edge of the door, causing it to swing open freely.

I rushed through the door and moved to clear my assigned sector. Each passing second became a moment long. Movements were exaggerated, similar to the slow-motion scenes of the many action-adventure movies I watched as a child.

From the blanket-covered window toward the floor on my left, a single ray of sunlight pierced through the darkened room, diagonally. Like microscopic ballerinas, particles of dust danced within the limits of the beam of light, each a hovering reminder that we were intruders in what was once a family's safe haven.

There was no furniture or light fixtures. No interior walls. No rooms. Blankets were scattered about the dirty floor, each likely used as bedding for those who dared to occupy the space. The stale smell of sweat and cordite melded with the unmistakable odor of adrenaline.

A man shot to his feet. He reached for a weapon that leaned against the wall at his side.

My finger tapped the trigger twice.

His hand released the rifle. His body remained erect, refusing to comply with the mind's recognition that his heart had stopped beating. His eyes the only part of him that seemed to recognize the truth of what had happened. Open and confused, they stared back at me.

A second man swung the barrel of a Kalashnikov in my direction.

My finger tapped the trigger twice.

He stumbled.

I tapped the trigger once again.

He slumped into the corner of the room. The weapon clanked against the floor, bounced, and came to rest at his side.

A woman screamed. She rushed to the fallen man's side. Her hands were obstructed by her hijab, the traditional Muslim dress.

"Raweenee edeek!" I shouted. "Show me your fucking hands! Raweenee edeek!"

Her empty hands emerged from beneath her dress. Relief washed over me. Then, she reached for the weapon.

"Asqat alsilah!" I shouted, standing no more than fifteen feet from her. "Drop the fucking weapon!"

She chose not to heed my command.

Two successive rounds from the M4 flattened the fabric of the hijab to her chest. Her body tumbled, landing mere inches from the man whose death she hoped to avenge. Face up, she remained motionless.

The dusty gray fabric draped her body from her shoulders to her toes. Frozen in place for what seemed like a lifetime, I watched as a river of blood darkened the hijab from her swollen breasts to the pronounced bump of what could only be that of a pregnant woman.

I shook my head from side to side, hoping to clear it of the memories I'd spent years trying to forget. Portrayed in lucid dreams, the events of my time in combat were returning, one after the other.

Jolted from my sleep, I stared at the ceiling for some time.

Confused as to where I was and what was going on, I tried to clear my head. After a moment, everything came to me. I was inflicted with a contagious disease and was quarantined to my bedroom.

I glanced around the room. Bottles of Gatorade were placed neatly on my nightstand. I rolled to the edge of the bed and reached for one of them. I struggled with the lid for some time. Upon twisting it free, I realized how debilitating the disease could be.

Unable to sit up and too weak to raise my head, I poured the sweet red liquid all over my face just to get a drink.

I was living wedged between two hells. One of my own making, and one created by a disease that had no cure.

Uncertain of which was worse, I closed my eyes and prayed for it to end.

I then wondered in what manner my prayers may be answered.

21

ANNA

Day eight

"Where's the fucking Corpsman?" Braxton shouted. "He's going to bleed out. I need a Corpsman and a fucking medevac."

I nearly jumped out of my skin. His voice was much different than normal. Deeper. More authoritative.

There was a brief moment of silence, and then the screaming began again. "God damn it, Wilson!" he bellowed. "I need that fucking Corpsman! I've got three wounded! Two critical!"

A few seconds of silence followed. I drew a deep breath, hoping that his nightmare would end.

"Wentz!" he barked. "Grab that M40 and get on that fucking sniper."

"Hold on, Pratt," he said in a much calmer voice. "That bird's on the way. Hear it? It's coming, Brother. Just hold on."

"Where's that fucking Medic!" he wailed, sounding as if he were in tears. "I need that medic, goddamn it!"

He'd been screaming on and off for eight hours. Some of it made sense. A good part of it was in lingo I couldn't decipher. I paced the floor and prayed that he'd fall back into a deep sleep. I felt miserable that there was nothing I could do.

After a few moments, he began moaning. I had no idea if he was in terrible pain, or if the moans were nothing more than his reaction to less vivid dreams. It continued for an hour.

The room fell silent.

His rhythmic breathing followed, leading me to believe that he'd finally fallen into a sound sleep.

Exhausted, I took a seat at the end of the couch.

I had no idea why our lives had collided, but I was grateful that they had. Despite the disease, his condition, or how he'd treated me before we made peace with one another, I enjoyed Braxton's company.

His charisma lured the unsuspecting toward him. From my interpretations of his dreams, he must have been a figure of authority in the Marines. I imagined the men who were following him into battle did so without hesitation, question, or remorse.

There was no doubt in my mind that men died in his command. I told myself that had anyone else been in charge, the loss of life would have been much worse.

No matter where we ended up when everything was over, I'd cherish the time I spent with him. Furthermore, I'd never forget listening to him day in and day out while he was sick.

I nestled into the corner of the couch and peeked through the window. Much to my surprise, it was dark outside.

The last I knew, it was 5:00 pm.

I told myself to get up and eat. I needed a little rest first. A small one. Just to close my eyes for a few minutes. I was asleep the instant my eyelids fell closed.

I was awakened by Braxton's moaning.

I sat up in my seat. The sun was rising over the top of the home across the street. I glanced around the room, uncertain of how much time had passed. I realized it had been hours since I'd heard anything from Braxton. I thanked God that he, too, had a few hours of sound sleep.

"I need a drink," he moaned. "Pratt, give me...your water... buffalo. Mine's empty."

He made smacking noises with his lips, moaned a little more, and then went silent.

It dawned on me that he might not have anything to drink. I assumed he did, but it was highly likely he didn't.

The only way for me to know would be to go inside his home.

If I did, I'd expose myself to the virus. I could possibly become infected, fall ill, and die. As ridiculous as it seemed to admit, I didn't care. Doctors and nurses came in contact with infected patients all day, every day. They'd been doing it for months.

If they could do it, I could do it.

All I needed was the courage. I prayed for God to provide me with an answer. A nudge. Anything.

"Pratt. That water...I'm dying, Brother."

Just like that, my prayers were answered.

22

ANNA

Day nine

Seeming annoyed, the pharmacist sauntered to the counter. He rubbed his bald head as if annoyed. The day was only beginning. He had no reason to have an attitude. At least not yet.

I grinned. "Hi."

He put his hands on his hips and looked me up and down. "Are you the consult?"

He was 40-ish, tall, and wore horn-rimmed glasses. He was also outwardly angry that I had taken a moment of his precious time.

I shrugged. "I guess so."

He pushed his glasses up the bridge of his nose. "How can I help you?"

"Well—"

He glanced at his watch.

I cocked my hip. "First, you could start by losing the attitude. Your time is not more precious than mine. Not one bit. This thing that's going on isn't easy for any of us, believe me. If I didn't have a problem that needed to be solved, I wouldn't have asked for you."

He forced a sigh. "I've been working overtime for—"

"I haven't slept since I don't know when," I snapped, even though I'd just awaken an hour beforehand. "Like I said, it's not easy for any of us."

His face was washed with surprise. "How can I help you?"

"I have a friend who is sick. I need to make sure he's getting whatever nutrients he needs. He's too weak to eat, but I think he can drink. What should I have for him to drink?"

"Does he have a fever?"

"I'm sure he does."

"You haven't taken his temperature?"

"I haven't," I replied. "He took it a few days ago and it was 103."

His eyes went wide. He took a step back. "Does he have a cough?"

I leaned against the counter just to make him nervous. He was a prick, he needed it. "A raspy cough," I said. "Oh, and chest pain. He's got some difficulty breathing, too. And a high fever."

He took a few more steps away from me. "He needs to be tested for—"

"He's been tested. That's an entirely different issue altogether," I said flatly. "I need to know what to get for him to drink. I see there's Pedialyte for adults." I gestured behind me. "But there's none on the shelf. Any recommendations?"

"We're sold out of Pedialyte," he said. "We're sold out of nearly everything. Pain relief, cold relief, vitamins..." His brows pinched together. "He didn't test positive. Right?"

"Actually, he did. Don't be worried. I haven't been in contact with him *yet*. He's in his house and I'm in mine. I'm listening to him through these." I tapped my finger against my right earbud. "He's reached a point that I need to check on him, so I thought I'd take plenty for him to drink. I don't want him to dehydrate."

"You haven't been in physical contact with him yet?"

I hadn't been within a hundred feet of Braxton in three weeks, so the pharmacist wasn't at risk. I didn't want to go into details, and I wasn't in the mood to be hated on, so I gave the quick and easy answer.

"Nope," I said. "No contact."

"But it's your intention to see him?"

"Yes."

"Is he at home? Quarantined?"

"He is."

"Does anyone else live in the home?"

"No, he lives alone."

He raised his index finger. "Just a moment."

He returned with two bulging plastic bags. "Here. Take these."

I glanced inside. In one, there was a pair of rose-colored scrubs. In the other, there were two masks, a package of disinfectant wipes, and a wad of blue rubber gloves.

The masks, wipes, and gloves were like gold. Hospitals were crying for the supplies and couldn't acquire them.

"What—"

"We just got a shipment in of gloves, wipes, and masks. We're donating everything to the hospitals. You'll need it as badly as they do, and they sure won't miss them." He nodded toward the aisle at my side. "Get some Gatorade. It's as good as the Pedialyte."

My heart swelled. "Thank you."

His lips thinned. "Look, I'm sorry." He shook his head in an apology, of sorts. "It's been a tough several weeks. If you don't have one, grab a digital thermometer on your way out. Be sure to take his temperature. If it's over 103, call an ambulance."

"Okay," I said. "I'll grab one on my way out."

"Take a trash bag with you when you go to see him," he said. "Put on the scrubs, gloves, and mask before you enter his home. If possible, wear something underneath the scrubs. Once inside the home, don't touch anything you don't have to. Preferably, nothing. When you exit the home, use one of those disinfectant wipes to close the door, then wipe the door handles down, both inside and out. Disrobe immediately, if possible. Place the gloves, the scrubs, and the used disinfectant wipe in the trash bag. Set the trash bag aside, put on a new pair of gloves, and then pick it back up. When you get home, handle the scrubs with the gloves. Wash the scrubs. Discard the gloves and the trash bag. Then, take a hot shower with soap."

"Oh my gosh. Thank you so much."

He grinned. "I'm glad I could help."

"Well, again, thank you."

"What's your name?"

"Anna."

"Your friend's name?"

"Braxton."

He gave a nod and turned away. "Stop in and see me when he's better, will you?" he asked over his shoulder.

"I sure will."

I prayed that one day I'd be able to fulfil the promise.

I pulled into my driveway. There was a truck blocking Braxton's drive. A man was standing on Braxton's porch, pounding his fist against the door like a madman.

I shoved the car into park, bringing it to a screeching halt. I flung my door open and jumped out.

"Hey!" I shouted.

He continued to pummel the door with the back side of his fist. I had no idea who the knucklehead was, but Braxton desperately needed his sleep.

"Hey!" I screamed, taking a few more steps toward him. "What the fuck do you think you're doing!?"

He faced me. "Oh. You must be—"

"Don't beat on that door." I walked in his direction. "You'll wake him up. He hasn't slept well in two days."

"What the fuck's he been doing?" he asked. "Not returning my calls, that's for sure."

I paused 30 feet from where he stood. He was tall, lean, and in good physical condition. Tattoos peppered each forearm. His hair was short and spiky, and his pronounced brow jutted forward like a rock ledge.

"Who are you?" I asked.

"Gordon Pratt," he replied. "Are you Annie?"

I was pleasantly surprised that Braxton had mentioned me. Even if his friend couldn't get my name right.

"Anna," I said proudly. "Please. Don't knock on the door. Braxton's sick."

His gaze narrowed. "He's not—"

"Yes," I said. "He is. I'm taking care of him."

He nervously stepped to the side, toward his truck. "He's got the virus?"

"Yes, he does," I replied. "So does his father. His father's in the hospital."

"Hap? Holy fucking shit." He rubbed his temples with his palms. "Seriously?"

"Seriously."

He tilted his head toward Braxton's house. "You've been in there?"

"I have not. But I'm going in there in a minute. He needs something to drink, so I bought him Gatorade." I gestured toward my car. "I got a thermometer, too. I want to take his temperature."

"If you haven't been in there, how...fuck, he could be...what if his lungs filled up with shit and he's dead?"

I brushed my hair behind my ear. "I'm on a phone call with him, listening to him twenty-four hours a day. I have been for a day and a half. I don't know what I'm going to do if it gets disconnected."

"You got a key to his place?"

"I do."

"If it gets disconnected, call me," he said, folding his arms over his broad chest. "I'll reconnect it."

I mentally rolled my eyes at his foolishness. "You'd have to go inside to reconnect it. He's infected."

"He saved my life," he said. "He could have been killed doing it, too. Been meaning for years to pay him back for what he did, but I never got the opportunity. I'll take the stuff in, I'll take his temperature, and I'll reconnect the phone if it gets disconnected."

A sigh of relief escaped me. "You will?"

He gave a sharp nod. "I sure will."

A light bulb went off. "Oh my God. You're *Pratt*! The guy that squashed the cookie sheet and the guy from his dreams."

He seemed confused. "What dreams?"

"His nightmares," I said. "He had them all night last night. He was talking in his sleep. I remember him saying your name. It came up over and over."

He lowered his arms to his side. "What did he say?"

"Uhhm. He said. Let me see. He said, 'Hold on Pratt. That bird. The bird is coming, can you hear it, Brother?' Something like that."

He swallowed heavily. Sweat burst from every pore in his brow. He began to speak several times but paused on each occasion, just before the first word passed his lips. I thought for a moment that he might break down.

"That was a long time ago." He wiped his brow with his forearm. "Seems like. Hell, it seems like yesterday, now."

"Can you tell me what happened?" I asked. "Can I ask? If I'm overstepping—"

"Sniper caught us while we were on patrol." He cleared his throat. "Fucker waited for us to all get where he could see us. Then, one by one, he started picking us off. Shot up the entire rifle squad pretty bad. Rourke was our Platoon Sergeant. I took one in the chest and went down, but I didn't realize Rourke—"

"One what?" I asked.

"A round," he said.

I stared blankly.

"A bullet." He pounded his clenched fist against his chest. "Right here. Missed my heart by about a centimeter."

I couldn't believe he got shot in the chest by a sniper and he'd lived to tell about it. Modern protective gear had probably saved more lives than I could imagine.

"But you had on a bullet-proof vest?" I asked.

He laughed. "Bullet-proof vests don't stop sniper rounds. Small arms fire? Sure. But not a rifle round. SAPI plates are designed to stop them, but they're too fucking heavy to wear, so we toss 'em."

Confused, I stared back at him wondering how he could have lived if he didn't have a bullet-proof vest.

I shook my head in disbelief. "How then. How did you live?"

"Rourke," he said. "Crazy fucker dragged me behind a burned-out Toyota. Was the only thing on that entire street to hide behind. Wasn't much, but it was better than nothing."

Everything clicked into place.

"Oh my God." I gasped. "The 'bird.' That's your lingo for a helicopter, right? He said he needed a medevac. You were that guy, weren't you?"

"Correct. I was one of 'em. By the time it was over, six of us were shot up, Rourke included. He was the first one. Took a round to the shoulder right before me. Never said a fucking word. Then, while we waited for the medevac, he took another in the back of his thigh. Refused to leave me, though. He got us all out of there. Every one of us. We didn't have one casualty."

"Was he in charge?" I asked.

"Who? Rourke?"

"Yeah. Was Braxton in charge?"

He laughed. "He was the one we listened to. I can tell you that. Our LT was a shit hat. Rourke made all the calls. Without him, we would have lost our entire platoon. Man's got a sixth sense. He knows things. About people. About situations. Kind of eerie the way he does it, too."

"He guessed my underwear color," I whispered. "I'll tell you about it some time when this is all over. Right now, I need to get him some water."

"Got any scissors?" he asked.

It seemed like an odd request. "Sure," I replied. "What do you need?"

"Scissors." He made a scissors motion with his index and middle finger. "I don't know. Do they come in different kinds?"

I laughed. "No. I meant what do you need them for?"

"I'm going to cut a mask out of my shirt," he replied. "Left my house so fast I forgot mine. Not looking to get infected if that fucker coughs on me."

"The pharmacist gave me a few masks and some rubber gloves. I've got some scrubs, too. I doubt they'd fit."

He looked at me like I was crazy. "I'm not going to snuggle with the grumpy bastard. I'll put some Gatorade beside him, take his temperature, and—it's not a rectal thermometer, is it?"

"It's all they had." I shrugged. "They were sold out of everything else."

He winced.

"I'm joking," I said. "It's one of those point and shoot deals."

"I was about to say you could don those scrubs and one of those masks and come with me. I'd spread his cheeks and you could poke it in."

"Reverse those roles, and I'm in," I said with a laugh.

"Not happening. Gimme the mask and gloves, and I'm good," he said. "If that prick infects me through that gear, it was meant to be."

Although I was willing to do what I must, I was apprehensive to enter Braxton's home. Now that Pratt had volunteered, I was able to exhale a sigh of relief. "You have no idea how much I appreciate this. I've been nervous all morning."

He pulled a lollipop from his back pocket and peeled off the wrapper. "Want one?"

"No, thank you."

"Got a box of 'em in the truck." He poked it in his mouth. "If you want one, I got every flavor these little fuckers come in."

I chuckled. "I'm good."

"Suit yourself." He chuckled. "Rourke got me to saying that. *Suit yourself*. He says it all the time." He gestured toward my car. "Go grab the stuff. I better get in there before I come to my senses."

"If you don't want to do it—"

He pulled the sucker from his mouth and wagged it in my direction. "Women, the elderly, and kids."

I was lost. His comment made no sense. "Huh?"

"Women, the elderly, or children. Can't let harm come to any of 'em, or Rourke would have my ass," he said. "One of his rules. You ain't a kid or elderly, but you're one hundred percent woman. I'm just trying to make sure Rourke don't furlough me for breaking the rules once he gets well."

I laughed. "Okay."

It was obvious the comments Marge made about Braxton a few days earlier were right. Contrary to what one might perceive from his sexual antics, Braxton was a good man on the inside.

I glanced at Pratt and then turned toward my car. His existence on earth was proof.

Braxton was a damned good man.

23

ANNA

Day ten

Pratt got home and had to come right back to reconnect Braxton's phone. Then, four hours later, Braxton had a fit while dreaming, and he disconnected the phone again. Pratt returned again, without one word of complaint. He moved the phone to the far side of the nightstand, so Braxton couldn't reach it as easily. After that, we hadn't had another incident.

All in all, I felt that things were improving. Braxton's wheezing was now sporadic instead of constant. His fits of coughing were shorter and sounded much less invasive. The bad dreams continued, but his fits of shouting often lasted for no longer than a few minutes. Those tense moments, for both of us, were hell.

Pratt said on the day he got shot that everything happened in a span of 3- or 4-minutes, total. Hundreds of rounds—if not thousands—had been fired, six men were wounded, and one sniper was killed. All in less time than it takes to fill a car's gas tank at the convenience store.

When it was over, the men didn't get to go home. The wounded were bandaged up and continued to fight as soon as they were willing. The fortunate few who weren't wounded were fighting in another battle on that same street thirty minutes later.

Pratt said he felt guilty during the time that he was prohibited from returning to battle. While he was in the hospital getting a blood transfusion, all he could think of was "when will they let me return to combat."

That mindset, from what he said, was typical of the good men.

The devoted.

I couldn't imagine one 24-hour day of war. An entire day—1,440 minutes—of being shot at, shooting back, and trying to stay clear of the roadside bombs that littered the roadways. From my count, Braxton endured that living hell for just shy of 4,000 days.

Ten horrific years.

His devotion was nothing short of unimaginable.

It was time for me to be devoted to him. To pay him back for what he'd done for the men and women of the country.

My days ran into my nights. My nights were sleepless. I realized Braxton had no days or nights, only the passing of time. When I became frustrated or felt like I couldn't stay awake a moment longer, I told myself *at least no one is shooting at me.*

It seemed to help.

I was convinced Braxton would overcome his illness in time. I wanted to make him as comfortable as I was able. Providing comfort from afar forced me to be creative.

"Wentz!" he bellowed. "Two o'clock. Second window from the left, third from the top. Pop that motherfucker!"

I nearly spilled my coffee. He's been silent for the past hour and a half, which was enough time for me to make a pot of coffee and scramble some eggs.

"Zebra, this is Echo-six," he said in a muffled tone. "We're taking fire. Repeat, taking fire. Two KIA, three wounded. Need an air strike, over."

A few seconds of silence followed. Then, he began pleading for help.

"Zebra, we are under heavy fire," he said, his voice etched with emotion. "Again, this is Echo-six, and we are under fire. Two KIA, four wounded. If no airstrike, we're requesting extraction, over."

I finished my coffee and walked to the living room. I desperately needed some sleep. Braxton did, too. Hoping to put us both to sleep, I rocked back and forth against the back of the couch and began to sing.

"Hush, little Braxton, don't you scream
Anna's gonna take you to a fishing stream
And if that stream don't have no fish
Anna's gonna let you make a wish
And if that wish don't make you grin
Anna's gonna let you try again
And if that wish is to hold her tight
Anna's gonna hold you with all her might
She'll hold you close and sing you songs
So you can sleep all night long..."

I paused.

A light snoring sound was his response to my lullaby.

I did a mental fist pump and closed my eyes.

Sleep well, my Dear.

24

ANNA

Day eleven

Braxton's nightmares continued on and off for four days. During his lulls from shouting I prayed that God would be gracious enough to release him from the disease's grasp long before it was too late.

As fond as I'd grown of Braxton, I knew only bits and pieces of what he may find solace in. Of those things, I was limited in what I could provide.

I walked past the three books he'd given me. A light bulb illuminated. I'd done everything except what he wanted to do on the day he became ill.

While he was in one of his periods of uninterrupted sleep, I picked up *The History of Love*.

I opened the cover, read the first few paragraphs to myself, and smiled. Then, I began to read the book out loud, to Braxton.

He was excited to provide me with the book, and equally eager for us to read them together. If his current state of being prevented him from reading it himself, it was only fitting that I read the book to him.

I read the first paragraph out loud, and then another. Before long, I'd finished a chapter. One chapter led to another. In no time I was submerged in the story and Braxton was lulled into a sound and uneventful sleep.

I continued to read long into the night. Driven in part by a wonderfully woven tale and in part by a feeling of necessity to comfort Braxton, I continued.

As the sun peeked from over the top of the Mediterranean home across the street, I realized I'd been reading to him for roughly ten hours. It was ten hours of uninterrupted sleep for him, which was nine more than he'd received for the past four days and nights.

When I finished the story a few moments later, it was obvious why he'd chosen the novel as an all-time favorite. The story—and the book—were things I'd cherish for a lifetime.

Exhausted, but unwilling to chance having Braxton slip back into his restlessness, I picked up *Angela's Ashes*.

"Are you ready for Frank McCourt?" I asked, speaking to him through the earbud's microphone.

I read the first chapter, and then the second. I had to stop after the second chapter, because I'd not only laughed so hard I nearly peed, I'd cried so violently I could no longer breathe.

Through my tears, I continued. "This one's going to be tough, Dear."

I realized I called Braxton *Dear*, out loud. I promptly dismissed it as being a snafu brought on by no sleep, little food, and hours upon hours of reading. Nevertheless, I liked the way it rolled off my tongue.

I made a cup of coffee, regained my composure, and continued. By the time four o'clock arrived, I was not quite halfway into the book. My emotions were all over the map. Frank McCourt's memoir was taking me for a ride I wasn't prepared for.

"We're going to take a break for a while, Dear." I had no more than spoken, and realized I'd done it, again. Feeling like a dork, I said an apology, even though I really didn't need to. "Sorry, that just spilled out. I didn't mean it." I cleared my throat. "I didn't mean for it to happen. I don't know what I'm trying to say. Just. We're taking a break. Let's leave it at that."

Exhausted, I set the book aside. I promptly marched up the street to Marge's house.

She was sitting on her stoop, drinking a glass of iced tea.

I sat down at her side. "No chores today?"

"I think I'm caught up for the moment." She glanced around the yard. "It feels nice." She reached to her side and produced another glass of tea. "Here, this one's for you."

"Oh." I took the glass from her grasp. "Thank you."

"It's peach," she said. "I like it strong."

I took a drink of the tea. It was wonderful, with neither the tea or the peaches overpowering the drink.

I looked at the glass. It appeared to be nothing more than a glass of tea. Its taste was far more complex than its looks, that was for sure.

"Is this something you made?" I asked.

"Of course," she replied. "It's black tea and peach simple syrup. The simple syrup is nothing more than cooked peaches, sugar, and water. After the tea is made, you add the syrup to your liking. I thought it was a little strong, but I like it that way."

"It's refreshing," I said.

"I'm glad you like it." She shifted her shoulders to face me. "How's our neighbor?"

"Much better," I replied. "I've been reading to him."

"Are you reading books you said he bought for you?"

I nodded. "I thought if he liked them enough to buy them for me, that he'd enjoy them just as much if I read them to him."

"I'm sure he finds your voice comforting." She raised her hand to my face and placed her palm against my cheek. "Sweetheart, you look like you haven't been sleeping well."

I sighed. "I was up all night. I haven't slept yet."

"Reading?"

Sipping the wonderful tea, I gave a nod.

She smiled. "Well, aren't you a doll."

"I'm trying my best."

"How's his breathing?" she asked.

"Much better."

"What about the nightmares?"

"Since I started reading to him, it seems like they're gone," I replied. "He hasn't been screaming at least."

"I'll thank the good Lord for that." She gazed across the street, toward Braxton's home. "I think that might have been the fever talking. Raymond used to wake up screaming all the time right after he got back from Korea. They said he was shell-shocked."

I had no idea if Braxton's dreaming was a product of the fever, or if it was something that happened all the time. I prayed that it wasn't something he had to deal with day after day.

"Did it ever get better?" I asked.

"It did. Over time." She sipped her tea as she seemed to recall the memories of her late husband. "He'd have episodes from time to time. Eventually, it all but stopped."

"I wondered if it was something he had to deal with all the time, or if it was because he was sick."

"It's hard to say, for sure." She patted my shoulder. "If his breathing is better and the nightmares are over with, he might be on the mend. That's what matters."

"I called him 'Dear' on accident," I murmured. "Twice."

Her brows raised. "Pardon me?"

"Dear," I said. "I called him *dear* when I was reading to him. Twice. I have no idea why."

She scowled playfully. "I do."

"You do what?"

"I know why."

"Why?"

She grinned. "Because he holds a special place in your heart."

"Before all this started, we were nothing but—" I swallowed heavily. "—nothing but neighbors."

"Sweetheart, when all of this is over, you'll be much more than neighbors. Wait and see." She raised her glass and held it between us. "Here's to his recovery."

I hoped that she was right. Clinging to that wish, I clanked my glass against hers.

25

BRAXTON

Day unknown

I wondered if a condition of the disease was losing one's sanity. I had to piss but wasn't sure where the bathroom was. Wrapped in damp bed linen, I rolled to my side.

I glanced around the room. Nothing looked familiar.

Empty plastic bottles were scattered about the floor. My phone was on the nightstand closest to me, sitting atop the wireless charger.

I had no recollection of putting it there.

I pressed my tongue to the roof of my mouth and tried to swallow but couldn't produce enough saliva to do so.

A half full bottle of Gatorade sat on the nightstand, beside my phone. I stretched my arm toward it and fell off the side of the bed in the process.

I hit the floor with a *thud!*

"Mother fucker," I groaned.

Tangled in my bedsheet, I couldn't immediately stand. As I began to unravel myself, a voice from the nightstand startled me.

"Are you okay? Is everything alright?"

Confused, my eyes darted to my phone. "Anna?"

"I'm here," she said. "Are you okay?"

"I was trying to get a drink and I fell out of bed," I said. "Hold on a second."

"Oh my God." She gasped. "Are you okay?'

"I'm fine."

"Are you sure?"

I peeled the sweat-soaked bedsheet away from my clammy skin and tossed it aside. I grabbed for the bottle of Gatorade. I took a drink, and then another.

"I'm sure," I said.

I was wearing nothing more than a pair of underwear. Wondering where my clothes had gone, I scanned the room. A tee shirt was draped over the headboard of my bed. A pair of sweatpants were on the floor half the distance to the bathroom, strewn across the carpet.

I took a step. My legs wobbled.

I wondered if I could make it to the bathroom. If I had to, I'd crawl.

"I've got to piss," I said. "Wish me luck."

"Excuse me?"

"Forget it," I said. "I'll be back in a minute."

Like a newborn giraffe, I stumbled toward the bathroom, one awkward step after the other. When I reached the doorway, I wanted to cheer. I didn't dare, though. I feared I might collapse if I exerted too much energy.

On my way to the toilet, I paused in front of the vanity. I glanced in the mirror.

I could count my ribs in my reflection. My beard was untrimmed. My hair was matted to the side of my head. Creases across my shoulder, chest, and forehead marked where the sheets had pressed against me while I slept.

I tried to count the days. My mind became a jumbled mess.

Bits and pieces of a masked nurse hovering over me came to

mind, but I fully realized I hadn't been to the hospital. I didn't think I had, at least.

I relieved my aching bladder, washed my face, and stumbled into the bedroom. I sat on the edge of the bed.

"Anna? Are you still there?" I asked.

"Yes," she said, answering almost immediately. "I'm here. Is everything okay?"

"I'm fine," I replied. "I think I'm confused."

"About what?"

"Did I go to the hospital at some point?"

"No," she replied. "You've been in your room all this time."

"I have this weird recollection of a nurse taking my temperature with one of those electric thermometers. She was wearing a respirator and her hair was in a bun. She kind of. She reminded me of you."

"I'll be darned," she said. "Probably just a weird dream."

"Speaking of dreams, I've been having fucking nightmares. Jesus Christ. Talk about vivid." I shook my head to clear it. "They were fucking awful."

"Is it common for you to have nightmares?" she asked.

"Not at all. Hell, I rarely dream at all, and never have nightmares."

She sighed. "I think nightmares are pretty common with a high fever. At least from what I've read."

"I think my fever might be gone," I said. "I don't feel chills any longer."

"You slept well last night," she said. "Almost no coughing at all."

"Before that?" I asked. "Was it bad?"

"It was just awful on the day before yesterday," she replied. "Maybe the worst. It might have been three days ago, I don't know. They're all kind of squished together. Have you been drinking plenty of Gatorade?"

I glanced at the floor. "Apparently, I have." I stared at the empty bottles that littered the floor in disbelief. "I must be going nuts."

"Why do you say that?"

"I don't remember buying this shit. The Gatorade. I have no idea where it came from."

"You're probably just confused," she said. "I'm sure everything will come back to you sooner or later."

"I hope so."

"Do you have any body aches?"

"I feel like I've been in a week-long boxing match," I replied. "My entire body aches, but not like before. It was so bad the other day that I was in tears. I think this is residual."

"Good, maybe you're on the downhill slope."

I'd read about victims who had felt they were on the road to recovery, only to have their symptoms worsen a day or so later. I took a drink of Gatorade, wondering if I'd slip back onto the living hell I'd been in since the day the books arrived.

I took another drink. "I just remembered the books. We started reading the one about Christopher."

"We did."

I took another drink. I glanced around the room. Bits and pieces of memories came to me like snippets of a movie clip.

"Did you read to me?" I asked.

"I did."

I chuckled. "I have a faint recollection of Leo Gursky and Bruno trying to bake a cake."

"I read it to you."

"That part?" I asked, taking another drink. "The beginning? That was at the beginning, wasn't it?"

"That part? Yeah. It seems like it was at the beginning," she replied. "I'm not sure. All the days kind of run into one another right now."

I was disappointed that we didn't get to read the books together. It was something I was looking forward to sharing with her.

"How much of it did you read?" I asked.

"I read the entire book."

"Did you enjoy it?"

"I did."

"All of it?"

"Every word," she replied. "It seemed to calm you. I know it calmed me."

I took my phone off the nightstand and cancelled the speaker. I raised it to my ear. "Wait, you read it to me?"

"I did."

"All of it?"

"Uh huh."

"Have you cracked the cover of *Angela's Ashes*?"

"I have."

I was fractionally disappointed. More so in myself than anything else. "I had visions of reading them together. Sharing the experience."

"We did share the experience," she replied.

"Don't tell me you read Angela's Ashes to me, too.'"

"I did."

"All of it?"

"Every chapter."

"Holy shit," I replied, rubbing my face with my hand. "I've been out of it."

"Yes," she said. "You sure have."

"Hold on a minute," I said. "I'm going to go weigh myself."

"Why?"

"When I was in the bathroom a minute ago, I looked like a skeleton. I want to see what I weigh."

"Okay."

I finished the bottle of Gatorade and set it on the nightstand. With my phone pressed to my ear I walked to the bathroom. Each step became much easier than the last. Excited that I was getting better, I got on the scale.

I stared at the digital readout like it was a lie. I got off, reset the scale, and got back on. The same number displayed.

"I've lost 18 pounds," I declared. "There's no fucking way. How long has it been?"

"Since the day you fell asleep?"

"Since the day we started reading," I replied. "That's the last day I remember."

"Let's see," she said. "Thirteen days since your diagnosis, and seven days since you got sick."

"I've been in bed for seven fucking days?"

"Uh huh."

"An entire week? Jesus." I glanced at the shower. "I'm going to try to take a shower. I'll call you when I'm done. Okay?"

"I'm sure a shower will feel good."

"Talk to you in a minute."

"Okay."

I started to hang up, and then paused. "Anna?"

"Yes?"

"Thank you."

"Don't worry about it," she said. "I enjoyed it."

I hung up the phone and placed it on the vanity. After brushing a week of yack from my teeth, I took a long, hot shower. As I washed my hair, I recalled bits and pieces of my time in bed. Hours upon hours of aching, periods of hot sweats, cold chills, and the endless nights of nightmares.

I stood in front of the mirror, drying myself with a towel. It came to me that my father was in the hospital. I'd all but forgotten. Frantic, I grabbed my phone from the vanity.

I opened the call log and thumbed through it. Missed calls from Pratt, missed calls from Anna, and calls I'd made to Anna—all of which were accepted—were the only calls on the log. I had no recollection of anything that was listed.

Dumbfounded, I called the hospital and asked about my father. According to the nurse, he was still listed as "stable", but that was all she could say.

I asked about the risk of exposing myself to others. I was advised if someone has been symptom-free for 3 days and they developed their first symptoms or were diagnosed more than 10 days prior, they were no longer considered to be infectious.

Naked, disappointed, and a little confused, I sauntered into the kitchen. I opened the fridge. It was filled with Gatorade. The milk, however, was gone.

I searched the trash. An empty milk carton was at the top. Beside it, a plastic bag from Ralph's.

I never shopped at Ralph's.

I lifted the bag from the container and opened it. A crumpled receipt was at the bottom. I retrieved the receipt, unfolded it, and looked at the purchase.

30 bottles of Gatorade @ $0.99 each

1 digital thermometer @ $51.47

1 8 oz can of Starbuck's Cold Brew @ 4.39

I folded the receipt neatly, discarded the trash bag, and got dressed. Feeling like recovery was well within my grasp, I picked up my bedroom, stripped the bed, and began washing the bedding.

I meandered past the kitchen. The three books I'd purchased were spread out beside one another in the island. I glanced at *The History of Love.*

I let out a long sigh.

Seven days of knocking on death's door changed my outlook, entirely. I was grateful for my health, my recovery, and above all, Anna.

I peered out my kitchen window toward my nurse, neighbor, and caregiver's home.

I couldn't believe I'd nearly let her slip away.

26

ANNA

Day fifteen

The doctor recommended waiting three more days before Braxton and I could be face-to-face with one another. I felt like I'd been released from prison but wasn't allowed to leave the compound. Frustrated, I rinsed my breakfast plate, put it in the dishwasher, and meandered to the bathroom.

Braxton had exposed himself to me unknowingly. I felt guilty. Like I'd read his diary or peered through his bedroom window without him knowing.

What I learned opened my eyes.

He, however, had no idea of the knowledge I'd gained. He knew not that he'd revealed his most sacred inner thoughts, feelings, and weaknesses to me.

Hoping to rid myself of the guilt, I showered. Feeling no less guilty, I searched for something to wear. My initial COVID-19 attire consisted of sweats, old tee shirts, and flip-flops. Meeting with Marge on a daily basis and making peace with Braxton caused me to realize I was living in a state of depression.

I now dressed like I was going out, even though I knew nothing could be further from the truth.

I rifled through my clothes, trying to find something suitable. After displaying all my clean articles of clothing on the foot of the bed, I realized my warm weather attire had nearly all been worn. In desperate need of doing a few loads of laundry, I selected a sports bra and my favorite jeans, knowing I'd change before I saw Marge.

I carried the dirty clothes to the laundry room and started a load in the washer. On my way to the bedroom, an idea came to me.

An idea that would either fuel Braxton's fire, or explode in my face.

I grabbed my jean jacket, bunched my hair into a messy bun, and put on my favorite pink hat. I planned to reveal a secret of my own and hoped it would make Braxton and I even. It made sense to me, anyway.

I placed the tripod on the end table in the living room and I secured my phone to it. Then, I called Braxton on Google's video app, *Duo*.

Wearing a grin, he answered. His gaunt face filled the phone's screen. He appeared happy.

"How are you feeling?" I asked.

"Good, thanks."

"Did you just wake up?"

"I woke up before the sun came up," he replied, standing. "I feel like its dinnertime."

He was wearing a pair of gray sweats and a tank top. His beard was in bad need of being trimmed. For once, he looked human.

His face moved closer to the camera. "Are you wearing a hat?"

I pulled it low on my head. "I am."

"Back up so I can see it."

I moved away from the camera, giving him a full view of my layered outfit.

"And a jacket?" he asked.

"Yep."

He smirked. "You look cute."

"So do you."

"Are you going somewhere?" he asked.

"No," I replied. "I just want to tell you something."

"I'm listening."

"It's a secret," I said, feeling slightly embarrassed. "I'm revealing something about myself that nobody knows."

"I'll keep it between you and me. How's that?"

"Perfect."

He smiled. "I'm listening."

"When I was in college, I needed money for basic stuff, and I didn't want to ask my parents. I felt it was time for me to become independent. So, I got a job stripping, in Kansas. I'd drive from my apartment across the border, and strip for tips."

He laughed. "Really?"

"Uh huh."

He chuckled. "That's awesome."

I was pleased that he didn't seem repulsed. The fact that he didn't call me a whore was a plus, too. I saw the profession as a way to survive the financial strain while in college, and nothing more. Not everyone looked at it the same, though.

"Wanna hear something funny?" I asked.

"Sure."

"I loved doing it."

He seemed puzzled. "Why?"

"It was sensual," I replied. "Sexy. Nobody touched me, and I didn't mingle with customers or give lap dances. All I did was strip, but it was so, so sexy."

"Down to a bikini?" he asked. "Or nude?"

"Topless," I replied. "We had to wear bottoms."

"Sounds sexy as hell."

"Hold on a sec," I said, moving out of the camera's eye.

I grabbed the television remote and selected the Pandora

application. Then, I selected the song *Leave Your Hat On*, by Joe Cocker. I walked in front of the camera, remote in hand.

Standing in clear view, I faced the phone. I unbuttoned my jacket, revealing my snow-white sports bra.

I grinned a guilty grin. "Are you ready?"

His face lit up. "Hell, yeah."

I pressed *play* and tossed the remote aside.

His eyes widened as I moved in perfect timing with the song.

When I stripped in college, I stepped onto the stage a different woman. The instant I was in front of a screaming crowd, I became Kandy Kane.

As I pulled off my jacket one seductive sleeve at a time, I was none other than Anna Wilson, Braxton Rourke's neighbor and very confused friend.

To get us both warmed up, I spent a moment gyrating my hips to the music in my bra. When I was soaked—and his eyes were glued to the screen—I unbuttoned my jeans and slowly slid my hands deep inside them. Watching the look on Braxton's face morph from a curious one to that of a horny man was worth the risk I'd taken in revealing my past.

After shedding my jeans, I lowered my left bra strap. Then, I lowered the left cup, revealing my erect nipple. I did the same with the right. Then, I removed the bra as slowly and seductively as I was able. I dropped the garment at my feet and covered my breasts with my cupped hands, feigning my best look of innocence.

Just to remind him that was still wearing panties, I backed away from the camera far enough for him to see.

Facing the camera, I was dressed in nothing but a pair of lace panties and my pink hat. Still gyrating to the music, I gave him my best performance, sliding my hand inside my panties and touching myself lightly.

I was beyond aroused, and my pussy was soaked, but the dance wasn't for me. It was a performance for a man I hoped would enjoy it.

Something to take his mind off his sick father and the deteriorating condition of the nation.

With a minute left in the song, I faced away from the camera, giving Braxton a full view of my best side. As I watched the song's remaining time on the television screen, I pushed my panties down my hips.

An inch at a time, I gave him more of me, until my panties were at my ankles.

With 20 seconds left, I was completely naked, short of my hat. Facing the television, I finished my performance and hoped he enjoyed it. As the song faded to nothing, I slowly faced the camera and titled my hat to the side.

I was fifteen feet from the phone, but it looked like he was masturbating.

I moved closer. Facing the camera with his cock in his hand, his shirt was off. His sweats were around his thighs.

Staring right at me, he was stroking his cock like his life depended on it. Turned on beyond measure and filled with a sense of self-pride for bringing him to that point of arousal, I watched as he finished his chore.

After erupting a geyser of cum into his cupped hand, he excused himself.

I'd trusted Braxton enough to reveal a secret about myself to him. Doing so cleansed me of my feelings of guilt, and it drew me even closer to the man I was slowly developing deep feelings for.

Feeling uncertain of where our relationship was headed, but pleased with where it was for the moment, I waited for him to return.

"Holy shit," he said, stepping in front of the camera. "That was sexy as fuck."

I grinned. "Do you feel better?"

"I do," he replied. "Do you?"

The guilt—and my clothes—were gone. Still naked, but as comfortable as if I were clothed, I offered him a heartfelt smile.

"Yes," I said. "I sure do."

27

ANNA

Day seventeen

I was tested for the virus and received negative results. Braxton drove to an independent laboratory to see if his body had developed antibodies against the disease. Although there was plenty of published data to support him no longer being contagious, he wanted scientific proof before he came in contact with others.

I yearned to be in Braxton's presence but wanted a doctor's clearance as much as he did. I didn't want to be the cause for another funeral with no attendees or become the subject of a *Dateline* story about a wannabe nurse who died taking care of her sexy COVID-19 infected neighbor.

I sat on the couch, waiting for Braxton to return. Accustomed to having him breathing in my ear or talking to me on a video chat, the silence of his absence was unnerving. Feeling anxious, I pieced together a timeline of our makeshift relationship.

He saved me from a criminal. I became starry-eyed. We had sex. I was infatuated. He resisted. I pressed on. We had sex again, which was interrupted by a Hollywood harlot. During that disruption, he left me for the harlot.

We didn't speak for two weeks.

He became infected with a life-threatening disease, which caused him to take a long, hard look at his life, and his actions. Thankfully, he had no symptoms.

He apologized for his actions.

Following his heartfelt apology, I felt much better about matters between us, and of the possibility that we could develop a valuable friendship.

Then, he fell ill.

Eleven days passed. During that time, the minutes seemed like hours. The hours resembled the longest of days, and the days dragged on like weeks. When it was over, my feelings about Braxton were far different than they were in the beginning.

In a week and a half, I learned who Braxton Rourke truly was. Throughout his illness, he unwillingly lost the layers of his protective armor, one by one. Eventually, he was exposed, alone, and in need of protection. I offered him shelter with the bedtime stories I read. I lulled him to sleep with songs. I absorbed each tear that he shed and wept for him when he was unable.

I now feared a friendship between us wouldn't suffice. My relationship clock had been ticking at a much different pace than Braxton's. During his sickness, I had spent a decade at his side reliving the horrors of war. That decade, however, was ten years that he had no idea I'd been a part of.

Unbeknownst to him, I'd accompanied him through battle. I held his virtual hand while he called in airstrikes. I sought shelter at his side on a dusty Iraqi road behind a burned-out Toyota while a sniper took pot shots at us. I waited impatiently in Afghanistan for a Corpsman that never came. As his brothers in arms drew their last dying breaths, I held him in my arms while he held them in his.

The familiar drone of his SUV's exhaust snatched me from my dreamlike state. Sitting in my spot at the end of the sofa, I faced the window and waited.

He turned into my drive and rolled to a stop.

I held my breath.

He stepped out of the vehicle. His tailored navy suit that once fit him like a second skin now hung from his shoulders like he'd selected it from Nordstrom's sale rack. He produced a sheet of paper from inside his coat pocket. He fumbled to unfold it, and then raised it high in the air.

I rushed to the front door and yanked it open. "What did they say? Is it...are you—"

A prideful grin covered his face. "I'm one hundred percent safe."

"One hundred percent as in—"

He stretched his arms wide. "One hundred percent as in, *come here.*"

We hadn't hugged yet. It would be our first.

I rushed through the yard and down the driveway. I leaped against him with such force that I nearly knocked him over.

He caught me mid-air and swung me in circles. Our actions resembled the scenes from the cheesy Lifetime movies that I used to watch at Christmastime while I was in college.

Only it was real.

Not knowing if we were merely celebrating his release from confinement with a hug, or if this was the beginning of something much bigger, I mentally struggled with where I should place my hands.

Fearing rejection, I chose to let them dangle at my sides.

I had questions I wanted to ask. There were answers I desperately needed to hear. I told myself to enjoy the moment until it was over. I closed my eyes and relished the comfort of being in his arms.

We stopped spinning. I opened my eyes.

His gaze met mine.

Held tight in his arms, my feet dangled six inches above the concrete. I searched his eyes for answers. They possessed a desire that I hadn't previously noticed.

Lost in admiration, I gazed into the glistening sea of brown and green, wondering just what my future held.

He traced the tip of his finger along the edge of my jaw. A tinge of anticipation ran though me.

He lifted my chin slightly.

Then, he answered all my questions with a kiss.

It wasn't a *thank you* kiss, nor was it one of appreciation. It was the type of kiss that all other kisses are compared to.

The kiss that defines kisses.

A kiss that forces the recipient to long for it more than they long for anything else in their lifetime.

One of his hands rested along the bottom of my butt. The other pressed firmly against the middle of my back. I draped mine over his shoulders and pulled him against me.

His lips melded to mine. Our tongues intertwined. The passage of time stopped altogether.

Suspended in that moment, we kissed each other as if our lives were dependent upon our successes.

When our mouths parted, I was mindless.

I knew one thing, however.

Braxton Rourke held my heart in his hands.

I prayed that he handled it with care this time.

28

BRAXTON

My fellow Marines were placed in two categories. The trustworthy and the incapable. While in combat, both groups of men faced the prospect of dying.

When placed at the crossroad of life and death, the trustworthy Marines stood firm in their convictions. They fought to uphold their system of beliefs; death be damned.

The incapable Marines were unwilling to devote themselves to a cause they were contractually—and morally—obligated to uphold. They were promptly deemed unreliable and disloyal.

The men who risked their lives received the same level of devotion in return. The men who were indecisive in the heat of battle never held my respect for a fleeting moment.

My experience in combat taught me many things. Most importantly, I learned that when a man is staring death in the face, the decisions he makes will define him.

Four days earlier, when I woke up from my sickness, I telephoned Pratt. I felt guilty for not informing him of my illness and embarrassed for haphazardly exposing myself to the virus. In short, I owed him an apology.

I called him and apologized. He explained what Anna had done. When faced with the prospect of forfeiting her life to save another, she made the decision without hesitation. She chose to run toward the threat instead of away from it.

Pratt may have prevented her from entering my home, but his choice didn't negate the decision she'd made when she was at the crossroad of life and death. Her decision, like the decisions of my fellow Marines, defined her.

There was only one thing left for her to prove.

When I reached the age that I found interest in women, my father offered mountains of advice. I never knew if my failure to secure the right woman was a result of my father's poor advice or my inability to make good decisions.

One piece of his advice now came to mind.

"Never choose a woman because she's good in the sack," he said.

"Why not?" I asked.

"Because good pussies aren't always attached to good women," he replied.

"So, what am I supposed to do?"

He looked at me like I was a complete idiot. "Choose a woman based on how she makes you feel when she's *not* fucking you."

I returned six months or so later, asking him to expand upon his advice.

"Human beings have a propensity to lie," he said. "But a kiss will always tell the truth."

He explained that the moment he kissed my mother he knew she was the one he'd spend the rest of his life loving, caring for, and building a family with. I laughed at his claim. Something as simple as a kiss revealed absolutely nothing about who a woman was.

Or, so I thought.

"Holy crap," Anna said. "What was..." She wiped her mouth with the back of her hand. "What was that about?"

"I guess it was a test."

She playfully batted her eyes. "Did I pass?"

Her curly brown hair glistened in the afternoon sun. Her face—which had worn the looks of either worry, wonder, or aggravation for the past month—now expressed delight. I gazed at her admiringly.

It was as if I was seeing her for the first time.

My father was right. Kissing her opened a door within my soul that I had no idea existed. When we kissed, Anna unknowingly stepped through it. She now resided in a place alongside my beloved Marines; protected, admired, and respected.

I needed to know if she felt the same way but had no idea how to ask. I continued my admiring observation. I didn't know what else to do.

"Hell-o," she said sarcastically. "Earth to Rourke, Braxton Rourke. Come in Rourke, Braxton Rourke."

I gazed at her blankly, wondering if it was a fluke. Had the disease compromised my ability to reason? I'd been immune to the feelings of attraction for more than ten years. I needed to know for sure before I made the commitment.

I lifted her chin. I pressed my lips against hers. We kissed. My head began to tingle. An indescribable sensation of contentment filled me, completely.

I pulled away.

She seemed surprised that I'd ended the kiss. "What's wrong?"

"Absolutely nothing." I gave her a quick once-over. "What do you want out of this?"

Her gaze narrowed a little. "What's *this*?"

"You and me," I replied. "Us."

"I don't know," she said. "Honestly, I hate to set my sights on something too glorious, because—"

"If you got to choose what happened between us, what would it be? Anything goes."

Her lips parted slightly. Seeming hesitant to speak her mind, she brushed her hair behind her ear. With worry in her eyes, she studied me.

"Anything," I said. "What would it be?"

"When we met? I liked you. You were intriguing. We had sex. It was amazing. I wanted more." Her gaze fell to the driveway. "More sex, really. I mean, I didn't like the idea of being rejected, but at that point it wasn't about anything but sex. When you got sick, I was your wannabe nurse. I spent every waking hour with you. I learned more about who you really are. I found out more about myself, too. I still like you, but now it's for all the right reasons. We can either be friends, or we can be lovers, but we can't be in between," She met my gaze. "If I get to pick, I want to be lovers."

"Lovers?" I asked. "We'd be in a full-fledged relationship?"

"Call it whatever makes you comfortable." She kicked an errant stone with the toe of her shoe. "But that's what I want. If I get to pick. If that's what we decide, there will be a few rules."

"Like what?"

"As far as sex goes, we're not jumping right back to where we were. Like I said, I want this to be for all the right reasons. To convince myself that it is, we need to start slow."

It wasn't much of a sacrifice. Kissing her was as good as any sex that I'd ever had. However, as right as it felt to kiss her, the thought of committing to a relationship scared the hell out of me.

"I've been shot twice, cut more times than I can count, lived through two IED explosions, had three bones broken, and had my skull fractured," I said. "Nothing was as painful as being cheated on. The pain of having that trust severed? It was—"

"I know," she said. "It's happened to me, too."

"You've been cheated on?"

"More times than I can count."

"You're trustworthy," I said, expressing my conscious thoughts before I could contain them.

She looked at me funny. "You're asking me, or telling me?"

"I don't know." I shrugged. "Maybe a little of both."

"Do you carry a knife?" she asked.

"Say again?"

"A knife," she said, looking me up and down. "Do you carry one? Most guys like you do."

It seemed like an odd request. I reached into my pocket. "I do."

"Can I see it?" she asked.

"Be careful," I said, handing it to her. "It's sharp as fuck."

She flicked the blade open, proving it wasn't the first knife of its kind that she'd ever handled. She extended her thumb. Before I could stop her, she sliced into the flesh.

Blood dripped from the tip of her thumb onto the driveway between us.

She handed me the knife. "Here."

"What the fuck are you doing?" I asked.

She nodded toward the knife. "Cut your thumb. We'll make a blood bond. It's like a pinkie promise for adults."

If she hoped to garner my attention, she'd certainly done it.

"What are we promising?" I asked.

"We're committing to one another that we're in this for the long haul. If you cheat on me, your word isn't worth steaming pile of shit." She tilted her head toward the distant freeway. "I'll buy a billboard and make sure the city knows it, too. 'Braxton, Braxton Rourke is a no good, lying asshole.' As long as you're faithful, you'll see that same level of commitment from me."

It seemed like an odd manner of committing to one another considering the world's current views regarding the ease of transmission of the disease.

I stared at her in disbelief. Instantly, she mistook my hesitation as an indication of fear.

"Don't be a fucking pussy," she said under her breath. "I'm not scared. You shouldn't be, either."

Imagining a life with her in it came easily. I tried to imagine a life without her. It was incomprehensible. Not a life I wanted to live, that much I was sure of.

Without further thought, I swept the knife's blade along the pad of my thumb. I squeezed out a droplet of blood. As it splashed onto the concrete between my feet, our eyes met.

"Now what?" I asked.

"When you're ready to make the commitment." She raised her thumb. "Press yours against mine."

"Thumb, or lips?" I asked.

She smirked. "Suit yourself."

Given the freedom to decide, I chose both.

29

ANNA

It was hard to believe I was giddy during a global pandemic, but it was true. In fact, I was so full of excitement I could barely contain myself. For me, being in a relationship with anyone was an accomplishment.

When that person was Braxton, Braxton Rourke. Yeah, it was epic. Anxious to get started on living life—even if we were confined to our homes—I fought to keep from letting the cat out of the bag with Marge.

To celebrate Braxton's release from the doctor, she invited us over for a dinner of homemade chicken and noodles, mashed potatoes, bread and corn. Braxton and I discussed it, and decided we wanted to wait until after dinner to break the exciting news to her.

Braxton said he didn't want her to choke on her food.

Marge sat at one side of the small table and Braxton and I were seated side by side, across from her. It was tough to argue our placement. The table was decorated with folded paper nametags. I added Marge's perfectly scribed cursive handwriting to the things I envied about her.

She looked at Braxton. "How's your father coming along?"

"I can't get any more than 'he's stable' out of them," he replied. "It's frustrating."

Marge lowered her eyes to the table. "It's disappointing they can't tell you more. Hopefully, the prognosis will change soon."

"It's been over two weeks." Braxton shoveled another bite in his mouth. "There's been no improvements as far as I know. No deterioration to his health, either. I guess that's good. It's tough, for sure. I feel helpless."

Braxton was on a mission to gain the 18 pounds he'd lost. From the looks of things, he was going to do it entirely on Marge's chicken and noodles.

"I'm going to start emailing the hospital's staff tomorrow, asking for a more thorough explanation of his father's condition," I interjected. "Hopefully, I'll get someone to respond. My dad always said, 'the squeaky wheel gets the grease.' If I make enough commotion, hopefully someone will give a response better than 'he's stable.' That's a pretty poor answer for someone's condition."

"It amazes me that they haven't come up with a medication yet," Braxton complained. "I understand they haven't had time to develop a cure, but it would be nice if they'd come up with something that could help out with the breathing."

"I agree," I chimed.

Marge reached for her glass of tea. "When I was a child, I thought chicken and noodles were as good at curing ailments as any medicine."

"I've never heard that," I said.

Shoveling noodles into his mouth at a breakneck pace, Braxton shook his head. "Me, neither."

"It was my mother's claim," Marge said, seeming as if she truly believed what she was saying. "Chicken and noodles were a cure for everything. If someone was sick, she made chicken and noodles. If a neighbor fell on financial trouble, chicken and noodles was the answer. When the Zander couple down the street began talking of divorce, chicken and noodles was the cure. I was convinced she was right. Chicken and noodles could fix anything." She glanced at Braxton. "Maybe you should take your father some chicken and noodles."

Braxton shook his head in frustration. "When I went to the doctor this morning, I drove by there. I couldn't get past the lobby. Hell, I was lucky to make it that far, to be honest. They've truly got the place locked down."

"It's hard to comprehend," Marge said. She picked at her food. "A son can't go visit his ailing father in the hospital."

"They told Braxton if he tried to go any further than the lobby, they'd arrest him," I said.

Marge looked up. "That's awful."

"It is, but I guess it's for the better," Braxton said. "I wouldn't wish this disease on anyone."

Marge glanced at Braxton and then did a double take. "Don't make yourself sick."

"Excuse me?"

"You're going to give yourself stomach cramps." Grinning, she gestured toward his plate "Slow down. No one's going to take it from you."

"I haven't eaten a meal like this in I don't know how long," Braxton admitted, mid-bite. "This is amazing."

Marge beamed with pride. "Thank you, Braxton."

Marge's home was a step back in time. Golds and greens were abundant throughout the living room. The kitchen was as neat as it could possibly be. The white Formica countertops and seafoam green cabinets gave the place the feel of an era long since passed. Seeing it flooded me with childhood memories from my grandmother's farmhouse.

"This kitchen reminds me of my grandmother's," I said. "Your food resembles hers, too."

"Was your grandmother a hack in the kitchen?" Marge asked, straight-faced.

"A hack?" I laughed. "Making noodles like this isn't the work of a hack. It takes years of experience."

"Eggs, flour, milk, and salt," she said. "A monkey could do it."

"Did you hear that Braxton?" I scooped up a perfect portion of noodles and mashed potatoes. "Sounds like you could add this to your arsenal."

"I'll have you know I can get by in the kitchen," Braxton said between bites. "I've been doing it for years."

"You two had a little cooking lesson before you went sick, didn't you?" Marge asked.

"We did." Braxton replied.

"I thought that was the sweetest thing," Marge said. "She was really looking after you, wasn't she?"

Braxton offered a half-assed shrug. "She did pretty good."

"Pretty good?" Marge scoffed. "From what I heard she gave you step-by-step instructions."

"That doesn't mean I needed them," Braxton said.

"The fact that she offered is what matters," Marge argued. She glanced at me and smiled. "Not many would have been so thoughtful."

"She's alright," Braxton deadpanned.

"Did she tell you that she owns a car dealership?" Marge asked.

"She did," Braxton muttered.

Marge picked up a morsel of mashed potatoes and paused. She shifted her eyes from her food to Braxton. "Quite an accomplishment, if you ask me."

"Thank you," I said.

It was obvious that Marge had every intention of trying to set us up. I was itching to tell her what we'd decided but refrained.

"I told her I didn't realize people in Oklahoma knew how to drive," Braxton said with a laugh. "I thought they still rode horses."

"Don't be a jerk," Marge said jokingly.

"He's just playing," I said.

"He needs to be sweet," Marge said. "Sarcasm does little to attract a woman."

Braxton coughed out a laugh. "Who says I want to attract her?"

Having heard enough of Braxton's nonsense, Marge lowered her fork and shot him a glare. "I'm saying you're a fool if you don't."

Braxton looked me over as if considering Marge's recommendation. He glanced at Marge. "She did a pretty good job of looking after me when I was sick."

"She sure did," Marge agreed.

"Did she tell you she read to me?"

"She sure did," Marge said, alternating glances between Braxton and me as she spoke. "She sang you a lullaby or two, as well. Did she tell you that?"

Braxton scraped his plate clean with his fork. "She may have mentioned it."

"I don't know that she slept much in that two-week period," Marge wiped her hands on her napkin. "She was far too concerned with your wellbeing to relax."

Braxton looked at me, and then at her. "It sounds like she did a pretty good job."

She scowled like one would expect a cute little old lady to scowl if she took exception to what someone said.

"She did better than pretty good," she stated.

Braxton pushed himself away from the table. He looked at Marge. "Do you think much can be told from a kiss?"

"What do you mean?" she asked.

"When a man and a woman kiss," he explained, "do you think the result of that kiss is any indication as to whether or not they're compatible?"

"I think a kiss tells everything," Marge replied. "A man and a woman can be attracted to one another, but if their kiss has no chemistry, they're doomed."

"If there's chemistry in a kiss, they're destined to last forever?" Braxton asked.

"There are no assurances in life," Marge said matter-of-factly. "Speaking from experience, I can say lasting forever requires a lot of work. Quite frankly, day in and day out, it's a struggle."

I didn't disagree with Marge's statement, but I was surprised to hear her admit it. I gave her a surprised look. "You and Raymond had difficulties?"

"Oh, heavens yes," she replied. "The happiest and the angriest I've ever been in my life was a result of something my Raymond did."

I laughed. "Really?"

"He went to the bar to 'have a few' with his friends from the Army one Thursday night. The VFW had beer specials on Thursdays, back then. He didn't come home until Monday. I was worried sick. Friday morning, I took a Taxi to the VFW. He wasn't there. I checked the police stations, the morgue, the jails, everywhere I could think. I came up empty-handed at every turn. When I got done checking with LA County, I checked Orange County. Then, San Diego County. I had nowhere else to go, so I started working my way up north. By the time I got to Santa Barbara County, it was Monday. He came stumbling through the door, drunker than a skunk. I nearly beaned him in the head with a skillet."

"I'm surprised you didn't." I gave Braxton a look, warning him of what his future held. "I probably would have."

"I smacked him a good one, more than once," Marge admitted. "Not with a skillet, but I popped him with a rolling pin, a hair brush a few times, and a spatula a time or two."

"What did you do to solve the problems?" I asked. "Like with the extended trip to the VFW?"

"I identified the problem and proposed a solution," she replied. "We didn't have cell phones back then. Calling me meant he had to ask to use the phone in the bar, which most men saw as embarrassing. I gave him the option to either give me the courtesy of a call or stop drinking. Eventually, he stopped drinking."

"So, it's not always easy?" I asked.

"At times? Sure. Always?" She laughed a cute little laugh.

"Sweetheart, I wish I could say yes but it would be a lie."

"For the right man, I think I could be forgiving, understanding—" I glanced at Braxton. "And devoted."

"The devotion is more important than anything," she said. "Everything else falls into place if you're devoted."

Braxton stood. He gestured toward the noodles, which were in a big stock pot on the stove. "Do you mind?"

"Help yourself," Marge replied. "Don't be bashful, I was just razzing you earlier."

"I'm never bashful when it comes to food," Braxton said with a grin.

He fixed another heaping plate and promptly returned. He slid the plate in front of his chair and then loomed over me.

I glanced up. "What?"

He brushed his salt-and-pepper locks away from his face. "I'm curious about something." He smirked. "Come here for a minute."

Wondering what he was up to, I reached for his extended hand. With his assistance, I rose to my feet.

"Wondering about what?" I asked.

Just like the scene from *Casablanca*, he pulled me close and kissed me. It wasn't at all what I was expecting.

In fact, the kiss rocked me to my core.

Standing on legs made of rubber, I gazed at him in complete shock. "Wow."

His hazel eyes glistened with satisfaction. "I was going to say the same thing."

I took a quick glance in Marge's direction. Her hands were clasped together. She was glowing with joy.

If our little charade was a complete improv, I decided to play the part to the best of my ability. I twisted my hips back and forth in mock excitement and batted my eyes. "Can we do that again?"

Braxton kissed me in response, ever so sweetly. When our lips parted our eyes met.

"Do you want to give this a try?" I asked.

"I think so," he replied.

I scowled. "You *think* so?"

As if pondering the subject, he cocked his head to the side and gazed down at the floor. Following a short pause, he looked up. "Let's do it."

"It's going to be a lot of work," I warned.

"For the right woman," he said. "It'll be worth it."

Reliving the moment for Marge's enjoyment was as satisfying the real thing.

Still looking right at Braxton, I raised my brows in false wonder. "Am I the right woman?"

"If that kiss is any indication," he replied. "You sure are."

"Alright," I said with a smile. "Let's do it."

Marge clapped her hands. "I think this is cause for a celebration," she said. "I have a cobbler in the oven and ice cream in the freezer."

Braxton flashed me a grin and then looked at Marge. "I need to finish my plate of food first."

"Well. Get to it," Marge said, standing from her seat. Attempting to hide her ear to ear grin, she gestured toward the kitchen. "Anna, would you like to come help me with the cobbler?"

"Sure."

I stood at her side as she prepared bowls of peach cobbler with vanilla ice cream. When she was finished, she wiped the countertop free of crumbs.

"It seems men are always slow to realize what's in front of them," she whispered. "Sometimes they need a little nudge. I'm just pleased my plan worked out."

"Plan?" I asked.

She glanced over her shoulder. Braxton was cleaning his plate. She patted her hand against the stock pot of noodles.

"The chicken and noodles, Honey." She picked up two bowls and nodded toward the third. "Like I said, they're a cure-all."

I had no intention of ever admitting anything to the contrary. I picked up the bowl of cobbler and smiled. "They sure are."

30

BRAXTON

When arguing or negotiating, I had a policy. I did so in person. It was never over the phone, by text, or email. The pandemic forced me to reconsider my methods.

I was sitting at the kitchen island in front of my laptop, negotiating *and* arguing over the phone with Pratt.

"It's not hard to understand if you stop talking for a minute," I explained. "Are you willing to shut the fuck up and pay attention?"

Pratt sighed into the speaker of his phone. "I heard you, asshole. Doesn't mean I agree with what you said."

"In hindsight," I said. "It's the right thing to do. Just shift the money to the business account."

"I understand the fifty grand for the sewing machines. I'm not arguing that," he said. "But I'm not following you on the ventilators. Where's that money come from?"

I'd advised Pratt that we needed to take the $100,000 in revenue from the sewing machines and purchase N95 masks from a source I'd found in Hawaii. I was then going to donate the masks to the local hospitals.

In addition, mainly because I felt like an inconsiderate prick for profiting on the pandemic, I wanted to donate 6 ventilators to the hospitals. They were going to cost another $100,000 which was coming out of our pockets.

"It comes out of your wallet," I said. "Look at it as a donation. Doing shit like this is supposed to make people feel good."

"That's where I was afraid you were headed," he muttered. "You're giving the same $50,000?"

"Actually, I'm giving $57,420, to be exact," I said. "In addition to my half of the sewing machine money."

"I'll give $49,000," he said, "because you owe me a grand. A bet's a bet."

"That'll work."

"Good karma brings good karma," he said. "Maybe I'll win the lottery."

"Maybe so," I said in agreement. "Transfer the money. Ninety-nine k, total."

"Take me with you when you donate this shit," he pleaded. "Maybe some smoking hot nurse will give me some pussy in appreciation."

"If I were you, the last person I'd be fucking right now would be a nurse," I said. "They're exposed to this infection all day, every day."

"They're not touching it with their twats," he argued.

"They're touching it with their hands, and then their wiping their twats after they piss, aren't they?"

"Son-of-a-bitch," he grumbled. "I can't win."

"Send the money. I need to pay for this stuff before someone else buys it."

"Will do," he said.

"Appreciate it, Pratt."

"Tell Annie I said hi."

"Anna."

"That's what I meant."

"I'll let you know when this deal's secure," I said.

"Talk to you later."

I hung up the phone and pushed it onto the island. "I hate talking on the phone with him. He's impossible to argue with in person."

Anna peered over the top of her laptop. "How many masks does $100,000 buy?"

"In the middle of this mess? They're $5.00 each. So, it ought to buy 20,000. On this deal, I talked him into accepting a pre-pandemic price. 80 cents each. Shipping is what's killing me."

"Are you friends with any of the people you work with?" she asked.

I wasn't really friends with anyone, other than Pratt.

"What do you mean?" I asked.

"Any of the Hollywood types? Are you on a first name basis with any of them?"

"Oh. Sure."

"A lot of them?"

I shrugged. "On a professional level, I'd say there are quite a few. Why?"

"Do you have an Instagram account?"

I gave her a look of sheer disbelief. "Do I look like I fuck with social media?"

"Well." She lifted her phone. "I do. And I've got several thousand followers on my dealership page. Get one of your Hollywood friends to donate their time or give you a signed movie poster or something or the other, and then use it to sweeten the pot with your supplier. See if he'll throw in shipping. You can tag the person who makes the donation on my Instagram account when you give the hospital the stuff. We'll do a fancy picture of you bumping elbows or something within the limits of the social distancing measures."

It sounded like a hell of an idea. "I like it," I said. "Let me see who will do what." I nodded toward her laptop. "How's the email campaign coming?"

"I'm just getting started."

Everyone I contacted was supportive of the stay at home order and wanted to do whatever they could to encourage others to follow the state's guidelines. Their support of first responders, medical workers, and caregivers was profound. After thirty minutes of text messages, I had more donations than I knew what to do with.

I chose two of the more appealing offers and included them as an incentive in my return email to the supplier. A few seconds after clicking the *send* button, my phone rang. It was my contact with the supplier.

Wearing a smirk, I answered the phone. "Rourke."

"A walk-in on a Kevin Hart movie?" he asked. "Seriously? You're telling me I'll have a part in the next Kevin Hart movie?"'

"That's what he said."

"And a guest spot on Ellen DeGeneres' show?"

"That is correct. But I'm giving you $200,000 even, and you're air freighting me 125,000 masks and 8 brand new ventilators."

"I said I'd provide 6."

"And, I'm saying you either need to provide 8, or I'll find someone else to do business with."

"Who the fuck do you think you are?" he asked. "The ventilators are bringing $20,000 each on the streets."

"If the feds catch you selling them for profit, you'll be doing 20 years in Lompoc."

"Well, you're not the feds."

"It's something to think about though. Men in the federal prison system are being infected at an astounding rate. Have you seen the numbers?"

"Enough about prison," he said. "I can't do 8. We need to stick with 6."

"Got any kids?" I asked.

"What the fuck's that got to do with anything?"

"Just wondering if any of your kids would like to be in a Shawn Mendez music video."

"Who the fuck's Shawn Mendez?"

"You must not have any kids."

"Is he popular?" he asked.

"He's an award-winning artist. He's got one music video that has over a billion views on YouTube."

"A fucking billion?" he asked. "With a 'B'?"

"Billion with a 'B'."

"Let me call you back."

"Make it quick," I warned. "In ten minutes, I'm going to someone else. Someone who knows who Shawn Mendez is."

I hung up the phone and set it aside. When I looked up, Anna was sitting at her computer with her mouth agape. Her eyes were as wide as saucers.

"You got Shawn Mendez to donate a music video spot?" she asked. "Shawn Mendez? Like *Seňorita* Shawn Mendez? Camila Cabello Shawn Mendez?"

"That'd be him."

"Hoe. Lee. Crap."

"We'll see if my Hawaiian connection wants it."

"Who wouldn't?"

The phone rang. I gestured to it and grinned. "Hopefully, he's got kids."

"If not, I guess you'll have to offer it to someone else. Someone will snatch that deal up."

I reached for the phone. "There is no one else."

I answered it. "Well?"

"This shit's for real?" he asked, seeming hesitant. "No bullshit?"

"You've got my personal guarantee that when this pandemic's over, you'll get what I've promised. Ask around the industry, I don't make promises I can't keep."

"Your reputation's sterling," he said. "Or we wouldn't be talking. Tell you what. You've got a deal."

"Email me the wire transfer information and I'll send you the money. This stuff better be on a plane this afternoon. I need it tomorrow. No exceptions."

"It'll be out today," he said. "You have my word."

I hung up the phone and glanced at Anna. "Well, that's a done deal."

"So, you're getting 125,000 N95 masks?"

"Correct."

"Can I use 10,000 of them as a bargaining chip?"

"For what?"

"I want a doctor from the hospital to call you and have a one-on-one conversation about your father. I think the masks might be enough of an incentive to get him to do so."

"Not a bad idea," I said. "Give it a try."

She leaned over her keyboard and began typing like her fingers were on fire. Since our agreement to be in a relationship, she'd been in my home non-stop. Six weeks earlier, I would have described such an event as torturous.

Now, I couldn't think of having it any other way.

She swept the hair away from her face a few times, and then twisted it into a bun. She went right back to typing as if nothing had happened. The corners of my mouth curled up. I couldn't help it.

"I don't want you to leave," I murmured.

She glanced up, but only for a second. "I wasn't planning on it."

"I mean at all," I said. "I want you to stay here. I wake up, I see you. I go to bed, you're at my side."

She looked up. "Really?"

"Really."

She smiled. "Sounds fun. I'm in."

She commenced with her email campaign. I watched her for a few moments, grinning all the while.

I shook my head in disbelief. "This is nuts."

"What?" she asked, not bothering to look up from her typing. "Getting the masks? I know, they're impossible to find. It's crazy you found them, huh?"

"No, not that," I replied.

She paused. "What, then?"

I pointed at her, and then at me. "This. Us."

She looked up. "What about it? Us? Whatever."

"It's just. I don't know." I rested my chin against my clasped hands. "It's easy."

"Oh." She smiled and then went right back to typing. "Yeah, it's good stuff, that's for sure."

I didn't know if it was Anna or the disease that opened my eyes, but they were open wider than they ever had been. The clarity of my vision allowed me to see a future with her that I never would have guessed could exist.

I hoped from deep within the limits of my soul that my father could be a part of it, also.

31

ANNA

A member of the news crew had a microphone on an aluminum pole that was six feet long. With his arm extended, the device was eight feet from where he stood. He positioned it beneath Braxton's chin.

We were at Scripps Mercy Hospital in San Diego, in the parking lot just beside the entrance. The moving van was parked at Braxton's side, and the news reporter had an open case of N95 masks at her feet.

Wearing his favorite Tom Ford suit, his Breitling watch, and a homemade mask, Braxton leaned forward slightly. His salt-and-pepper beard was trimmed neatly, and his hair was freshly cut by yours truly.

"I can't say enough to accurately express my appreciation for what the medical workers are doing in an effort to combat this disease," Braxton said into the fur-covered device. "I felt this gesture would allow them to safely continue their quest to provide care to those who are suffering."

The bubbly brunette reporter raised a small cardboard box of masks so the second cameraman could get it in the picture. "The filter in the N95 mask is made of thousands of nonwoven fibers, each of which is smaller than a human hair," she explained through her cotton mask. "It is that complex filtration system that provides peace of mind to the many healthcare workers who are devoted to caring for those who are struggling to survive this deadly disease."

She lowered the box and looked at Braxton. "It's our understanding that you father is here? In Mercy?"

"He is."

"Infected with COVID-19?"

"That is correct."

"Any word on his expected recovery?"

"He's on a ventilator," Braxton replied. "He's stable. That's really all we know."

"So many lives are dependent upon the ventilators, which are also in short supply," she said. "This brings us to another chapter in this book of selfless acts. You've donated 2 ventilators to this facility as well?"

"I have," Braxton replied. "They're in high demand and in short supply."

The reporter faced the second camera. "Shy of their capacity in the ICU, Mercy was forced to turn away COVID-19 patients with critical respiratory issues, as their stock of ventilators was being utilized by men and women who were fighting respiratory failure. There's no doubt that the ventilators donated will save many lives throughout this pandemic, which is only getting started here in San Diego County." She turned to Braxton. "It's our further understanding that you didn't assemble this donation by yourself. What can you share about how this came together?"

"I couldn't have done any of this without the help of a few generous and very thoughtful people," Braxton replied.

"Can you name them?" she asked.

"I can," Braxton said. "Ellen DeGeneres, Kevin Hart, and Shawn Mendez each made unnamed contributions, but none of this could have been done without Anna Wilson. When I was at an impasse in negotiations, it was her idea to include celebrity endorsements. Those endorsements sealed the deal."

My heart swelled so much I could barely breathe. Then, my face went flush.

"We're familiar with the first three names," the reported said. "But the third? Is she new on the Hollywood scene?"

Braxton extended his right arm toward me. "Anna?"

Embarrassed, grateful, and shocked beyond belief, I stepped in front of the camera. Braxton draped his arm over my shoulder.

"Can you explain your thought process on putting this amazing deal together, Miss Wilson?" the reporter asked.

"This disease does not discriminate," I replied. "Young, old, compromised health, or the epitome of health, we're all at risk. To spread the word of this disease's contagion and seriousness, I thought someone with a strong social media presence would be best."

"Well, you've certainly found those people with DeGeneres, Hart, and Mendez," she said, turning to face the second camera. "From Hollywood fixer, to Hospital fixer, Braxton Rourke and company have left their mark on Scripps Mercy. The medical staff, the community, and all of us at KGTV San Diego would like to express our sincere thanks. This is Meghan Murphy reminding you to stay safe, stay six feet apart, and stay strong."

Following a few still shots of the delivery van, Braxton, and me, thanks was given by the entire news crew from afar. The medical staff then expressed their gratitude from inside the facility in the form of hand-written signs they held high in the air.

MASKS SAVE LIVES - THANK YOU

As the news crew loaded their equipment, Braxton faced me. "I'm glad this is over."

"You looked like you were annoyed," I said.

"Never cared much for having my picture taken."

"Mister Rourke," A voice from behind us said.

We both turned around. A gentleman dressed in blue scrubs was standing on the top steps of the entrance, twenty feet from where we stood. A plastic face shield and a cotton mask obstructed his face, but they did little to hide his exhaustion.

"Good morning," Braxton said.

"I'm Doctor Betz," the man said. "I wanted to bring you up to speed on your father's condition."

"I'd appreciate anything you can share," Braxton said.

"As Doctor Ziminov advised you, your father's condition hadn't worsened, nor had it improved. He remained stable, but reliant upon the ventilator to breathe. This morning, based on your discussions of late yesterday, we opted to try an experimental drug, *Remdesivir*. Since the drug's administration, we've seen major improvements in your father's oxygenation. We've also recorded a significant decrease in his lung edema. He remains on the ventilator, but we have expectation that he'll be off of it before day's end."

I gasped.

"Breathing on his own?" Braxton asked excitedly.

"This is our first experiment with this drug," the doctor admitted, checking his watch as he spoke. "Believe me, we're as excited as you are. Although we have chosen to leave him on the ventilator for now, we believe he will be breathing on his own soon."

Braxton exhaled. "Is there any way you can keep me posted on his—"

"I have your cell phone number," the doctor replied. "May I—"

Braxton nodded. "Absolutely."

The doctor checked his watch. "I need to go."

"Thanks, Doc," Braxton said. "For everything."

"The instant something changes," The doctor said. "You'll hear from me."

Braxton held me tight against his shoulder. "Thanks again."

The doctor gave a curt nod and turned away. As he disappeared through the hospital's doors, Braxton exhaled. "Maybe Pratt's right."

"About what?"

"He said good karma brings good karma."

"I believe hatred breeds hatred, and love can only blossom by and through love," I said. "It sounds like he and I think alike."

"Pratt doesn't think like anyone," he retorted. "He wanted to come here and see if he could get a nurse to fuck him. It wasn't until I warned him about the possibility of getting infected that he finally decided it wasn't a good idea."

I gave Braxton a quick once-over.

I smirked. "He sounds like someone else I know."

"That was the old me," he said. "The new me isn't like that."

"Oh, he's not?" I asked with a note of sarcasm.

"No, he's not." He kissed me. "The new me only fucks wannabe nurses, not real ones."

32

BRAXTON

We had driven from Los Angeles to San Diego to pick up my father. The day after they administered the experimental medication, he was capable of breathing on his own. Two days later, they were ready to release him. Although he hadn't fully recovered, staying in the hospital was no longer necessary. He didn't know it yet, but he was going to be living at my home until I felt he was strong enough to be on his own.

My father was like the THC-laced edibles peddled in So-Cal's many marijuana shops. A little bit of him made most people smile, but a large dose could end catastrophically.

As we approached the hospital, the thought of having him in the home was proving to be more than I could bear.

"Is it the excitement, or is there something wrong?" Anna asked. "You seem, I don't know, tense."

I stared straight ahead. Visions of him going on a rampage about how I'd infected him with the disease came to mind. They were promptly replaced with vivid recollections of how he treated my ex-wife.

They got along like a mongoose and a snake.

I glanced in Anna's direction. "Nothing's wrong—"

"Why do you seem so anxious?"

I hadn't lived with him since I was eighteen years old. As excited as I was to see him, the thought of having him in my home—especially with Anna present—made me as nervous.

"He's just. He can be overwhelming," I said. "He's very opinionated."

"You guys get along well, though. Right?"

I'd seen my father every Sunday for as long as I could remember. I couldn't imagine life any other way. Having him in my home on a semi-permanent basis was a different story altogether. I wanted to explain matters to Anna but doing so without making him sound like an absolute asshole would be impossible.

"We do and we don't. He's...I don't know how to explain it. He's got an opinion about everything."

"Most elderly men do," she said. "I know my father did."

"It's not as simple as that. I guess you'll just have to see."

"All you've done for three weeks is complain because he's in the hospital," she gave me a condescending look. "I think you should be happy."

"I am happy. I'm just. I guess," I stammered. "I don't know. I'm worried."

She laughed out loud. "Worried? You? Mister 'I've been shot, stabbed, and survived roadside bombs' is worried?"

I shifted my eyes from the freeway to her. "I'd rather be shot again than have him living with me. Us. This is going to be interesting I'll promise you that."

She gave me an apologetic look. "I don't have to stay at your house. I can go home, you know."

My desire to have Anna stay was as strong as my desire to have my father elsewhere.

"You're staying." I shot her a glare. "End. Of. Discussion."

"Okay, *Boss*."

As instructed by the hospital's staff, we pulled up to the

administration entrance of the hospital. The vehicle rolled to a stop. I glanced at the building. The hospital's western-facing glass was tinted, but not so much that I couldn't see through it. A tall mask-wearing orderly was standing beside a wheelchair. My father's arms were waving in every direction, and his mouth was moving a mile a minute. An armed security guard at their side appeared to be taking mental notes of the event.

"See that?" I asked.

Anna shifted her attention from the parking lot to the hospital. "What?"

"Inside." I nodded toward the commotion. "Right beside that potted palm. You can't miss it."

She scanned the area. Her eyes locked on the three men. "The two guys arguing?"

"One of them is arguing," I said with a laugh. "The other is just listening. It looks like the guard is acting as the referee."

"Is that—"

"You guessed it," I said. "That's Hap."

She peered toward the three men. She squinted. "I thought he was a frail little old man. He doesn't look frail, little, or old. He's tall and he looks physically fit, especially for being comatose for three weeks."

She was right. Considering the length of time he was confined to a bed, he looked like he was in remarkable condition.

"There's nothing little about him." I got out of the car and glanced at Anna. "I'll be right back."

She shot me a look while reaching for her door. "I'm coming."

"Suit yourself," I murmured.

We walked to the entrance side by side. The automatic doors slid open, revealing an amused guard, an argumentative Hap, and an extremely accepting young orderly, who appeared to be offering the old man a wheelchair.

They were thirty feet from where we stood. Consumed with the argument, they had no idea we'd walked through the door.

Hap looked like a blind two-year-old had fitted his mask. It was askew, with one of the elastic straps barely attached to the top of his ear. His left hand clutched a plastic bag marked with the hospital's logo.

"Painfully fucking obvious you can't hear," Hap snarled. He gave the kid a side-eyed look. "Is English your native language?"

The kid was as white as a sheet. His hair was as red as a fire truck. I don't know what other language he may have spoken. Hoping to diffuse the situation, I started to walk in their direction. Anna held out her arm and stopped me from taking the first step.

"Yes, it is," the kid responded. "Like I said a moment ago, this is policy, Sir. I'm supposed to—"

"You can go fuck a goat," Hap said, motioning to the wheelchair. "You get in that fucking thing, and I'll push your dumb red-headed ass out into the parking lot."

The orderly sighed. "The hospital's policy for departing ICU—"

"Here's my policy," Hap snapped, interrupting the orderly mid-sentence. "When my dipshit son gets here, I'm walking through those doors like a man."

"Leave him alone, Old Man," I said. "He's just trying to do his job."

Hap's attention shot from the orderly to me. His face contorted. "What in the hell happened to you?" he looked me up and down. "You go on a cabbage soup diet or something? You look like hammered shit."

"Get in the wheelchair, Old Man." I motioned to the SUV with my thumb. "Let's go."

His eyes thinned. "You get in the wheelchair, Dipshit."

Anna brushed past me. "How about if I push you?" she asked. "We can do wheelies on the way."

Hap's eyes widened. "Who might you be?"

She tilted her head toward me. "I'm with him."

Hap looked her over good. "Are you the fiery Italian gal from next door?"

"How'd you know I was Italian?" she asked.

Hap laughed. He looked at me. "I told you."

Anna glanced at each of us. "Told him what?"

"I told Dipshit you were Italian," Hap replied. "I knew you were either a wop or a Mexican."

"I'm half wop," Anna said, seeming unoffended by the derogatory term.

Knowing nothing would be off-limits to the old man, I scanned my memory for anything I'd revealed that I wouldn't want him repeating. While I tried to recall everything we'd discussed, Anna sauntered to the wheelchair.

Anna smiled at the orderly. "Is it okay if I drive?"

Outwardly relieved the incident was concluding, the kid struggled to hide a smile. "Absolutely."

Anna motioned to the wheelchair with a wave of her hand. "Get in."

Hap folded his 6'-3" frame into the wheelchair like it was his idea to do so all along. Anna grabbed the handles and turned the chair in my direction.

"My mother's parents were Italian immigrants," she explained, pushing the chair past me. "While my father was in New York staying with his uncle, he met my mother. He was supposed to come home at the end of the summer, but he ended up staying for two years because of her."

"What was your mother's last name?" Hap asked.

"Regio."

"I knew it was something like that." Hap glanced up. "Did you put dumbass on a diet? Or did he do that on his own?"

"He lost weight when he was—"

I got Anna's attention and mouthed the words *don't tell him*. Anna pushed the wheelchair to the SUV and set the wheel brake.

"When he was what?" Hap asked.

Anna seemed confused. "Excuse me?"

"You said 'he lost the weight when he was', and then you

stopped," Hap replied. He got out of the wheelchair. "When he was what?"

"When he was waiting for you to get out of here," she replied. "He was so worried he could barely eat."

"Well, isn't that sweet." Hap said in a snide tone. He faced the orderly. "Satisfied?"

The orderly reached for the wheelchair and flashed a smile. "Extremely."

I opened the back door and motioned inside. "Get in, Old Man."

He gave me a look. "Are you taking me home?"

"You're coming to my house for a while."

"You can go fuck a goat, too," he said. He looked at Anna. "Take me home. Dipshit can tell you how to get there."

"I'm driving," I said.

Hap slid into the seat. "When you drive it makes me sick to my stomach. You want me to barf all over this pretty British piece of shit?"

"I'll drive," Anna said. "But you're staying with us."

Hap's brows raised. "Us?"

Anna nodded. "Us."

Hap looked at me. "Us?"

I nodded. "Anna and me."

Hap chuckled. "Did hell freeze over while I was sick?"

"I've got a woman in my house, and you're coming to stay with me," I replied. "It must have."

33

ANNA

Braxton may have been frustrated with his father's presence, but I wasn't. Hap had only been around for an hour and I could claim that I'd never been so entertained in all my life. He and Braxton were like Laurel and Hardy, Dean Martin and Jerry Lewis, or Cheech and Chong. Their love was undeniable and the chemistry between them was irrefutable.

Hap didn't look—or act—like he was in his mid-seventies. His arms were bulging with muscles, his chest was broad, and his waist was trim. He walked like Braxton, expressing confidence with each step he took.

The similarities between the two men stopped there. Braxton was quiet, choosing to talk when spoken to. Hap never stopped talking. He seemed to enjoy choosing subjects that got beneath Braxton's skin. He'd then talk about them until they ended up in an argument.

It seemed that each argument had purpose, at least to Hap. That beneath all the "fuck you, Son" and "dipshit" jabs he made, there was a deeper meaning. If nothing else, the subject matter he chose to argue about was worth listening to.

Hap strolled past the living room wearing a clean pair of khakis and a white tee shirt that we picked up from his home.

I looked up from season four, episode six of *Mad Men*. "Feel better?"

"I needed that shower," he replied, pausing in the doorway. "All that hospital doled out were whore baths."

"Whore baths are good when there's no other option."

He scowled. "Are you always so upbeat?"

I smiled. "Most of the time."

He disappeared. In an instant, he returned. "Dipshit go to get my meds?"

"Yes, he did."

He vanished. His footsteps went from room to room, opening and closing every door, closet, cupboard, and drawer. Fifteen minutes into his quest, the slamming of doors ceased.

He peeked into the living room. "Have you been here long enough to know where he keeps things?"

"I know where some things are," I replied. "You're supposed to stay out of the refrigerator, though. There's a surprise in there."

"He already warned me about the fridge," he grunted. "Where's he keep his hammer?"

It seemed like an odd request. There wasn't anything in the house that I could think of that Braxton would want his father beating on.

I turned to face him. "I know he has a hammer, but I don't think he wants you working on anything. You're supposed to be taking it easy."

"I'm going to smack something once, and then I'll be done," he said. "Do you know where he keeps it?"

"He used it to tenderize chicken the other day. He said he kept it in the garage."

He looked at me like I was out of my mind. "He used a hammer on a piece of chicken?"

"A rubber mallet," I replied. "He tenderized a chicken breast with it. It was covered with plastic."

"A rubber mallet?" His face lit up. "That's exactly what I need."

"What are you going to do?" I asked.

He disappeared for a moment without responding. When he returned, he was grinning like the cat that ate the canary.

"Did you find it?" I asked.

He stepped between me and the television. "Do you know if he's got hair clippers?"

"He does." I paused the television. "He bought an entire kit the other day and had it delivered."

He scratched the sides of his head. "Do you know how to give a proper crewcut?"

"I think so."

He crossed his arms. His look went serious. "You think so, or you know so?"

"I used to cut my dad's hair all the time," I replied. "He didn't wear a crewcut, but he kept it short. I can watch a YouTube video and make sure. It can't be that difficult."

"Either you know, or you don't." He gave me a flippant look. "Sounds like you don't."

"Just a minute." I grabbed my phone. I Googled *crewcut* and selected the first video. I watched thirty seconds of the tutorial and looked up. "I can do it."

"This isn't a good time for you to be betting on a *maybe*," he said, seeming annoyed. "I don't want a haircut with a bunch of fucking holes in it."

"I'm positive."

"Well..." He put his hands on his hips. "Are you going to sit there and look pretty, or are we going to get this done?"

"Oh." I set the remote on the end table. "You want to do it now?"

"This shit's going in every direction." He mussed his hair with his fingertips. "I look like an Iowa farmhand that just got done fucking one of the unwilling sheep."

He looked like a mad scientist. Choking on a laugh, I sprung from my seat. "I'll be right back."

When I returned, he was sitting at the kitchen island with his arms crossed. He studied me as I walked toward him, almost as if evaluating me. Feeling nervous, I stepped to his side and presented the tools of the trade.

"I've got it all," I declared. "Cape, clippers, comb, and scissors. I've even got a mirror."

"Where do you want to do this?"

"In here is fine," I replied. "The lighting is good, but you'll have to sit on one of those short chairs. I can't see the top of your head if you're on a stool."

He slid off the edge of the stool. He gave me a once-over. "How tall are you?"

"Five-two."

His visual inspection continued. He paused when he reached my hair. "Is that your natural hair color?""

"It is."

He sauntered to the dining table and pulled out a chair. He glanced at the table before sitting down. "Restaurants are closed until who knows when. What have you two been doing for food?"

"I've been cooking," I replied. "I'd rather cook than go out, anyway."

"No guard on the sides," he said. "Fade into a number one, and scissor cut on top, just long enough to make me look mean."

I grinned. "One haircut with mean intentions, coming right up."

I fitted the cape around his neck. Clutching to the hope that I didn't make a haircut 'with a bunch of fucking holes in it', I began shaving off his thick silver locks.

"Ever been arrested?" he asked.

The question came from nowhere. It took me by complete surprise. Luckily, I wasn't cutting his hair at the moment.

I turned off the clippers. "Yes, once."

"What for?"

"Resisting arrest."

"What were they arresting you for in the first place?"

"That's the exact same question I asked the judge. I wasn't really resisting *arrest*. It was more just me being resistant to an overbearing cop's attitude."

"Let's hear the story," he said.

I grinned at the thought of it. "I got pulled over for speeding out in the middle of nowhere. I was test driving a customer's car before taking it in on trade. I wanted to see if it had any drivability issues. On an open stretch of road outside of Tulsa, I got up to 160 miles an hour. Just as I was getting ready to slow down, I whooshed past this cornfield. There was a cop backed into the farmer's entrance, eating a barbeque sandwich and clocking—"

"If you were going 160, how do you know what he was eating?"

"Because it was all over his shirt when he pulled me over five minutes later."

"Proceed with the story, my dear."

I liked it that he called me *my dear*. My father did it regularly, and I missed it.

I smiled. "I slowed down to a crawl, and he pulled me over five or six miles down the road. He came walking up the car with his hand on his gun and barbeque sauce from one end of him to the other. The first thing he said—even before 'do you know how fast you were going' or 'can I see your driver's license?' was, 'I'll be taking this purty blue sum bitch to the impound yard.' I threw a fit. He told me to settle down. I didn't. It really wasn't a big deal."

"Had you hit the brakes before you blew past him?"

"No, I was still on the gas."

"How fast did he clock you?"

"168."

"Jesus H. Christ," he said with a laugh. "What were you driving?"

"A Lamborghini Aventador. Someone was trading it in on a Ferrari."

"Do you always drive customer's cars like that?"

"Supercars?" I asked. "Sure. I need to make sure they don't problems. If I took one on trade, giving a customer $200,000 for it, and then when the next customer took possession he brought it in and said, 'hey this thing wobbles and makes weird noises at 160, I'd might be spending 20 grand for a suspension overhaul."

"Sounds reasonable," he said. "So, when the cop said he was going to tow it, you threw a fit?"

"Pretty much. After he made his comment about the impound yard, I said, 'hold on a minute.' He said he had the right to tow it. I said, 'You might have the right, but you don't have my permission.' He said, 'You're not in charge, Missy.' I said, 'My name is *Anna*.' He smirked a shitty little smile, showing me the bits of pulled pork that were still stuck in his teeth, and said, 'Well, Anna, I'll be taking this shiny blue sum bitch to the impound yard, like it or not.'"

"He sounds like a horse's ass."

"He was," I said. "I explained that I could have someone there to get it in five minutes. It only had about two inches of ground clearance, and I didn't want them to damage it when they tried to load it on a truck. He called for a tow truck, anyway. That's when I called him a fat sloppy piece of shit."

He coughed out a laugh. "Calling a cop a fat sloppy piece of shit is like calling the first base umpire a cocksucker. It's a surefire way to expose their bad side." He glanced over his shoulder. "Did they tow the car?"

"They did. It had $4,000 worth of damage when I got it back."

"You're not afraid of standing up for yourself," he said. "That's a quality not often found in a woman."

"If anything, I have a problem keeping my opinions to myself."

"How much was the speeding ticket?"

"$4,000 damage to the car, I lost my driver's license for a year, paid a $2,500 fine, and did 160 hours of community service."

"Holy hell," he exclaimed. "Out here people drive that fast on their way to work."

"I know. In bumper-to-bumper traffic, too."

He patted the side of his head. "Get back to work, Missy."

Hap was a hard man to read. I hoped the battery of questions meant that he liked me. I doubted he'd admit it, even if he did. After a few swipes with the clippers, the next question came.

"You're successful, pretty, and you've got spunk. Why aren't you married?"

"I was at one point," I replied, gliding the clippers up the back of his head as I spoke. "I divorced him."

"Just get tired of him, or what?"

"He couldn't keep his prick in his pants," I replied. "I swore off men and sex after that. When I came here, I was on a two-year hiatus."

"From relationships or sex?"

"Both."

He digested my response for a few moments.

He was a much different person than my father, but he reminded me of him. It may have been that he had hit me with a barrage of questions. Every time I visited my parents, it seemed my father had random things to ask about my life. I wondered if asking random questions was an age-related thing, or a more of a fatherly trait.

While I mulled it over, he continued.

"Is your business profitable, or is it more for fun?"

"It's profitable," I replied proudly. "Very, actually."

"Lot of high-end cars around here," he said. "Dumb bastards trade 'em in every six months. Seems most of these rich pricks have more money than sense."

"I'm sure there's quite a few," I replied. "I haven't got out much, so I haven't noticed."

"Can't swing a dead cat in LA County without smacking a new Rolls, Bentley, or Lambo. Dip-shits drive 'em like they're pickup trucks. See them at the store all the time with shopping carts laying against them."

In and around Tulsa, there was oil money, and only the

extremely fortunate drove such cars. Luckily, there were enough oil barons to keep me afloat.

"That's a shame," I said, brushing the hair clippings off his ears. "About the shopping carts."

"Siblings?" he asked.

"Nope," I said. "Just me."

"Brax told me about your parents. Shame any time something like that happens. Glad to have you here, but I'm sorry that's what brought you."

"Thank you," I said. "Life isn't always easy, I guess. That's one of those things I'll probably never understand."

"Were you able to get the funerals taken care of before they banned public gatherings?"

"They asked to be cremated. It's all been taken care of."

"That's what I want, too. Something about being buried doesn't set very well with me."

"Me, neither."

"Leave any kids back in Oklahoma?"

"Kids?" I chuckled. "Nope."

"Kids get in the way of living life," he muttered.

It seemed like an inconsiderate thing to say, considering Braxton was willing to pick him up from the hospital, take care of him, and run to get his prescriptions.

"I don't know about that," I replied. "Can you imagine life without Braxton?"

"I dream about it sometimes. Then, I have a nightmare. One where he's still around. Snatches me right out of my sleep in a cold sweat."

I turned off the clippers and stepped in front of him. "That's crap," I argued. "And you know it."

He let out a heavy sigh. "Kids are like big feet. They're with you for a lifetime no matter how much you hate looking at 'em."

"You're evil," I said.

He grinned. "Thank you."

Like most women, my early dreams included having children. The hope faded a little with each failed relationship. When I passed my mid-thirties, I wondered if it would ever happen. After my divorce, I felt fortunate that I wasn't another single mother raising children without a father in their lives.

"When I was younger, I wanted children," I admitted. "Looking back on things now, I can't think of anyone I'd liked to have had them with. I guess it wasn't meant to be. Back to my understanding life comment. It's not always easy."

He patted the side of his head. "It sure isn't."

After a few more careful swipes of the clippers, I was nearly done. Using the comb as a guide, I blended the sides of his hair to the top. After snipping a few stray strands, everything looked good.

I handed Hap the mirror. "Well?"

He held the mirror in one hand while brushing the palm of his free hand up each side of his head. "Looks good, feels good," he said with a nod. "You did a fine job."

I took the mirror and removed his cape, being careful not to get hair on him. "Thank you."

He brushed his hands against the thighs of his pants and then looked up. "When this virus is over, are you staying or going back to Oklahoma?"

Of all the things he could have asked, I wish he wouldn't have asked that. It was a tough question to answer, truthfully. I'd like to think I'd be staying but had no idea how things with Braxton might change once the stay at home order was lifted.

"I haven't decided," I replied.

"What's preventing you from deciding?"

The sound of Braxton's SUV caught my attention. I found his arrival ironic.

"Uncertainty," I replied.

He cocked his head to the side and raised his brows. "Of what?"

I didn't want to admit that things might not last between Braxton and me, therefore, I didn't care to answer the question.

The front door opened. I glanced at Braxton, forced a smile, and then looked at Hap.

He met my gaze, held it for a second, and then patted me on the shoulder. "No need to respond," he said. "You just gave me all the answer I need."

34

BRAXTON

The three of us stood at the dining room table, eyeing the "Welcome Home" meal Anna prepared. Hap had been acting like he had a burr up his ass since I got home from the pharmacy. I hoped the homecooked meal brought him out of his bad mood.

Anna gestured toward the food. "We better start before it gets cold."

I kissed Anna. "Thank you."

Hap's favorite meal was roast with carrots, onions and potatoes. He demanded my mother serve it with quartered yellow potatoes *and* mashed potatoes with gravy. Anna had done her best to replicate the meal, even baking homemade bread for him to mop up the gravy with.

Sporting a fresh haircut, Hap leaned over the table. He looked everything over and closed his eyes. He drew a long, slow breath through his nose.

Anna took her chair. "I hope everyone enjoys it."

I sat down beside her.

Hap took his seat. "Smells divine."

I glanced at the various offerings that were on display. It was the maiden voyage for the serving platters and a good portion of the dishes we were using. To be honest, I had no idea where most of the dinnerware came from.

I looked at Hap. I realized it was the first time he had eaten in my home.

Excluding Christmas and Easter, the last time I could recall eating a meal with my father that wasn't out of a takeout container was when my brother was alive.

He'd been gone for over thirty years.

When I lived at home, we sat down every night and ate at the dinner table, as a family. We said *please* and *thank you.* No one got up from the table without being excused, and we didn't complain about quality or quantity, regardless of what was served.

Yes, Sir and *no, Ma'am* were as common as *pass the potatoes, please.* We didn't need to ask when dinnertime was, because it was at the same time every night, without fail.

5:30.

After my brother died, the Marine Corps became my only family. It wasn't by choice. By design, every moment was consumed by training, combat, and travel, leaving no time for my blood family.

By the time my military career ended, my mother was gone. Although I loved my father dearly, I never felt that he and I comprised a *family.* We were merely two men who were bound by blood. Together, we were a father and son team. A family, we were not.

"Mind passing me that roast?" Hap asked.

"Not at all," Anna replied.

Each item was passed from person to person until our plates were filled with all that Anna had prepared. When the last platter was set into its place, Hap cleared his throat.

"Are we saying grace, or just digging in?" he asked. "I feel like I ought to be thanking him for letting me make it to this meal."

When I was a kid, my mother said grace before every meal. When I left home, the tradition stopped. Short of Anna saying a prayer before we ate the parmesan chicken, I hadn't blessed a meal in over thirty years.

I was surprised Hap asked.

"I'll say grace," Anna replied. "If it's okay."

"Probably be best if you did it," Hap replied. "I doubt Dipshit and the man upstairs are on speaking terms, and it's been so long since I said anything over a plate of food, I'll likely embarrass myself."

Anna said a quick prayer, and we began to eat. The meal was as good as I remember it being when my mother cooked it, if not better. After I'd taken time to taste everything, I looked up. Hap was mopping gravy off his plate with a piece of bread.

"What do you think, Old Man?"

"I think it's been a long time since I ate anything this good." He looked at Anna. "You're a damned fine cook, young lady."

"Thank you," she said, beaming with pride. "For the young lady comment, and about the food."

Hap poked the gravy-soaked bread in his mouth. "What are you pushing?" He eyed her up and down. "About thirty?"

"Add ten," she said.

"You don't look it," Hap said, shaking his head in disbelief. "Keep doing what you're doing, it's working well."

Hap filled his plate and returned to the table. He gave the food an admiring look. "My appetite's coming back. I'll pick up a couple of lost pounds right here."

"I need to pick up a few," I admitted.

Hap pierced a potato and paused. He lifted his chin and looked right at me. "You end up with this shit, Son?"

"What shit?" I asked, although I knew exactly what he wanted to know.

"The virus." He poked the spud in his mouth. "Did you have it?"

I set my fork aside. Out of my peripheral I noticed Anna stopped chewing. I wiped my hands on my napkin and set it aside.

"I did," I said.

"Serves you right." He swallowed. He poked another potato. "You're an inconsiderate prick on a good day."

It went better than I expected. "You're right," I said. "I'm sorry."

"Sorry don't cut it on a deal like this," he said. "Being selfish almost cost my life, and yours, too. Life isn't just about you, Son. There's two people at this table that you need to be worried about other than yourself. In fact, right now? There's a whole nation of people you ought to be considering."

"You're right," I said. "I was inconsiderate."

"There comes a point in time in a man's life when he's got to take a good hard look at himself, and at his life," he said. "I'm of the opinion you're at that point."

I'd managed to reach that place when I was sick. When I finally crawled out of bed, it dawned on me that the lifetime I had left to live was going to be miserable if I continued in the same fashion.

"I think I was there two weeks or so ago, when I woke up from being sick. I'd been battling nightmares for a week straight. When my fever broke, I realized a lot of things."

He leaned his fork against the edge of his plate. "When you took a look at yourself, what did you see?"

"A selfish prick."

"Are you saying that to satisfy me, or because you believe it?"

I hated to admit it, but it was true. I hadn't just been selfish when it came to the virus, I'd been selfish my entire life. It was easy to see, all I had to do was take a look at the highlights.

Devoting my life to the military while being married to a woman who never got the opportunity to see her husband.

Leaving my father alone following the death of my mother by volunteering to be overseas for years after my obligatory 15-month combat tour.

Depriving my father of a grandchild because I'd rather spare myself potential heartache than take a chance with a relationship.

"Because it's true," I said. "I've been a selfish prick."

He tilted his head toward Anna. "What about her?"

"What about her?" I asked.

"When they lift the order to stay at home, what are you going to do?"

"About what?"

"About her," he growled. "If you're planning on doing anything other than what you're doing, I highly suggest you be honest and tell her now. If you lead her to believe you're doing one thing, and you end up going back to being you, you'll break her heart."

"Nothing's going to change," I said.

He scowled. "You sure?"

I'd never been surer of anything in my life.

"I'm positive," I said.

"You've got shit for experience with women," he said in a spiteful tone. "How can you be sure of anything?"

"Because," I said. "Human beings have a propensity to lie. But a kiss will always tell the truth."

He grinned a prideful grin. He got up and sauntered into the kitchen. He opened the cabinet underneath the sink and pulled something out. With his hand hidden behind his back, he walked back to where we were seated.

He dropped the object beside the mashed potatoes. It hit the table with a *bang!*, bounced, and the handle landed in the mashed potatoes.

"See that?" he asked, nodding toward the table while holding my gaze.

"Can't help but see it," I replied. "It's two feet long, bright red, and in the mashed potatoes."

He picked it up and wiped the potatoes with his finger. He admired the hammer before licking his finger clean. "Guess what I was going to do with it."

"I have no idea."

"I was planning on whacking you in your rock-hard head with it."

"You're out of your—"

He leaned over the table. "That's exactly what I told you I was going to do if you got me infected," he argued. "I hoped it'd knock some sense into you, too. It was going to be a two for one. Payback for making me sick, and maybe I'd knock the dumb out of you at the same time."

"Put the hammer away, Old Man," I said with a laugh. "I've already apologized and the dumb's long gone."

He glanced at Anna, grinned, and then gave me a condescending look.

"Guess time will tell." He took his seat. "But if you do anything stupid, remember, I know where you keep the hammer."

35

ANNA

Abstinence was oddly reassuring. It eliminated sex from the relationship's equation. As a result, I was left to believe that Braxton wanted me there for reasons other than satisfying his sexual desires.

Until we had the celebration dinner, I wondered how much of my presence in Braxton's life was due to his appreciation for what I'd done while he was sick, and how much might have been out of guilt's sake.

Following Hap's presentation of the hammer, I believed I was where I was for one reason, and one reason only.

Braxton cared about me.

The moon's faint blue glow was all that prevented the bedroom from being completely dark. On my back with my head buried deeply into my down pillow, I stared at the ceiling fan for some time contemplating my future.

Many of Hap's remarks from earlier in the day came to mind. I wondered if they were seeds that he'd intentionally planted, or if I only perceived them as such. I decided it didn't matter. The end result was the same.

I rolled to my side and tapped Braxton on the shoulder. "Are you awake?"

"I am."

"Remember after you got your test and you kissed me and then we talked about being in a relationship but I said there were going to be rules and you asked what those rules were and then I told you that we weren't going to have sex until it was the right time?"

"That was a run-on sentence if I ever heard one," he replied.

I slapped my hand against his bare chest. My open palm hit him with a *thwack!*

"Answer," I demanded.

"Vaguely."

I slapped him again.

He sat up. "Yes," he said. "I remember."

"It's time," I said.

He peered down at me. "For another conversation?"

"No," I replied. "It's time to fuck."

"Is it?"

I sat up. "It is."

He kissed me.

The act had become so commonplace that it no longer took me by surprise. It didn't make me appreciate it any less. Our kisses were special. Neither the passing of time nor the frequency of the embrace would change things. That much I knew.

As we kissed, I blindly fumbled along the thigh of his flannel pajamas until my fingers found the fly. I reached inside. He was aroused beyond measure.

It didn't surprise me. When he kissed me deeply, I'd be soaking wet before we broke our embrace. It amazed me that something as simple as a kiss could evoke such emotion. Time after time, however, it did.

Eager for our lovemaking session to begin, I stroked his length. Sensing my desires, he pulled away.

He lowered both of us to the bed. With his chest pressed to mine, he kissed me deeply. I was dwarfed by his size. Yet. Beneath him I didn't feel powerless.

I felt protected.

I spread my legs wide.

Lost in a sea of euphoria, my eyes fell closed. My hands groped and grabbed; my mind unwilling to accept that there was any one place that they should land. His back, arms, and chest were as firm as stone, yet his lips were as soft as butter.

His hips wedged between my thighs. We kissed like enthusiastic teens, savagely taking in each other's taste and scent. Eager fingers explored places we had been too shy to find during the previous opportunities we had to do so.

His swollen tip penetrated me. Slowly, his length followed, one careful inch at a time. Glued to one another, we made love, neither of us willing to break the kiss.

On every occasion that we came up for air I stole a glance at his moonlit face, just to make sure I wasn't dreaming.

His hips rowed back and forth rhythmically. His length explored places I had no idea I possessed. Each well-timed stroke pushed me closer to the brink.

His girth swelled. I clawed my nails into the flesh of his back. The pressure within me grew until I feared I'd explode into a million little pieces.

My ears began to ring. With each thrust of his hips our moans of pleasure became more distant, until they were almost unintelligible. Emotion cascaded over me like a waterfall, eventually encompassing me entirely.

Coinciding with his final thrusts, his satisfaction erupted into me. I sank my teeth into his lower lip, stifling the desire to scream my pleasure into the room. Frantically, my hands slapped against the bedding. Every muscle tensed. I'd reached the pinnacle. I clenched the fabric in my fists as if my life depended on it.

I clung to the cliff's edge, uncertain if I could survive the fall.

Our eyes met. He buried his length into me fully, holding it in place while he gazed into my eyes. Prepared to meet my fate, I released the bedding.

Waves of euphoria rushed through me, each causing my entire body to shudder. Mentally, I screamed and shouted as I fell to earth, but no sound escaped me. When my mind returned, Braxton was laying at my side.

I gazed at the ceiling, incapable of doing much else. I now knew the difference between making love and fucking. I tilted my head to the side. He swept the hair away from my face with the tip of his finger.

"I love you," he said.

My heart faltered.

I felt the same way but hadn't expressed my feelings for fear of rejection. Now that the door had been opened, a flood of emotion rushed through me.

"I love you, too," I said, the words coming on the heels of a breath that shot from my lungs.

"Are you okay?" he asked.

"Okay?" I laughed. "No. I'll never be okay. Not after that."

"What do you mean?" he asked.

"I'm ruined."

He kissed me. "Well, at least you're not alone."

36

BRAXTON

Being confined to a home for an extended period of time wasn't an easy thing to do. To keep from going bonkers, we each developed routines. Every afternoon, Anna visited with the neighbor across the street. Hap exercised four days a week. I alternated cardio and weight-training, seven days a week.

The three of us agreed on a day-to-day schedule. On Mondays, we binge watched *90 Day Fiancé*. Tuesdays were reserved for various board games. Wednesdays were a free for all, with each of us doing whatever we preferred. Thursdays were consumed with a drive to nowhere, generally a cruise around Los Angeles Counties many neighborhoods, or to the Mexican border and back. Friday was movie night, alternating who was able to select the movie from week to week. On Saturdays we ordered groceries and watched random shows on Hulu, Netflix, and Amazon Prime. Each Sunday, Anna prepared a feast for a king, and we ate like royalty.

Knowing in advance what each day held allowed Hap to glide through the weeks without much to complain about. Anna seemed to be along for the ride, happy with whatever we were doing, as long as we were doing it as a family. Life was easy for me.

If Anna was happy, I was happy.

"What kind of dumb fuck would spend $150,000 to chat with a Russian chick online, and then claim he fell in love without ever actually talking to her on the phone or meeting her?" Hap asked during the commercial break.

"He thinks he fell in love with a chick," I replied. "He's talking to some 13-year-old boy in Moscow who's posing as a girl. The kid probably makes 10 bucks a week working for the dating service, and they charge that guy in Las Vegas $2,000 a month to chat."

Anna shoveled a fistful of popcorn into her mouth. "I think it's funny that he only has one picture of her, he's never met her, and he's never spoken to her, but he claims he wants to propose to her."

"Goes to show you how gullible people can be," Hap said. "This guy's an absolute imbecile."

"I think it shows how much we all want to believe in love," Anna offered.

The premise of the television show was simple. It followed various couples through the process of bringing someone they met over the internet into the United States on a K-1 Visa. The law required that they get married before the visa's 90 days expired. At the end of 90 days if they weren't married, the rejected lover had to go back to their country of origin, never to return again.

One of the men in the show's current season was a retired computer tech from Las Vegas. He'd been chatting online with a Russian girl for seven years, spending $2,000 a month to subscribe to the chat service she used. He traveled to Russia three times to meet her, and on each occasion, she didn't show up. He'd even booked a cruise with her and she failed to arrive, leaving him embarking on his vacation alone.

Despite all the warning signals, he was returning to Russia, hoping to meet her and propose marriage.

"This dumb fuck's journey through Russia is like a compound bone fracture," Hap said. "It's gut-wrenching to see, but for some reason you can't force yourself to look away."

Anna shoved her hand deep into her bowl of popcorn. "It's like a train wreck."

I glanced at Anna, who was sitting beside me on the couch. Two months earlier, falling in love was incomprehensible. I tried to imagine it happening without meeting her. To chat online, develop a feel for who she was, and allow myself to become attached to her. To me, it made no sense, whatsoever.

Touching her. Feeling her skin against mine. Holding her in my arms. Seeing her smile when I spoke. The warmth I felt when she looked at me for answers, and the joy I saw in her eyes when I complimented her on yet another spectacular meal. All absent. The sensation that rushed through me when we kissed, non-existent.

I'd never felt such desire—or necessity—to have another person be part of my life. It was unimaginable to live a life without her in it.

"Anna," I muttered.

She took a quick glance in my direction. "What?"

"I didn't love her," I said.

Her face washed with confusion. "What?"

"My first wife," I said. "I never loved her."

"What are you talking about?" she asked.

"Yeah," Hap chimed. "What the fuck are you talking about?"

"I didn't love her," I said, glancing at Hap and then at Anna. "Now that I know what love is, I know I never lover her. This is a first for me. That's all. No big deal."

"Shut your pie hole, lovebird," Hap said. "Show's back on."

Anna kissed me. "I love you."

"I love you, too."

The show's next scene followed the travels of "Big Ed", a mid-fifties So-Cal native from San Diego who had fallen in love with "Rose", a Filipina twenty-year-old woman who had one child from a previous relationship.

Rose expressed during their Facebook chats—prior to meeting face-to-face—that she wished to have more children. At the time, Ed took no objection to her desires. After flying to the Philippines, having sex with her, and spending time with her family, he admitted that it was his intention all along to get a vasectomy as soon as he returned to Southern California.

"That fat little prick needs his cock snipped, not his balls," Hap seethed. "Sick fucking bastard flew down there to knock off a young piece of Filipino ass, that's all. Take a look at her face." He pointed at the television. "She's done. It's over between them."

"I agree," Anna said. "Rose isn't coming back from this one. Ed lied to her one too many times."

"I thought she was done when that little troll handed her a toothbrush and said, 'Here, your breath stinks.'" Hap added. "He's got no tact, whatsoever."

"It's pretty obvious to me that the people on this show are of two types," I said. "The US citizen who is unlikely to find anyone interested in them through the normal course of living life, and the foreigner who wants to become a US citizen and is willing to get married to do so."

"Agreed," Hap said. "They're getting married to obtain citizenship. They ought to do a follow up and show us how many of these nitwits are still married five years down the road. It'd be void of any participants."

"They have another show," Anna said excitedly. "It's called *After the 90 Days*."

"I'm guessing this short little mayonnaise-haired no-neck having prick isn't going to be on that show," Hap snarled. "Because these two aren't getting married in the first place. There's no love between these two."

"This show's entertaining, but none of them are going to make it," I interjected. "They've got 90 days. That's not enough time to commit marriage to one another."

"Neither love nor marriage has a time requirement," Hap argued as he watched Big Ed and Rose argue. "Two people can fall in love over a weekend together. If they're willing to make the commitment, they could get married the next weekend. A marriage's success requires two elements. Love, and a willingness to fulfil a commitment. Time doesn't enter into the equation."

I gave Hap a look. "I'm confused, Old Man. You're saying these people can or can't be in love?"

"This show is filled with deficiencies." He shifted his attention from the television to me. "Love ought to be developed, naturally. Claiming it happens online with someone you've never met is wishful thinking on the part of the numbskull who's thinking it. Fucktards like this give love a bad name. Doesn't say much about the covenant of marriage, either."

"Love lessons from Hap Rourke," I said with a laugh.

"Faithful to your mother for forty-plus years." He pridefully puffed his chest. "Ought to be enough of an accomplishment to get a little recognition from a man who admits that he didn't even love his first wife, that's for goddamned sure."

"I was joking," I said.

His wiry brows raised. "About the time necessary to fall in love, about your first marriage, or about my inability to give love lessons?"

"Don't be difficult, Old Man."

"Nothing difficult about what I said, or how I said it," he argued. "Marriage isn't something that should ever be done for the sake of convenience or financial gain."

"If that's the case, none of the people on this show ought to be getting married. Is that your opinion? That they shouldn't be allowed to?"

"Marriage should be set aside for those who are in love." He wagged his finger at me. "But only if they're willing to devote themselves to a lifetime of commitment and sacrifice. If they are, and they do, the rewards are monumental. If they're not, they end up fifty years old with a shitty head of hair, a physique they're not proud of, and a respective other who is out searching for someone better each time she goes to get groceries."

"My physique's improving," I declared. "I've gained 7 pounds."

"I'm not talking about you, Dipshit," he snarled. "I was talking about the dipshit on television."

"Oh."

"You two ought to be married," he said, rising from his seat as he spoke. "Even a blind man could see that you're in love. All it gets down to is your willingness to commit." He gave me a lingering look before glancing at Anna. "Pause that idiot box my dear, it's dinnertime."

I looked at Anna, and she at me. Without speaking, we shared a moment.

If my father were right, Anna and I could spend the rest of our lives together. If he were wrong, I'd suffer a heartbreak.

I had no idea if he were wrong or right, but I knew I couldn't survive another broken heart.

37

ANNA

"This staying at home business might be frustrating," Marge said, pausing from her task of sweeping the sidewalk. "But no matter how bad things get, there's always a grain of good amongst the pebbles of bad. It's only a matter of finding it."

"I suppose."

She patted me on the shoulder. "You're frustrated, but you're not alone. The entire country is frustrated. They're revolting in Michigan, demanding that the governor open up the state."

"But people are still being infected—and dying—at an alarming rate."

"This disease has divided the nation," she said, shaking her head in sorrow. "There's the group that believes the threat is real, and the group that believes it's nothing more than the common flu. My brother has lost lifelong friends over his support of our governor's position. It's sad, really."

"So, where's the grain of good in this?" I asked.

"Honey." She leaned against her broom handle. Her mouth curled into a shallow grin. "Your grain weighs 200 pounds, and his name is Braxton. Enjoy the time you have with him while you're able."

"I am," I replied. "I just. I want to live a real life with him. Not one where we're forced to be in the house together."

"If it were the way it used to be, he'd be coming and going at an alarming rate," she argued. "His absence would have nothing to do with his love for you. It would be business as usual." Her brows raised. "Is that what you want?"

"I suppose not."

"We're all frustrated, sweetheart." She leaned the broom against the porch and gave me a hug. "It's hard, I know. One day, this too, shall pass."

She leaned away and looked me in the eyes. "Any time you want to talk, I'm here. It doesn't have to be at four o'clock."

"I like our little routine," I replied.

She smiled. "I do, too."

"Maybe I need to find something to do with my spare time. I've got a lot of it when Braxton and Hap are exercising. I run on Braxton's treadmill for 30 minutes, but those two exercise for *hours*."

"There's always things you could be doing," she said. "I used to crochet."

Crocheting would be a natural sedative. In no time I'd be face-down on the couch with a needle in my hand, slobbering on my bicep.

"I don't think that's for me," I said.

"Write a book. Maybe talking about your frustrations might do you some good."

I let out a sigh of frustration. "I can't write a book."

She scowled playfully. "You could if you wanted to."

Since our Instagram story about the donations, I'd gained a few hundred thousand followers. Instagram wasn't known for its inspirational posts, but maybe I could start writing something every day in a post. Something that would lift people's spirits.

"I might do some writing," I said. "Not a book, but something."

"I think that'll do you some good."

"I think it will, too," I admitted. "I'm just ready for this to end."

"We're all ready, sweetheart."

Not knowing what else to say, but unwilling to cut my visitation short, I looked around. Hap was at the end of the hill, decompressing from his 3-mile run with a brisk walk. I looked at Marge.

"I know I love Braxton, and I'm sure he loves me, but I want to make sure everything's happening for all the right reasons."

"I'm sure you're just gun shy," she said. "Every relationship you've had has ended because of infidelity. It makes sense you'd be apprehensive. If it helps, I've never known Braxton to be in a relationship other than his marriage, and that was a long, long time ago. The fact that he's in one with you means something's changed inside of him."

"Did you see the movie *The Breakfast Club*?" I asked.

"Sweetheart, I don't think so," she replied. "It sure doesn't sound familiar."

"There were five high school kids who were all given detention at the same time," I explained. "There was a criminal, an athlete, a prom queen, a nerd, and a manically depressed girl. Needless to say, they weren't remotely close to one another when they started their little venture. But in the end, they were all, like, best friends. They ended up liking each other because they were locked up together for 9 hours in the lunchroom. If they were left to their own devices, they would have never met, and they certainly wouldn't have become friends."

"What brings a couple together is of little value," she said without giving the matter much time for thought. "The common ground that's shared between them becomes the glue that holds them together."

"That's a concern." I lowered my head. "We haven't been able to explore each other's likes and dislikes much because we've been confined to the house."

"Sweetheart, you're worrying about what hasn't happened instead of being grateful for what has." She lifted my head with her weathered hand. "Keep your chin up."

I smiled. The world's voice of reason came from the elderly. Their time on earth allowed them to give advice based on experience, not opinion. She was right. I needed to appreciate what I had instead of grieving over what I didn't.

"Thank you," I said.

She nodded toward my house. Her face wore a look of sheer satisfaction. "How long is he staying?"

I glanced over my shoulder. Dressed in a pair of gray shorts, a white tee shirt, and running shoes, Hap was stretching his arms over his head.

"Oh. I'm not sure." I chuckled. "Until he pisses Braxton off, I'm sure. I like having him around. He reminds me of my dad."

She waved her hand toward Braxton's house. "Why don't you run along, sweetheart. I'm going to see if that poor soul needs a glass of tea. He looks dehydrated."

"I'll see you tomorrow," I said with a laugh. "I'm going to see if Braxton and I have any common ground."

"I'm going to do the same thing," she said. "With him."

38

BRAXTON

The drive along the Pacific Coast Highway was one of the most scenic drives in the United States. With time on our hands, we voted to drive north, turn around, and then drive all the way from San Francisco to San Diego, along the coast.

With most of the state's businesses still shut down, traffic was nearly non-existent. The 12-hour drive was reduced to just over 7 hours. It allowed us to make the drive without worrying about taking the time to see a few of the sights.

Starting from the Golden Gate Park, we began the journey. It was the first time Anna had seen the Golden Gate Bridge. She cried tears of joy upon seeing it, but it seemed lately that nearly everything made her cry.

Monterey was our next stop, with Monterey Bay and Point Lobos State National Reserve being the major points of interest. I stared at the highway ahead in disbelief of the open road. It was something I'd never seen in Southern California.

"Now that the state is declining on death count and infections, it won't be long before this highway is packed again," I said. "We better enjoy this while we can. One of these day's it's going to be bumper to bumper traffic again."

Anna peered beyond the rock cliffs, toward the vast sea of indigo blue. "Now I know why people move to California. This is completely different than Sherman Oaks."

"It sure as fuck is," Hap agreed. "This is God's country."

"It's beautiful," Anna said, wiping the corner of her eye with the knuckle of her index finger.

"Are you okay?" I asked.

"I'm fine," she replied. "I've been cooped up too long." She gestured toward the ocean. "This is breathtaking. I mean, really. What do you expect?"

It had been a lifetime since I'd driven the length of the PCH. I'd nearly forgotten just how beautiful it was. The pandemic forced me to pause and take a look at many things, not all of which were beautiful to see. I was grateful I was able to view each and every one of them with open eyes.

"Wait till you see Big Sur from the Bixby Bridge." I gave her a kiss. "You'll bawl like a baby."

The entire drive was scenic, but parts of it were far more beautiful than others. For 600 miles, the highway followed the coast, taking the most natural route along the edge of the countryside's valleys, hills, cliffs, and mountains.

When driving south, the left side of the vehicle gave views of rock ledges, homes that overlooked the sea, small fishing villages, and sprawling cities. On the right, the Pacific Ocean lashed against the California coast.

I looked at Hap. "When was the last time you took this drive? All the way?"

His gaze fell to the ground between his feet. When he looked up, he bore an odd sense of content. "I'm going to guess it was with you and your brother. Two days before you left for boot camp."

It was the last time I could recall seeing my brother alive. I was sure I saw him between our coastal drive and when I left for basic training, but my mind had no recollection of it.

Recalling the trip along the coast was easy. The four of us sat in silence, taking everything in until we reached San Clemente, at which point we ate dinner together at a local Mexican restaurant.

I gazed blankly beyond Hap, at the ocean. The meal was the last time we'd eaten together as a family.

"Remember Brandon betting me he could eat that hot pepper?" I asked. "Spit the fucker out and ran to the bathroom after one bite?"

"Drank half a gallon of milk trying to make that burn go away," Hap said with a laugh. "What kind of brother dares his only sibling to eat an entire habanero, anyway?"

I shifted my focus from the coast to Hap. "That was a good trip."

"One of my favorites," he agreed.

I nodded in agreement. "Last time we were—"

I paused, not knowing what I intended to say.

Hap cleared his throat. "Let's get this show on the road. If we don't, we won't be home 'till dark."

We continued south, slowing to take photos of the Bixby Bridge. We gawked at Big Sur's beauty, admired the rock formations off the coast of San Luis Obispo, and paused to take in the sand dunes at Montaña de Oro State Park. Morrow Bay and Morrow Rock caused Anna to shed another tear.

It seemed if she wasn't crying, she was snapping pictures with her cell phone, hoping to keep them to jog her memory at some point in the future.

I glanced in the rearview mirror, at Hap. "Did you keep all the pictures you took of us on that trip?"

"When we drove this the last time?" he asked.

I nodded.

"Sure did. Have 'em at home," he replied. "Maybe we could grab 'em when we're that way."

"I'd like that."

Anna patted her hand against my right thigh. "I love you."

"I love you, too."

Anna glanced over her shoulder. "How has Marge been?"

"Why don't you tell me?" Hap grunted. "You're the one that's over there all afternoon."

"I go over there for an hour," she rebutted. "That's not all day."

"Well," Hap replied. "I may or may not stop by for long enough to get a glass of tea. I don't think that constitutes a conversation."

"Fine," Anna huffed.

Hap glanced out the window. "It's going to have to be," he retorted. "Because my business isn't your business."

"Next time you ask me something, you're going to get a big fat nothing in return," Anna said. "No-thing. Zero. Zilch. Nada."

"You vomit information like a compromised dam spews water," Hap said with a laugh. "You'll leak out enough to keep me entertained."

"Not anymore," she warned.

I liked seeing Hap argue with her. It let me know that he'd accepted her into his life, and into his heart.

We continued along the coast until we reached San Diego, with Anna talking nearly all the way. After stopping at Hap's house to pick up a box of photographs, we took the freeway back to Los Angeles.

Upon reaching our home, we each fixed a plate of leftover meatloaf and sat at the dinner table.

Hap ate with one hand as he pilfered through the photos with the other. He flipped one across the table.

"Remember that?" he asked.

It was a picture of my brother's bloody forearm.

I'd caught a four-foot long kingsnake and was teasing Brandon with it. As soon as I released its head, it bit him on the forearm so hard it drew blood. Hap ended up taking him to the doctor, primarily due to my mother's insistence that the snake was possibly poisonous.

"Mom was madder than hell about that," I said.

"She sure was."

"How old was I?"

"Well, I bought you that shirt on the Christmas before your thirteenth birthday, so I'm going to guess you were about thirteen. Give or take."

"Probably right," I agreed. "Brian Hudson got me interested in snakes and he moved away at the end of eighth grade."

"What about this?" he asked, flipping another across the table.

I handed Anna the picture of Brandon's arm and reached for the other one.

It was a picture of us on Halloween. We couldn't have been much older than four and five. I was dressed as a cowboy, and Brandon was dressed as an Indian. His face was marked with warpaint. A headband that covered nearly all his forehead was fitted with three turkey feathers.

Still looking at the picture of my brother and I, I laughed. "I kind of remember that. Not really. I remember Halloween with him, though. We'd make you walk so far behind us that no one knew you were with us."

"It didn't really matter if I was there or not, nobody in the neighborhood would have let anything happen to you little shits. Everyone knew everyone. Hell, the neighbors used to call us and say, 'Isn't it time to eat, Hap? Your two turds are in our back yard looking for horned toads.'"

"Things have sure changed," I agreed. "Can't wear an Indian costume these days. Somebody'd call the news and turn you in for race shaming. Times were different back then, no doubt."

I looked over the photo and handed it to Anna.

"Here," he flipped another across the table. "What about that?"

The photo was faded so much that gray and yellow were the only prominent colors. It was a photo of my mother, holding a baby.

"Is that Brandon?" I asked.

"It's you."

"Bullshit," I said. "That's got to be—"

"Turn it over," Hap said.

I turned over the photo. On the back, it was marked with block lettering, in pen. "Brax, 13 months."

I grinned. "You called me Brax back then?"

He nodded. "Drove your mother insane. She said it wasn't your name. That's why she wanted to name your brother Brandon and not Brayden. She knew if it was Brayden, I'd call you Brax and him Bray. She knew I wouldn't call your brother Bran, so she picked Brandon."

"That's funny," Anna said.

"I never knew that," I admitted.

We continued going through photos long into the night. When we finally retired to bed, I'd resurrected many memories from my past.

I'd also learned several things about my father, mother, and my brother.

And a lot about what I wanted my future to hold.

39

ANNA

I stretched my left arm toward Braxton, who was seated at my side. "Would you pass the salad, please?"

He lifted the bowl and placed it between us. "There you go. It's good, huh?"

It consisted of raw cauliflower, pickled red onions, bacon, and a creamy parmesan dressing. It was simple, but I couldn't stop eating it.

"It is," I said. "I like that recipe. I got it from Chrissy Teigen's Twitter. She said she loved it."

"Does she follow you?"

I forked a piece of cauliflower into my mouth. "I think so."

"You don't know?"

"She does." I gave him an apologetic look. "I don't think it's good to brag about such things."

"There's a difference between walking into a bar, sitting down, and saying, 'Oh, look, Chrissy Teigen sent me a personal message,' to the bartender, and answering a question I asked you."

"Okay. Chrissy Teigen follows me."

"I think it's good that you've established a faithful following," he said. "It might come in handy someday."

"Like when?"

He shrugged. "You never know."

I picked at my salad, and then at the chicken. The home seemed quiet. Empty. Eerily lonely.

"It seems weird," I said, gesturing to Hap's seat. "Not having Hap here."

"He's not big on chicken, anyway, so it's all for the better," he said. "Wonder what they're eating?"

Hap was having dinner at Marge's. After two weeks of sharing afternoon tea, they spent a week talking in the evenings while taking short walks. Eventually, Marge invited him over for dinner. I thought it was cute, but I really wanted to be a part of it. It frustrated me that I didn't get to see them together.

"Maybe we can include her in our Sunday dinners in the future," I said. "What do you think? Maybe, like every other week or something?"

"Okay by me," Braxton said.

"They're supposed to be holding a press conference on Monday about lifting the stay at home order. Did you see that?"

He nodded. "Pratt told me."

"If they do, what are you going to do?"

He continued to eat his chicken without skipping a beat. "About what?"

"About everything?"

He paused. "Like?"

"Work? Home? Me? You? Sunday Dinners? Hap?"

The shoveling of food commenced. With a mouth full of salad and a forkful of chicken, he shrugged as if it were no big deal. "Nothing, probably."

"Nothing?" I lowered my fork and raised my brows. "What do you mean, nothing?"

He poked the chicken in his mouth. "Nothing."

I slapped his bicep with the back of my hand. "Can you stop eating for a minute?"

He gave me a dismissive glance. "Sure." He set his fork down and wiped his hands on his napkin. "What?"

"You're going back to work, aren't you?"

"I haven't decided."

My heart skipped a beat. "What? Why? What's—"

"I like this," he said, glancing around the dining room. "It's nice. Spending time together. Having a family. I didn't realize how much I needed this until I got it. Now that I've got it, I don't know that I'm willing to give it up."

"I'm going to have to do *something*. I've got a little nest egg, but I don't want to—"

"Look," he said. "If you want to work, that's fine. I've got enough money for both of us, so there's nothing to worry about when it comes to finances."

"Why haven't we talked about this?" I asked.

"We're talking about it now, aren't we?"

"We're talking about it because I pressed the issue."

He reached for his fork. "Well, we're talking about it, and that's what matters."

The thought of working at my leisure was exciting. I despised the thought of giving up my dealership in Oklahoma, but I hated thinking about leaving Los Angeles even more.

Being closer to the beach was my dream. I tried to contain myself. "Are you planning on staying here forever?" I asked dryly.

"California? I can't think of living anywhere else."

"No," I replied. "Sherman Oaks."

He made a funny face. "No."

"You're thinking about leaving?"

He poked a piece of chicken in his mouth. "Yeah. Been thinking about it."

"Why haven't we talked about that?" I asked.

He shrugged. "Didn't get to it yet, I guess."

"All we talk about is what's on television, how funny your dad is, and what's for dinner," I said. "We never talk about our future."

He poked a piece of cauliflower in his mouth. "I'm not much of a talker."

I widened my eyes as if he'd made a grand revelation. "Oh, really?"

"Go to hell," he said, laughing over a mouthful of food. "I've never been a talker."

"Well, it's time to start," I declared. "Where were you thinking about moving to?"

"Hadn't given it a tremendous amount of thought." He swallowed his food and glanced over his left shoulder. "What do you think about moving closer to the beach?"

My heart raced. I tried to hide my excitement. I nervously poked at a piece of chicken. "I think that would be nice. I like the beach. It's peaceful. Are you thinking a little closer, or a lot closer?"

I slid my left hand under the table and crossed my fingers.

"I don't know," he said. "I was thinking if we could find a place in Santa Monica, Hermosa Beach, or Malibu that was on the beach that I might consider it."

We?

I swallowed hard. "*On* the beach?"

"Not much sense in being *close* to the beach." He chuckled. "Hell, we just as well stay in this shit-hole. I want to wake up and be able to look out my window and see it. I forgot how much I enjoyed the ocean until this pandemic started. Driving along the highway to San Diego once a week makes me want to get the hell out of here."

Truthfully, I could live in Dumpwater, Arkansas and be happy, as long as it was with Braxton.

"I think I'd settle for whatever made you happy," I said, reserving hope that he'd continue his desire to live on the beach. "You decide what you want, and I'm along for the ride."

"I think I might be ready for a change," he said. "Hap's a prick, but he's a happy prick. I don't want to live the rest of my life chasing life's loose ends and end up old and angry. I want to be like the Old Man."

I laughed. "You'd rather be a happy prick?"

"I would."

I picked at my food, dreaming of living along the coast. In a matter of moments, I became so excited I could barely contain myself.

The front door swung open.

We both looked up.

Hap stopped dead in his tracks and gave each of us a little jolt of his laser sharp glare. "What are you two dipshits looking at?" he asked. "Never seen an old man walk through a door?"

"Evening, Pop," Braxton said.

"Fuck you," Hap snarled. "It's none of your business."

Braxton gave him a flippant look. "I didn't ask a thing."

"You were getting ready to." He shifted his eyes to me. "And so were you."

"I wasn't going to say—"

"Keep your yap shut," Hap said, taking long strides toward his bedroom. "You're not sweet talking me out of anything."

"That's fine," I said. "I'll just talk to Marge tomorrow."

He laughed as he walked past. "We've taken an oath of secrecy."

"Girl code trumps any oath between a man and a woman," I said.

He paused and turned to face me. He glared. "Is there such a thing? Girl code?"

"Oh yeah," I said. "It's an unbreakable bond we all share."

"If you'll agree to leave her alone about it, I'll tell you this, and no more." He looked at Braxton and then at me. "Agreed?"

I nodded. "Sure."

He grinned. "If having fun is a crime, I ought to be doing life in Folsom Prison."

"I'm glad you had fun," I said, trying not to smile too much.

"So am I," Braxton added.

"What were you two blabbing about?" Hap took a moment to look at each of us. "You look like a couple of numbskulls that are plotting to rob a bank."

"We're just trying to decide what's for dinner tomorrow night," I lied.

"You two are either a couple of morons or a couple of liars," he said, alternating glances between us. "Tomorrow's Taco Tuesday. On Taco Tuesday, we have fucking tacos."

"Thanks," I said. "All the days kind of run into one another."

"Think nothing of it," he said with a wave of his hand.

Halfway to his room, he paused. "Oh. Almost forgot," he said over his shoulder. "Fix another plate for tomorrow night. We've got someone joining us."

"Is she staying for Scrabble?" I asked.

"Well, there's not much sense in giving her the boot as soon as we get done with dinner, is there?"

"I suppose not," I said.

"Then she'll be staying for Scrabble."

"Are you going to join us?" I asked. "You can have a seat and help us with our bank robbery plot."

"Nope, the neighbor gal and I are going to make hand gestures at each other through the window," he replied. "Have a good night."

His bedroom door closed. I smirked. Hap may have been a prick, but he was a very likeable prick.

I went back to picking at my food. Moving to the beach together may not have been a big deal to Braxton, but it was a huge deal to me. If we were moving into a new home together, it confirmed Braxton's commitment to me, and to our relationship.

I was eager to discuss it further.

"Sounds like that went well." I poked a piece of cauliflower and then glanced at Braxton. "Where were we?"

"We were moving to the beach," he deadpanned.

"Oh, that's right," I said, fighting a smile. "I almost forgot."

40

BRAXTON

The governor announced the stay at home order was lifted. The state rejoiced. Free travel was allowed, and all businesses were able to reopen. Things were much different following the pandemic. The experts claimed this was the way it would be for the foreseeable future.

Basketball, football, and soccer were now played privately, in what were formerly public venues. They were televised live. Attending sporting events was something of the past.

Buffets were no more. The chance of infection being transferred from person to person through the shared silverware, serving pans, and countertops was far too great. Casinos were ghost towns, due to the elimination of slot machines. As it was impossible to clean a machine after each use, they were banned from public use. Las Vegas was a ghost town.

The floors in grocery stores were marked with arrows, allowing traffic along the food aisles to travel in one direction, only. Lines were marked on the floors at the checkout aisles, six feet apart. See-through plastic walls separated the cashier from the customer.

Restaurants used throw-away menus, reduced their seating

capacity to 50% of the former allowances, and the servers wore gloves and masks. Tablecloths were paper, discarded by gloved workers after each use.

Airlines were forced to revamp their planes, changing the seating capacity and adding sneeze guards between seats. Due to the reduced seating capacity, the cost to fly went up 300%. Flying was now for the rich, and for those willing to take the risk to be confined to a petri dish in the air.

Rental cars were disinfected with chemicals and steam cleaned upon their return. A certificate of compliance was provided to the renter upon signing the contract.

Ride sharing was limited to two persons per vehicle seating row, regardless of the designed seating capacity for the row. No more 3 people fitting in a back seat of an Uber.

Working from home was commonplace, and would remain in effect for many corporations, making office space a thing of the past. Companies weren't willing to risk lawsuits for placing workers' lives at risk.

Social distancing measures remained in place. Masks were to be worn in public. Violators were fined for the first offense and jailed following the second.

Conspiracy theorists claimed the virus was developed in a laboratory and inflicted on mankind to allow the changes to be made. Yet others claimed it wasn't as bad as the news media claimed it to be. I wasn't sure one way or another. All I knew for sure was that I contracted COVID-19, and that the illness took me to death's door. It was while standing at the razor's edge between life and death that I realized I didn't want to live my life in the manner I'd been living it.

Labeling it COVID-19, the flu, or a spiritual awakening didn't matter. I saw that changes needed to be made in me, and the way I was living life. That's all that was important.

It was now time to implement those changes.

"C'mon, Old Man," I complained. "The freeways are going to be bumper to bumper if we wait. She said to be there at noon."

"Fuck her," he shouted from the bathroom. "My nose hairs are unruly."

"You've had two months to fix your nose hairs."

"And you've had a lifetime to fix that nasty-ass beard you wear, but you haven't. Fuck off, I'm almost done."

"Which one is this?" Anna asked.

"The one in Playa del Rey that your friend told you about. 6 bedrooms, 5 bathrooms, and the back yard is sand, straight out to the beach."

She mussed her hair. "The expensive one?"

"It's a little pricey, but the view? It's gorgeous."

She rubbed her hands together. "It's too much money, but I'm so excited to see it."

"I'm not excited one bit," Hap said as he walked out of the bathroom. "Sand gets in everything. In 'Nam, I got that shit in the tip of my Johnson. Ended up with an infection that—"

"We don't need 'Nam dick stories," I said with a laugh.

He patted me on the shoulder. "I'm excited for you."

"For us," Anna clarified.

"For us," Hap agreed.

We drove to the home in question, arriving 20 minutes after we left. It ended up that *bad traffic* wasn't all that bad.

Anna's friend, Giselle, was waiting in the drive.

From the street, the modern-looking 3-story contemporary home was attractive. A detached 2-car garage was connected to the home by a covered breezeway. Beside the garage was a wide concrete driveway that would easily allow parking for 10.

"Has a big garage," Hap said. "Lots of parking, too."

Anna laughed. "Not having covered garage space is something I'll have to get used to. My home in Oklahoma has a 3-car garage. Here? Most homes don't have a garage at all."

"You're lucky to get a 1-car garage in Southern California," I said.

The realtor, a friend of Anna's from before the pandemic, led us into the home, pointing out the various flooring used, the choices in trim, and the type of marble countertops used in the recent remodel.

The home was breathtaking, as was the view.

She, Hap, and Anna continued through the house, moving their way toward the kitchen. I stood dead in my tracks and stared through the glass wall that faced the beach.

"Are you coming?" Anna asked over her shoulder.

I dreamed of watching the sunsets from the living room with Anna resting her head against my shoulder. Listening to the waves crash ashore from the deck while drinking a glass of wine. Walking from the back deck to the beach, barefoot through the sand, with the woman I loved. Taking morning jogs along the beach with the Old Man.

"Come here," I said.

She turned around and walked to where I stood. "What are you doing?"

I gestured toward the beach. "Look."

"I know," she murmured. "It's crazy." She tugged my arm. "C'mon, let's at least entertain her."

My mind was made up. Nevertheless, I decided to play as if I could care less. "Okay."

We toured the home, spending time in each of the 6 remodeled bedrooms, 5 gorgeous bathrooms, and the 3 resurfaced decks that faced the beach. In my eyes, the home was nothing short of heaven on earth. When we ended the walkthrough, we were back where we started.

I looked at Hap. "What do you think, Old Man?"

He scratched the sides of his head. "It's one hell of a house."

I glanced at Anna. "Anna?"

"I love it but—"

"What are they asking for it, again?" I asked Giselle.

"$5,900,000," she replied.

"How long has it been on the market?"

"This listing isn't on the MLS yet," she replied. "It's officially for sale this weekend. The owners are currently out of town and are expected to return Friday. It will list on Saturday."

"Do you think they'll negotiate?"

"Personally, I think they'd be fools to. This home will be sold within a few days of being listed. Other than me, you're the first one to see it. They were preparing to list it before the pandemic hit. It was going to be $8,000,000, which was already a great price."

I looked at Anna.

She shrugged. "I don't know what you want me to say."

"Do you like it?" I asked.

"Who wouldn't?"

"Can you see yourself living here?"

"Not really."

"Why not?" I asked.

"Because it's a mansion." Her shoulders slumped a little. "An expensive mansion."

I cocked an eyebrow. "If price were no object, would this home be one of interest?"

"Like I said," she replied. "I love it."

"Would it please you to live here?"

She gave me a funny look. "If money were no object?"

I forced out a dramatic sigh. "If every home on the coast were the same price, would this one interest you?"

"Absolutely," she said excitedly. "I love that it has beach access and a beach view from every room. So many of them don't have beach access, they've just got a view. This has both."

I looked at Hap. "What about you, Old Man?"

"If I had $6,000,000 I wanted to spend on a home," he replied. "I'd buy this cocksucker right now."

I'd spend $60,000,000 on a home if it made Anna happy. Money was of no use to me if the woman I loved wasn't satisfied with the place she called home.

I turned toward Giselle. "Sounds like a unanimous vote. Tell them it's sold."

"What?!" Anna screeched.

I looked at her and grinned. "You said you wanted it."

"Yeah, but—"

I kissed her. "Yeah, but nothing. I love it. If you like it, and the Old Man can live with one of the upstairs bedrooms for a while, there's no sense in looking at anything else. Agreed?"

She kissed me. "Agreed." She looked at Hap. "Are you going to be staying with us for a while?"

"Maybe for a bit," he said. "I'd hate to be driving back and forth to San Diego just to have dinner at Marge's. Hell, I'd be on the road 8 hours a day now that they've opened up the freeways."

"Any contingencies?" Giselle asked.

"15-day occupancy, full ask, all cash, no inspection, no contingencies."

"Jesus," Hap said, whistling through his teeth. "Rubbing elbows with the stars has its privileges."

"It has a few," I said. "Might have to come out of retirement after this buy."

He laughed. "I know you well enough to know you're not spending your last dime on this house."

I grinned. "You know me well."

"I'll tell them the news," Giselle said. "I'll be in touch."

I glanced around the home. It was perfect. "Call them and tell them now," I said. "I want an answer before we leave."

She excused herself and walked onto the deck.

"This is insane," Anna said the instant Giselle was gone. "I can't believe we might be living here."

"We *will* be living here," I said. "In 2 weeks."

She looked ill. "It's just. It's hard to believe. I feel like I'm going to barf."

Giselle opened the sliding glass door. She looked at me and smiled. "They accepted your offer. Congratulations."

I looked at Anna. "Congratulations, my dear."

She dove against my chest.

I nearly toppled over.

She kissed me. "Thank you. It's going to take some time for this to sink in." She glanced over her shoulder and gazed toward the watery horizon. "It still feels like this is all a dream."

"If it seems like a dream now, just wait 13 days," I said. "You're going to faint."

Giselle cleared her throat. "I thought you said 15-day close?"

"I did."

"I'm confused," she said.

Anna looked at me funny. "Me, too."

"Makes perfect sense to me," Hap said.

It made perfect sense to me, too.

For the time being, that's all that mattered.

41

ANNA

Although the stay at home order was lifted, most of our routines remained. If nothing else, the pandemic taught us the value of doing things together, as a family.

It was our last Sunday in Sherman Oaks. In two more days, we'd be moving into our new home. As excited as I was to move to the beach, leaving the place where everything changed wasn't going to be easy. I took every inch of the home into view, coming to terms with the fact that the next Sunday dinner would be in a different place.

Marge pressed the tines of her fork through her lasagna. "It smells wonderful, Anna."

"She cooks a mean lasagna," Hap said. "But it's no surprise. She's half wop."

"Hap Rourke!" Marge barked. "That was uncalled for."

"It's okay," I said.

"It most certainly is not," Marge argued.

"What do you want me to do?" Hap laughed. "Apologize?"

"I don't want an apology," I said, glancing at Marge. "That's just Hap being Hap."

"Well," Marge said, directing her disappointment to Hap. "You should refrain from calling people derogatory names."

"I'll keep that in mind," Hap said. "When I'm exposed to public scrutiny."

Marge shook her head in mock disgust.

It was nice to have everyone at the dinner table. I knew Marge wasn't Braxton's mother and that Hap wasn't my father, but they were as close to our parents as we were going to get. Being at the Sunday dinner table was almost like I was at home in Oklahoma, on the farm.

Filled with the warmth of what only a family could offer, I checked everyone's plate. Hap, as always, was shoveling food in his mouth like a prisoner in the institution's chow hall. Braxton was picking at his food, but it wasn't surprising. He'd gained all the weight that he'd lost, and then some. According to him, he needed to be on a diet. Marge was being Marge. Eating tiny bites while she talked, she made no effort to set any records regarding food consumption.

Marge dipped her bread in the lasagna's sauce. She lifted it to her mouth. "When's the big day?"

Before I answered, Braxton started choking.

"Are you okay?" I asked.

After coughing himself red-faced, he finally caught his breath. He reached for his wine with one hand and pointed to his throat with the other. "Went down…wrong."

I shifted my attention from him to Marge. "We close on the home the day after tomorrow," I replied.

"Then you're off to Oklahoma to get your things?"

"We've already rented the U-Haul," I replied. "It'll be a fun road trip. We're bringing back the things I can't live without, and we're meeting with 2 different people who are interested in buying the dealership. We're figuring 3 days to get there, 3 days in Tulsa, and 3 to get back."

"I've got the house to myself for 9 days," Hap said, grinning a sly grin. "I'll be watching those sunsets naked as a jaybird."

Marge shot Hap a glare and then looked at me. "I hope the sale goes well."

"Me, too," I replied. "It's sad and exciting at the same time. Closing one chapter and opening another."

The thought of selling the dealership was disheartening. It was my life's accomplishment. I glanced at Braxton. Losing the dealership allowed me to gain a partner for life. It was a trade I'd make 1,000 times over.

Marge nibbled at her bread. "You can always start another dealership here. If that's your desire."

"I know. I'm not sure what I'll do. For now, I'll be decorating the new home. There are bedrooms galore."

"I'm excited to see it," she said.

"I'm excited for you to see it. You'll have to stay over and watch the sunset."

She smiled. "Sounds like a date."

I was so excited about the new home I was having a hard time falling asleep at night. Then, when morning arrived, I was exhausted and felt sick to my stomach. I needed to get back on track. I hoped once we moved in that my mind would settle down.

Hap looked at Braxton. "What time is—"

Braxton shot Hap a glare. "5:50."

"Are you okay?" I asked, looking him over. "You seem tense. You haven't even touched your food."

"Baby, I'm just like you." His intensity softened. "I'm excited about the house. That's all."

"I'm getting another plate," I announced. "Does anyone need anything?"

Hap stood. "I'll join you."

We filled our plates with another serving of lasagna, salad, and bread.

Hap nodded at my plate. "I have no idea where your food's been going. You've been eating like a horse and staying skinny as hell."

"Skinny?" I smacked myself on the ass. "Everywhere but here."

He smirked. "No comment."

On my way to the table I picked at my lasagna. By the time I took my seat, it was nearly gone. My appetite seemed endless.

Braxton gestured toward my plate. "You should have got two slices."

He was right. I should have. "I'm famished," I said. "I can't get enough."

"Probably that new workout you started. What's it called? Beach body something?"

"Beach Body Workout," I replied.

"It must be working," he said, looking me up and down. "You've been eating like a horse, and you're not gaining an ounce."

The doorbell rang. I glanced at the door. "Who—"

Braxton shot from his seat. "Pratt was coming by to get a few things for work."

Pratt was going to continue to operate as a Hollywood fixer, taking over the reins of Braxton's company.

I poked the remaining piece of lasagna in my mouth and stood. I faced Pratt and opened my arms wide. "Give me a hug, you big dork."

He hugged me like he hadn't seen me in years. In reality, it had only been a few days. He broke our embrace and looked me over. "How's it going, Annie?"

To Pratt, I'd always be Annie. I didn't bother me or Braxton to hear him say it. It made Hap angry, though.

"Good," I replied. "Just finishing dinner."

He glanced at the pan of lasagna. "Smells good."

"Want me to fix you a plate?"

"He can fix his own," Hap barked. He glanced at Pratt. "How's it going, *Prott*?"

Pratt sauntered toward the kitchen island. "Go to hell, Old Man." He glanced over his shoulder as he passed the table. "Evening, Marge."

"Good evening, Gordon."

Pratt fixed a plate and meandered to the other side of the table. "I like your top, Marge," he said, taking a seat beside her. "Purple's my favorite color."

Marge was wearing a pair of green pants, white open-toed sandals, and a purple short-sleeved top. As always, she looked adorable.

She adjusted herself in her seat and offered Pratt a grin. "Thank you, Gordon."

"Lasagna's good as fuck, Annie," Pratt muttered.

"Gordon Pratt!" Marge hissed. "Not at the dinner table, please."

Pratt lowered his head in shame. "Sorry, Marge."

We finished our dinner, discussing the changes we'd seen, the changes we expected to see as everyone implemented the new recommendations from the Center for Disease Control, and what we hoped the future held.

When everyone was done, Pratt and Braxton went to the garage while Marge and I served the tiramisu.

"I'll go get the dipshits," Hap said, leaning over my shoulder to get a look at the size of ice cream he was being served. "Give me one more scoop, just like that one."

I glanced over my shoulder. "You'll have to run an extra mile."

"It'll be worth it," he said. "This is a special night."

"Is it?"

"Last Sunday dinner," he said, looking around the room. "Here, anyway."

I gave him another scoop of ice cream. The other bowls seemed lop-sided. After deciding everyone needed 2 scoops of ice cream, Marge and I carried the bowls to the table.

When the men returned, everyone took their seats. Everyone except Braxton, that is. He paced the floor to my immediate right, like a nervous cat.

"What is wrong with you?" I asked. "You've been a wreck all night. Sit down and eat your ice cream before it melts."

"I've got something I need to say."

I poked a forkful of tiramisu into my mouth. "Say it after you eat."

"If I wait, I'll puke."

"Did the lasagna upset your stomach?"

"No, it's—"

I looked him over. "What then?"

"Jesus H. Christ!" Hap snarled. "Let the man speak."

"Hap Rourke!" Marge snapped. "Of all times."

"Well, he's doing his best," Hap retorted. "And she's trying to shove goddamned ice cream down his throat."

"Take a drink of wine," Pratt offered. "Alcohol always calms my nerves."

Braxton gulped his wine. Holding the empty glass, he stroked his beard with the web of his free hand.

He set the glass down at the end of the table. "The day I woke up from being sick, I realized something. I knew I didn't want to die living my life in the manner I'd been living it. I wanted—I needed—to make some changes."

He glanced at each of us.

"Work had lost its importance," he continued. "Living alone no longer had its appeal. There was someone I'd developed feelings for, but I'd disappointed her so greatly that I wondered if she'd forgive me. I took a chance and apologized, later asking if she'd consider being my lover. She—"

I alternated glances between Marge, Hap, and Pratt. "That's not exactly how it happened."

Hap's jaw tensed. "Let. The. Man. Speak."

Braxton grabbed his stomach. "I'm going to throw up."

"Don't you fucking dare," Hap barked, jumping from his seat. He rushed to Braxton's side. He draped his arm over Braxton's shoulder. "Suck it up, Son."

Braxton swallowed heavily. He swallowed again. After wiping his brow, he drew a long breath.

Hap released him.

Braxton stepped to my side. "My life's better than it was, but I still see it as an incomplete mess. The only thing that will make it complete is if you'll commit to take the rest of this journey with me." He looked me in the eyes. "Anna, I don't know what I'm going to do with the rest of my life, but whatever I do, I want to do it with you."

"I love you," I said.

"Anna, will you take this journey with me?" He reached for my hand. "As my wife?"

I was speechless. His words took me by complete surprise. I thought he was giving some wordy drunken speech. I wasn't expecting a proposal, at all.

I swallowed heavily.

My mind was screaming *yes*, but I couldn't formulate a response.

Hap cleared his throat. "Ring, Dipshit! Give her the goddamned ring."

"Hap Rourke!" Marge barked.

Braxton reached into his pocket and presented a gorgeous diamond ring. "Will you?" he asked. "Marry me?"

"Yes," I said pridefully. "I will."

My journey to find the man of my dreams wasn't simple. I didn't want simple. Settling for simple made me cry when I was a teen. Simple prevented me from marrying early in life. Simple got me a divorce.

Peeling away Braxton's layers took time, effort, and courage. What was beneath, however, was well worth the effort.

One by one, they gave congratulations and ogled the ring. It seemed everyone knew about the event except for me.

As we ate our melted ice cream and tiramisu, I took a moment and looked around. With Hap's shouting, Braxton nearly barfing, and my inability to understand what was happening, the proposal was an absolute shit show.

When I searched my mind for the events that got me there, I realized the journey was a shit show, too. Nevertheless, given the opportunity, I wouldn't change a thing.

Life was never perfect. If anyone knew that, it was the five of us.
A family of five.
By choice.

EPILOGUE

"Anna Rourke, line one," Karen said over the intercom. "Anna Rourke, you have an international call on line one."

On my way to lock the front doors and call it another successful day, I turned toward my office. The 60-second trek took 5 minutes.

Winded, I answered the phone. "Anna Rourke."

"Mrs. Rourke, this is Karl Koser in Madrid. I purchased the Enzo Ferrari last week. Sorry to call so late on a Saturday, but I'd like to speak to you regarding shipping. Have you a moment?"

He'd purchased a Ferrari for $2,300,000. I'd take whatever time I needed to satisfy him. I gave a nod although I knew he couldn't see it. "Sure."

"Is it possible to have a container devoted to the vehicle?" he asked. "The thought of shipping it alongside others makes me cringe."

"It was my understanding you were arranging the shipping," I replied. "Is that not the—"

"The thought of a one-owner Enzo being scratched or scuffed sickens me," he said. "My efforts to have the vehicle shipped in a satisfactory fashion have failed. I need your people to take every step possible to assure that it arrives at my port in the same condition that it leaves Los Angeles."

I fidgeted in my seat. "I can have my technicians personally load it, secure it, and then cover it with a lambswool blanket. The containers we use are fitted with weatherproof seals. It will arrive unscathed."

"The cost?" he asked.

"All I ask is for your return business," I replied.

"Anna, you're a class act."

I fanned my face with the latest copy of *Automobile.* "Thank you."

"Make the arrangements, if you will."

"I will," I said.

"I hate to ask, but the car isn't out in the rain, is it?'"

"Heavens no," I replied. "For one, it hasn't rained in five months. Secondly, my facility's vehicles are kept indoors at all times. Yours is in the detail shop."

"What a relief."

"I'll email you photographs as we reach the milestones."

"Thank you."

"The pleasure's mine," I said.

"I look forward to seeing those emails."

"They'll be coming forthwith," I said. "We'll talk again, soon."

An exotic dealership in Los Angeles was nothing like one in Oklahoma. $200,000 Lamborghinis were seen as high-end supercars in Oklahoma. In Los Angeles, they weren't of interest to the city's wealthy.

My customers wanted cars they couldn't find elsewhere. Special colors, bespoke interiors, one-off collector cars, and special edition hyper cars were my specialty.

Instead of $200,000 a month in revenue at a high margin, I was doing $10,000,000 a month at a low margin. A good percentage of my customers were celebrities who followed me on Instagram.

"Mrs. Rourke?" Karen asked over my phone's intercom. "I'm sorry, but I have a Miss Germanotta here to see you. The front door was unlocked."

Regardless of the time of day, I hated to turn away anyone.

"Send her in," I said.

I stood, tugged the wrinkles from my dress, and looked at my reflection in the glass. Whoever she was, she'd have to accept me in other than presentable condition.

A platinum blonde peeked through my office door. "Mrs. Rourke?"

She was wearing a wide-brimmed black hat, a white shawl, and cat eye sunglasses. She looked like money and had a New York accent.

"Call me Anna," I said.

She removed her glasses.

Oh. My God.

Upon realizing who she was, my heart thrashed against my ribs. Incapable of processing what was happening, I gripped the edge of my desk to keep myself from falling.

The room began to spin. Everything went black, but only for a second.

"Are you okay?" she asked, rushing to my side.

"I—" I fanned my face with my hand. "I need some air."

She removed her hat and fanned me with it. "How far along are you?"

"I'm scheduled to be induced next week." I rubbed the sides of my massive stomach with my palms. "On Monday."

She took a step back and looked me over. Her gaze fell to the floor between us. "Uhhm. Your water just broke."

"Oh My God," I gasped. "I'm so sorry."

"What—" She swallowed heavily. "—What do you want me to do?"

"These two are my first," I said. "I'm a little lost."

"Two?" she asked.

"We're having twins." I waddled to the guest chair and grabbed my purse. I handed her my phone. "If you don't mind, call 'HUBBY.' I'm sorry, I'm a little scatterbrained right now."

She scrolled through my contacts and made the call. "Hi. No. She's right here, though. No. It's Stefani Germanotta. Remember, we met a few—yeah. Lady Gaga. No. Her water broke. Okay. I don't know. UCLA Health, in Westwood? Sure. A dark gray G-Wagon. Okay. I don't know. Ten minutes? We'll see you there."

She handed me the phone. "Here, he wants to talk to you." She reached for my free hand. "C'mon, I'm driving you to the hospital."

I gasped. "You're what?!"

"He asked me if I'd drive you there." She tugged against my hand.

"By the time an ambulance gets here, it'll be too late. We can be there in five minutes."

I lifted the phone to my ear. "Hi," I said. "My water broke, and I feel like I'm going to puke. I love you."

"Keep your knees together," he said. "I mean it. If I miss this, there's going to be hell to pay."

"Okay."

"I mean it, Anna."

"Knees together," I said. "Got it."

"I'll see you there. I love you."

"I love you, too."

I hung up my phone and dropped it in my purse. I was ridiculously excited about giving birth, but at the moment, my only living idol was leading me to my car by the hand. It didn't make sense. I needed a few answers.

"Can I ask why you're here?"

"Chrissy Teigen sent me," she replied, leading me through the lobby. "She told me you sold her and John a new AMG G-Wagon. I need a new one, so I thought I'd come by and see what you had."

"You changed my life," I said, waddling along at her side. "You inspired me to wait for the right man."

"I don't...I don't know what to say," she stammered. "Thank you."

I didn't know her, and I'd only been in her presence for a few minutes, but I could tell she was genuine. Knowing that about her was reassuring.

She opened the door and helped me into the seat. "You look...uncomfortable."

"It feels weird," I said, lightly touching my stomach. "There's lots of pressure."

She rushed to her side of the SUV and got in.

With my legs spread as wide as I could get them and my belly between my thighs, I tried to extract the seatbelt to buckle it. No matter where I reached, either my tits or my belly was in my way.

After my third failed attempt, she helped me get it fastened. My failure to complete the task on my own reminded me of the day I met Braxton, and the issues I had with the seatbelt in his car in the diner's parking lot.

The ride to the hospital was horrific. Surprised that I made it without going into labor, I commented on her poor driving skills as she screeched to a stop at the entrance.

Braxton snatched the door open. "Are you okay?"

I was sprawled out in the seat like a beached Manatee. "I feel like a toad."

He helped me from the car. "You're gorgeous."

"You're a liar."

He peered beyond me, toward the other side of the car. "Thank you."

"You helped me once," she said. "Now, I've helped you."

"It'd mean the world to her if you could stay," he said. "She idolizes you."

"Hell-o." I gave him a look. "I'm standing right here."

"Sure," she muttered. "I can stay for a little while."

Excited that Lady Gaga was joining us, but more excited to meet my new babies, I waddled toward the birthing center's entrance with Lady Gaga on my left, and Braxton on my right.

Thirty minutes later, the excitement had been replaced with anger and disappointment.

Giving birth—or attempting to give birth—was a nightmare. There was nothing easy about it. If everyone knew how mind-numbingly difficult it was to push a child out of their twat, nobody would be having unprotected sex.

I gazed mindlessly at the television on the far wall. I was exhausted. I was drenched in sweat. My legs were numb. I felt like I'd pissed myself. Enough was enough.

I was on the cusp of throwing in the towel.

"I really need you to push this time," Braxton said. "Come on, Baby."

"I have been pushing," I complained. "It's hard."

"You don't want them to cut you, Anna. Believe me, I've been cut, and it's not fun. You'll be embarrassed every time you wear your bikini."

He was right. I didn't want to be cut. The unsightly scar would haunt me in my dreams.

I let out a long sigh. "Okay."

"We'll try one more time," the doctor warned. "After this, we may have to do the cesarean."

I shifted my gaze from the television to Braxton. "Give me your hand," I said. "We can do this."

Braxton gripped my right hand in his. I scanned the room. There were two nurses, a doctor, and Hap, all waiting for me to perform.

I looked at Hap. "Grab my other hand, Dad."

"You've got it, Kiddo," he replied.

With my only father on one side and my only lover on the other, I waited. In a moment, the doctor made the announcement.

"Here we go," he said. "One, two, three. PUSH!"

I pushed with every ounce of my being, screaming like a mental patient the entire time.

The room fell silent. My vision blurred. Everything went black. There was no pain, only an odd sensation that my nearly numb lower region was dissolving. Then, it ended. I felt slight relief, but in a very odd sense. I craned my neck to see of something happened, but my eyes couldn't come into focus.

A baby's crying filled the room.

My eyes welled with tears.

Our first born was an adorable little boy. We'd already decided to name him Brandon, after Braxton's brother. We'd chosen several girl's names but hadn't been able to make up our minds. I said when the time came, we'd see which name we felt fit her the best.

A few minutes later, our little girl was born.

"Any ideas on names?" Braxton asked, cradling her in his arms.

Beyond him, Hap held little Brandon. His face glowed with a

golden tan from his daily runs along the beach with Braxton. His eyes, glistening with admiration, were fixed on his first grandson.

I met Braxton's gaze. "Ally," I said. "After Ally Campano, in the movie."

Braxton grinned. "I should have known."

After everyone was checked out and cleaned up, Brandon was nestled in the valley between my right arm and my breast. Ally rested in the same place on my left side. I gave each of them an admiring look. My journey was only beginning. Our family was growing.

I felt as if I were dreaming.

I'd just given birth to two healthy twins. My husband stood proudly on one side of me, and my father-in-law stood beaming with pride on the other. All of our prayers, in their entirety, had been answered.

"Alright," I said. "Send them in."

Pratt and Marge came through the door. Upon seeing the babies, their faces lit up with joy. Behind them was Lady Gaga, the woman who gave me the courage to take the journey.

I glanced at my newborn babies, and then at each of the people who surrounded me. High on the wall behind Hap, the news played silently on the television. On the screen was the weather forecast.

No rain for the next 7 days. Only sunshine.

The corners of my mouth curled into a grin. My mother was right. We were beginning our sixth month of a drought.

And I was living a dream.

Printed in Poland
by Amazon Fulfillment
Poland Sp. z o.o., Wrocław

60994245R00181